PRAISE FOR
TEN THOUSAND TRIES

★ "Makechnie (*The Unforgettable Guinevere
St. Clair*) breathes life into both soccer scenes and
contemporary struggles in this emotional tour de
force centering family, love, grief, and death."
—*Publishers Weekly*, starred review

★ "A touching tale about family, love, and grief. . . .
Whether or not they are a fan of soccer, this title is
sure to make readers laugh and cry. An excellent
read-alike for Gary D. Schmidt's *Pay Attention,
Carter Jones*, 2019."
—*Booklist*, starred review

"A warm-hearted sports story about a kid learning
to accept the painful limitations and also unexpected
glories of passionate determination."
—*Bulletin of the Center for Children's Books*

TEN THOUSAND TRIES

Amy Makechnie

atheneum

Atheneum Books for Young Readers

NEW YORK LONDON TORONTO SYDNEY NEW DELHI

ATHENEUM BOOKS FOR YOUNG READERS
An imprint of Simon & Schuster Children's Publishing Division
1230 Avenue of the Americas, New York, New York 10020
This book is a work of fiction. Any references to historical events, real people, or real places are used fictitiously. Other names, characters, places, and events are products of the author's imagination, and any resemblance to actual events or places or persons, living or dead, is entirely coincidental.
Text © 2021 by Amy Makechnie
Cover illustration © 2021 by Abigail Dela Cruz
Cover design © 2021 by Simon & Schuster, Inc.
All rights reserved, including the right of reproduction in whole or in part in any form.
ATHENEUM BOOKS FOR YOUNG READERS is a registered trademark of Simon & Schuster, Inc. Atheneum logo is a trademark of Simon & Schuster, Inc.
For information about special discounts for bulk purchases, please contact Simon & Schuster Special Sales at 1-866-506-1949 or business@simonandschuster.com.
The Simon & Schuster Speakers Bureau can bring authors to your live event. For more information or to book an event, contact the Simon & Schuster Speakers Bureau at 1-866-248-3049 or visit our website at www.simonspeakers.com.
Also available in an Atheneum Books for Young Readers hardcover edition
Interior design by Irene Metaxatos
The text for this book was set in Adobe Caslon Pro.
Manufactured in the United States of America
0422 OFF
First Atheneum Books for Young Readers paperback edition May 2022
10 9 8 7 6 5 4 3 2 1
The Library of Congress has cataloged the hardcover edition as follows:
Names: Makechnie, Amy, author.
Title: Ten thousand tries / Amy Makechnie.
Description: First edition. | New York : Atheneum Books for Young Readers, [2021] | Audience: Ages 8 to 12. | Summary: Twelve-year-old Golden Maroni starts eighth grade determined to be master of his universe, but learns he cannot control everything on the soccer field, in his friendships, and especially in facing his father's incurable disease.
Identifiers: LCCN 2020044410 | ISBN 9781534482296 (hardcover) | ISBN 9781534482302 (pbk) | ISBN 9781534482319 (ebook)
Subjects: CYAC: Amyotrophic lateral sclerosis—Fiction. | Family life—Fiction. | Soccer—Fiction. | Friendship—Fiction
Classification: LCC PZ7.1.M34685 Ten 2021 | DDC [Fic]—dc2
LC record available at https://lccn.loc.gov/2020044410

TO NELSON, MY GOLDEN BOY

You can overcome anything, if and only if you love something enough.

—LIONEL MESSI

The Back-to-School Physical

When you saw him you would think: this kid
can't play ball.... He's too fragile, too small.
But immediately you'd realize that he was born
different, that he was a phenomenon and that he was
going to be impressive.

—ADRIÁN CORIA ON HIS FIRST
IMPRESSION OF TWELVE-YEAR-OLD LIONEL MESSI, SOCCER PHENOM

Every time Lionel Messi scores a goal, there's literally a small earthquake, an actual seismic shift. The crowd loves him so much that when he scores, they go completely nuts. They scream, stomp, and jump so hard that the earth actually moves under their feet. Some people call it a footquake, but I like Messiquake better.

When I dream, I become like my idol. The crowd loves me that much. *Golden, Golden, Golden!* Lucy passes me the ball, her blond hair flying. Benny sprints to the corner flag just in case I need him, giving me the assist. The ball is at my feet. I'm the dribbling maestro, faking out three defenders (it's sick, man). Three seconds on the clock. Left foot plants, right leg swings. Like a rocket, my shot spirals forward, the ball soaring above the goalie's fingertips. The crowd is on their feet, leaning forward, ready to shake the world. Time slows. Just before the ball hits the back of the net . . .

. . . a small chattering squirrel pounces on me.

I open my eyes to see the jaws of death—well, minus the two front teeth—a mere two inches from my face.

"Your breath smells like a dragon," the squirrel says.

"Get off, Roma!"

"Golden!" Mom yells from downstairs. "Let's go!"

My family has yet to recognize the greatness in their midst.

When my six-year-old sister doesn't move, I push past her and stumble down the stairs, consoling myself that even Messi, greatest soccer player in the world, probably has to have a yearly physical.

My last year of middle school officially starts with the annual visit to Dr. Arun. Which is fine except for shots and the whole let's-see-what's-going-on-down-there part. And of course that Mom and my two little sisters—Whitney and Roma—aka the Squirrels, are with me.

"Oooh, I like your dress," Roma says admiringly.

"It's a *gown*," I say before realizing that doesn't sound much better.

I'm wearing a small hospital gown printed with trains, the same one I've been wearing for every physical since age three. It has one useless tie in back that doesn't stop it from showcasing my bony spine and underwear.

Dr. Arun is a train fanatic. He's built a suspended track that travels the perimeter of the room, while an actual train chugs around the ceiling on it. When I was little, I couldn't wait to visit Dr. Arun because it was the coolest thing.

Actually, it's still the coolest thing, but when the nurse comes in to take my temperature and blood pressure, I pretend I wasn't looking at it and put a bored face on.

My older sister, Jaimes, says that everything for me is broken down into two categories: cool and uncool. For instance:

Cool: I'm starting eighth grade, so I'm finally gonna be THE MAN.

Uncool: Smallest boy in eighth grade. BY FAR.

Cool: I'm getting *bigger stronger faster*.

Uncool: Yesterday Jaimes called me a small furry rodent.

Cool: My comeback—"Your *legs* look like a small furry rodent!"

Oh, get wrecked, Jaimes!

"Mom," I say. "I'm going to ask Dr. Arun a question today and I need you to not interrupt."

"What is it?" Whitney asks.

"How intriguing," Mom says, raising an eyebrow and turning a page of her book.

"Mom, for real."

The door opens, the Squirrels exit to the waiting room for stickers and coloring, and in walks Dr. Arun. He's followed by a woman wearing a white doctor's jacket and a stethoscope around her neck like a boss.

"This is Hazel, a med student," Dr. Arun says. "Mind if she shadows me today?"

Hazel is so pretty that I find myself turning red and starting to sweat. Super uncool. To cover, I cough and pound on my chest as if I swallowed wrong.

"That's fine." My voice cracks. Uncool again. I start praying that Dr. Arun will not utter the words "Let's see what's going on down there" until Hazel is gone. Like, in a galaxy far, far away gone.

"What's your favorite subject in school?" he asks, listening to my heart.

"Gym?"

He laughs. "Favorite sport?"

I can't help but grin. "Soccer is why I'm living and breathing on planet Earth."

Mom smiles as Dr. Arun continues.

"Favorite player?" he asks, checking my ears.

"Uh, Messi, of course."

Which reminds me. I give Mom a warning look to not talk.

I clear my throat. "Could I get a . . . growth hormone prescription?"

Mom mouths *WHAT?*

"Messi took it as a kid," I continue. "'Cause he was small too."

Hazel smiles at me, showing straight white teeth, while Dr. Arun laughs again and tells me to stand.

I take that as a no.

Super uncool.

"Touch your toes." Dr. Arun turns me around so he can trace my spine with his gloved finger.

"You don't need growth hormone," Dr. Arun says, motioning for me to stand up straight. He glances at my chart. "Your growth is following a normal—and upward—trajectory. Besides, even with growth hormone Messi was always small and underrated, but look what he did anyway!"

"True," I say, brightening. "People used to call him a dwarf, said he was too fragile and small to play."

"And then?" Dr. Arun prods, feeling my lymph nodes.

"And then you'd watch him and know he was born to be the greatest of all time!"

"There you go," Dr. Arun says. "So don't worry. You'll grow. And your parents have some height. How tall is your dad?"

I glance at Mom.

"Five-ten," she answers, sounding totally normal.

"What position do you play?" Dr. Arun asks, and pats the table for me to sit.

"Forward, mostly."

"Ah, you must be fast."

I shrug like it's no big deal, like I haven't been training like crazy to be Messi fast.

"You like your coach?"

"He adores her," Mom says with a wave of her hand.

"You're eating fruits and vegetables?" Dr. Arun asks, switching back to boring health stuff.

"Yep." In addition to being a soccer fanatic, Mom's also become a vegetable freak.

"How's your dad doing? Everything all right?"

The silence that follows feels loud in my ears.

"He's good!" I say too loudly to fill it.

"All right then!" Dr. Arun says, turning to make a note. I'm filled with relief, no mortifying finale. Megacool.

Hazel takes over, asking Mom questions.

Anyone smoke? No.

Screen time limited to less than two hours a day? Yes.

Does Golden wear a helmet? Yes.

I accidentally laugh out loud. The three adults look at me strangely.

If Dad was here, we would discuss the word "irony." All

these safety questions, all these things we do to prevent bad things from happening, when Dad always wore a helmet. He ate fruits and vegetables. He never smoked. He's, like, the biggest, strongest, fastest, healthiest person I know. He can do 111 push-ups in less than three minutes—that's in the *extraordinary* category. And, well . . .

"Any changes in the household this past year?" Hazel continues.

"You could say that," Mom says. What she could have said: *Changes? More like a massive upheaval, thanks for asking.*

Dr. Arun nods, claps a hand on my shoulder, and shakes my hand for the first time.

I stand up straighter, puffing out my chest slightly.

"All set. Good luck, Golden."

"Thank you," I say, looking him right in the eye like Dad taught me.

Luck?

The odds might not look like they're in my favor, but actually? Destiny is about to deliver the best year of my life. I'm sure of it.

Dr. Arun turns to go.

"Uh . . . Doctor?" Hazel asks, pointing to something on my chart.

"Oh, right," he says. "Last thing. Can you drop your drawers?"

Drawers? For a second I look around the room for a dresser.

"Huh?"

"We'll take a look *down there*."

I feel my face grow hot.

Hazel doesn't move to leave and geez, *nothing* about today is cool.

The Wicked Cool Armbands

The harder you work, the luckier you get.

—DAD

So, I'm back home with no growth hormone prescription.

Dad says that whenever we encounter a setback, we should "bounce," or pivot to the next solution. "The impossible is always possible," he says. "You just have to find a way."

So without growth hormone I guess I just have to work even harder on my own: extra push-ups, crunches, and squats every single day. I carefully keep track on a wall calendar, next to my "ten thousand hours of soccer training" chart—which is the most important piece of paper in the house. Ten thousand hours is based on a theory Mom and Dad once told me about: you have to put in ten thousand hours before you become a master at anything.

For every hour of practice, I make a tiny tally mark. Every time I get a thousand, I circle it with a red Sharpie.

So let's say that since age one, I've touched the ball for one hour every day, six days a week, for twelve years. That's 3,744 hours.

After this summer I figure I have 6,256 hours left to becoming Messi. If I can log about a thousand hours every year between now and age eighteen, well, I'll basically be Master of the Universe. At least enough to be recruited to play in college. And after that? Going pro like Dad.

It's in between sets of crunches that I see them in the soccer catalog Mom left in the bathroom: captain armbands. Messi wears a captain's armband and it's the coolest. Therefore I want them, *need* them, more than I've ever wanted or needed anything. Well, you know, besides *the dad stuff*.

I send a picture to my best friends, Benny Ho and Lucy Littlehouse, in our group chat before looking out my bedroom window to Lucy's, just in case she's magically home early. Because it's Lucy, and knowing her, she might try to arrive in a hot-air balloon powered by the breath of her imaginary trolls in the forest.

But she isn't.

Her white roller skates look lonely, parked on her porch, waiting for her return.

Like me.

We've never been apart this long—almost the entire summer.

Sure, I have sisters, but Lucy's more like the twin sister I actually want. We've known each other since birth—no joke. We were born on the same day in the same hospital. There's even a framed picture of us on her fridge. I was bald but *very* cute, naturally.

The house next door remains dark except for the glowing amber eyes of her fat cat, Curtis Meowfield, as he slinks around the property. But something else catches my eyes as it moves near our shared driveway: a sleek silver car stopped in front, idling in the road. Curtis sees it too and freezes like a statue, one paw in the air. I peer closer but the car windows are tinted black, so I can't see inside.

My new-to-me, Jaimes's-hand-me-down-phone-that-does-exactly-one-thing buzzes with a text. It's Benny: GET THE ARMBANDS!

I'm on it.

"Mom," I say, running downstairs. "We have to get these."

"What?" she says absently, removing a plate from the dishwasher.

"Captain armbands!"

She doesn't even bother to glance at the catalog before she shakes her head.

"Why not?" I demand.

"Tone, Golden."

I morph into Polite Son.

"Please, Mother dear?"

"Why?"

"It's a thing. Every professional soccer team has them. . . ."

I'm distracted from my killer sales pitch by the long silver car now driving up the driveway and turning toward Lucy's house. A woman gets out. Her short silver hair matches her car, and she's wearing dark sunglasses and a black suit like some sort of secret agent.

"Look at you, you adorable feline!" Her deep husky voice comes in through the open window. Obviously, this woman does not know Curtis very well. But Curtis trots over to her and curls around her legs.

"Who's that?" I ask Mom.

She looks out the window and doesn't answer.

No one should be subjected to the terror of that cat without supervision, so I step out onto the porch as the stranger picks Curtis up and holds him like a baby, rubbing his belly and talking baby talk. "Sweet Curtis Meowfield, I've been *dying* to meet you."

"You can have him," I call out.

I briefly hope she'll kidnap Curtis, but since I'm the one who's supposed to be watching and feeding him, Lucy would never forgive me.

The woman gives a deep throaty laugh, showing white teeth that remind me of a wolf's.

"And you must be Golden. Lucy told me you and Curtis have a . . . tenuous and tempestuous relationship." I'm not confused by her big words. My dad's an English teacher. I'm confused because I've never seen this woman before, yet she knows about my "tenuous" and "tempestuous" relationship with Lucy's furball.

"Just checking on the house! I'll be seeing a lot of you later," she says. "Ta-ta!"

She's back in the driver's seat before I can even ask what that means, rumbling down the driveway, her fancy car kicking up dirt and dust. Curtis meows at me, and I run inside before he can follow me.

"That lady outside Lucy's was weird," I announce.

"Weird how?" Mom says.

"Well, for one, she adores Curtis Meowfield."

Mom laughs and begins cutting vegetables.

"Also, why is she checking on the house? We check on the house!"

"Can you put silverware on the table?" Mom says, distracted already. Big surprise. I don't complain about the silverware, even though it's Roma's job. Must Keep Mom in Good Mood.

"Mom," I say, separating the forks from the spoons from the knives. "Captain armbands. Haven't you noticed

15

that all the captains in the World Cup wear one?"

"Haven't been watching much World Cup, Goldie."

"Watch more, read less."

"You're not really selling me."

"Well, it's like a rule and these are totally legit. Benny agrees."

"Rayna?" Dad calls from upstairs.

Mom exhales a small breath. "Finish these?" She leaves the dishwasher open and the vegetables half cut. Dad probably needs help getting down the stairs or in the bathroom, which is kind of embarrassing but not as embarrassing as Dr. Arun looking *down there*. I shudder and try to block out the memory.

"Jaimes," Mom calls as she heads up the stairs. "Help your brother, please."

"You don't need captain armbands," Jaimes says, making zero movement away from her phone.

"*Your* captains wear them."

"Exactly, honey, and I'm in high school."

"Don't call me honey. And so what?"

"So, soccer is more *legit* in high school."

"You're supposed to be helping me." I squeeze the sink lip so I won't throw a wet, smelly dishrag at her face. Must Keep Mom in Good Mood.

Jaimes walks over and unloads exactly one cup while still staring at her screen.

"Jaimes! Focus on what's important here—soccer!" We used to play and talk soccer all the time, but now we never play and she hardly talks to me at all.

"I know soccer is important," she says. "I'm a junior—it's the most important season of my life."

She finally puts her phone down to set the table—and even finds a few reasons why the Mudbury Middle School Magpies need captains who wear legit armbands.

Then Mom and Dad come downstairs, Mom carefully watching their footing.

I ready myself but don't get a chance to bring it back up until we finally sit down to eat.

"It's a responsibility thing," I say, taking a bite of rice and something dark green and wilted. "Captain armbands build future leaders of Mudbury."

Jaimes rolls her eyes, even though I am directly quoting her. But my parents' eyes light up at the words "responsibility" and "leader." I feel a surge of power. One point for me.

"Responsibility?" Whitney asks. "Have you seen Golden's room lately?"

"Shut it, Squirrel—I mean, dear Whitney," I say, patting her head.

Thankfully, Dad raises a forkful of rice with his hand, and it distracts everyone from my not-so-polite-tone slipup. The fork inches up, up, a small wobble, but then it's on the move again, toward his open mouth—up, up, almost in—score! Well, it's close, half of the rice makes it into his mouth. The rest spills onto the table. We're going to have to work on that.

"It's okay, Dad!" Roma says cheerfully. "You can't help that you're messy."

"He's not messy," Whitney says. "He has ALS. His muscles didn't get the memo, right, Dad?"

"Right," he says matter-of-factly. Mom smooths his naturally wavy hair—the same hair I have—which is getting long and wild.

"The both of you need a haircut," she says.

Dad smiles at Mom with dark chocolate-brown eyes that also match mine, except his are oddly misty.

"Responsibility," I interrupt. "The captain is the leader. He—"

"He *and* she," Jaimes corrects. "Remember, there's always a male and female captain."

"Maybe Lucy will be captain," says Roma, looking out the window at Lucy's house.

"If you're the captain it'll be like you're married," says Whitney.

Jaimes starts to laugh. "Oh my gosh, I totally didn't make the connection. Golden, *you* want to be captain? Do you even know what that means?"

"Your arrogance will be your demise," I hiss.

"Jaimes," Mom says. "Be kind."

"Anyway," I say loudly. *"I'm* voting for Benny. Captain bands are just a way to . . . help my team."

"Uh-huh. Live in that dream world for a while," Jaimes says.

"Ow!" Jaimes registers my kick under the table, but no one else does, since I keep a very positive look on my face.

"I like the armband idea," Dad says as Mom patiently dabs his mouth with a thin paper napkin. "Golden's right. An armband signifies responsibility to teammates. It takes a special kid to pull captain off." I feel my hands get clammy, my breath quicken.

"With great power great responsibility comes," Jaimes says in a Yoda voice.

This prompts me to make my best Wookiee noise. I'm pretty good at it and it always makes Mom laugh. This time is no exception.

That's when I go in for the kill. "Pack of three. Eleven bucks—steal of a deal!"

Ten minutes later, Mom clicks buy and confirm.

Ten thousand points for me.

The Day I Don't Let Benny in the House

I'm sorry, Benny. And I mean it.
For everything.

—GOLDEN

Less than a week later, and two weeks before preseason, two packages arrive at our doorstep.

I run up to my room with them, slamming the door behind me. They're here, just in time.

I stare at the boxes, relishing the moment—until my door creaks open and I turn around to find four brown eyes staring at me through the crack. I also hear a meow.

You'd think that because I'm the only boy I'd have privacy or at least my own room. But oh no, Jaimes moved in this summer because her new room in the basement isn't finished and I was feeling charitable since the Squirrels were driving her nuts in their room. But I must've been the one who's nuts. Now even when Jaimes isn't around, the Squirrels are always busting in, wiggling and rolling and chattering with food in their mouths.

"Presents!" Whitney singsongs.

"We saw you run up here with them. Can I open one?" Roma says, pushing the door wide. In her arms she's holding Curtis Meowfield.

"No cats!"

"Shh!" Roma says. "You'll hurt Curtis's feelings."

But it's too late because Curtis jumps out of Roma's arms and onto my bed. He curls up on my pillow, his tail lazily swishing. Honestly. His yellow eyes stare at me, cool and impassive. I go between loathing Curtis Meowfield and admiring his unflappable boldness.

"Sit," I tell my sisters. "You can stay, but I'm opening them."

Miraculously, Roma and Whitney sit in unison.

"It's no big deal," I say, taking the scissors and slicing down the clear tape of the first box, which is slightly heavier than the second.

"*I* think it's a big deal," says Whitney. "What if *you* were voted captain?"

"Then I'd die a happy death," I say dramatically.

Roma looks horrified.

"Kidding, Squirrel," I say. "It's a joke. I'm not going to be captain *or* die."

"Is Dad going to die?"

"What? No!"

"Everyone will die someday," Whitney says, patting Roma's arm.

"But we won't for a long time. Including Dad," I say firmly, opening the cardboard flaps.

"Oooooh . . . ," Roma breathes, forgetting death.

"Hurry," Whitney whispers as I look inside, but my stomach plummets.

"Wrong box," I say quickly. "Just a boring book for Mom about . . . broccoli." A cold fear tries to paralyze me when I look again at the book that's actually inside. But I won't let it! I toss the box away from the Squirrels.

The second box thankfully does contain the armbands. They look just like the picture, except now they're real: red-and-white-striped elastic bands that perfectly match our uniforms, the word "Captain" printed in black across the middle of a white stripe. They're so beautiful I can almost forget what I saw.

"Whoa," the Squirrels say reverently as I lift them out, fingering the thin plastic covering around them.

I can't help myself.

I unwrap a band and carefully slide it up my arm and turn to look in the mirror. When I flex, the "Captain" letters stretch slightly, like my very small bicep was meant to wear this band—just like Messi.

"Can I try it on?" Roma asks.

"No. Only captains."

"But you're not captain."

I ignore this. "Do I look like Messi?"

Roma suddenly grabs the other armband and runs downstairs.

"Mom, armbands are here!" I say, chasing Roma into the living room with Whitney and Curtis Meowfield hot on my heels.

I stop short upon seeing a woman in scrubs in the living room with Mom and Dad.

"This is Verity," Mom says. "She's a nurse. Dad's having a home appointment today."

Verity the nurse smiles and tells Dad, "Hold my hands and don't let me pull you forward."

They tug back and forth until he's up.

Mom told us a nurse would start coming to the house eventually, but she didn't say it was happening *now*.

Seven months ago Dad asked me to clip his toenails. I was *really* bad at it. Dad bled all over the rug and said he'd take his pedicures from Roma in the future.

Six months ago Dad needed help lifting my bike into the back of his truck.

Five months ago he didn't kick the soccer ball back to me in the kitchen.

And then four months ago, Dad said, "Hey, can you reach the cereal boxes?"

I thought it was weird since he was, like, standing in front of the cupboards.

"Okay, lazybones," I said. But when I saw his face I realized he wasn't being lazy. He just couldn't raise his right arm like he could the day before.

A week after that he couldn't lift his left arm above his head, either.

But we've been working hard on all that. I guess we need to take it up a notch.

"Dad," I say. "We need to lift more weights."

"Maybe not," Verity says, and I instantly dislike her. "Any trouble walking?"

"A little."

"Lick your lips counterclockwise. . . . Good. Do you notice any drooling?"

Drooling?!

I snatch the armband from Roma and wander away to look blindly in the refrigerator. I hear Verity express surprise that Dad still plans on working this fall (ha!). She also tells Dad that he should consider "banking his voice" in an audio recording for his children.

"For me?" Roma asks, pleased.

"Yes," Verity says. "To tell you all the things he loves about you and wants you to know—and so that you'll always be able to hear his voice."

"Will Dad not be able to talk soon?" Whitney asks.

"Ah, you know Mom says I talk too much anyway," Dad says.

I peek around the fridge door. Dad is sticking his tongue out at Whitney.

"Let me show you something else you can help your dad practice," Verity says. "When it's too hard to talk, Dad can blink once for yes and twice for no. Do you want to try it?" Roma and Whitney start blinking fast at each other, giggling.

I'm about to tell her we're not going to need to talk in blinks, but a knock on the door stops me.

I open it, then immediately slam it back shut.

"Hello?" a voice says. "Golden?"

"Hey, Benny!" I squeak.

I open the door again, step onto the porch, and quickly pull it shut behind me.

"Hey," Benny says. "What's up . . . ?" His eyes go wide as he zeroes in on the armband around my bicep.

"They came today! I was just trying it on. . . ."

"Sick," Benny says, touching it. He holds up a bag.

"Dumplings?" I breathe. "Bless you."

"And egg rolls. From Grandma Ho."

I fist-pump the air. "Yes! I'm so hungry I've almost eaten Curtis a few times."

Benny laughs and looks behind me expectantly. "Can I come in?"

Trouble walking? Lick your lips? Drooling?

"Uh . . . can't right now."

Benny moves to the window to look in, but I jump in front of him.

"A nurse is visiting Dad."

Benny looks alarmed. "Is he okay?"

"Oh yeah! But the rest of the house is a mess and . . . maybe next week?"

I mean, it's true. The house *is* a mess.

"I used to practically live here," he says. "I know what your house looks like messy."

"Yeah." I nod but don't open the door.

"Okay," he says slowly. "Want to play soccer . . . or Wiffle ball . . . or ride bikes to the lake? We haven't been all summer."

"Uh, I wish, but . . . my tire is still flat. Next time. Thanks for the food."

We stand awkwardly on the porch until he finally turns to walk away. As I open the door again, I almost change my mind. But then I hear the nurse ask, "Any trouble swallowing?"

So instead I just shout, "Bye, Benny! You'll be wearing the armband soon! I'm voting for you!"

He holds up his hand in a wave and keeps walking, doesn't even turn around.

Curtis curls himself around my leg, sniffing the food.

"*Meow.*"

I pull the dumplings to my chest. "Don't even think about it, cat."

That night after the most delicious meal we've had in weeks, I'm tiptoeing across the hallway to my parents' bedroom with the stupid first package when I hear Mom talking to Dad downstairs.

"I just don't want him to be devastated," she says. "I know that every one of those boys, including Golden, is dreaming about being voted captain and wearing that armband. Life is hard enough for him right now." I crane my neck to hear more, but Dad's voice is lowered and more muffled. I hope he's not crying. He's more emotional now, an odd and puzzling ALS symptom from all the neurons in his head shriveling into nothing.

But it doesn't matter. Sometimes Mom just doesn't get it.

Life is *not* hard for me right now—soccer is starting!

I mean, I know better than a lot of people that bad things happen, but not during soccer season. I'm going to be so good at preseason that I'll earn the Messi position— starting forward.

As for the captain thing? I never told Mom I wanted to be captain.

But she's right. It's true. I do.

Just like Messi.

If I can follow in his shoes, we'll be unbeatable.

"Hey, Golden," Mom calls from downstairs, making me jump. "Come help for a second?"

I slide back across the hallway in my socks to my bedroom before I go. Instead of tossing Mom's package onto her bed like I planned, I defiantly shove it under my bed so she'll never find a book entitled *How to Talk to Your Kids About Dying*. A book nobody in this family needs.

Poor Mom.

Doesn't she know Dad's unbeatable too?

It Happened Like This

Look, I'm not totally delusional.

Dad has ALS.

I know that.

We found out one year and six months ago. It was just after Valentine's. Lucy, Benny, and I had just come in from sledding.

"Where's Mom and Dad?" I asked.

"How do you *not* know where they are?" Jaimes asked.

"They're still not back?"

She shook her head and looked out the window.

"Party!" I shouted. Jaimes looked at me, daggers in her eyes, but I didn't know why she was so touchy. It was just a doctor's appointment. Yeah, it was in Boston, which was weird, but Dad was in the best shape of anyone I knew. All the other dads joked about Dad's superhuman fitness.

So Lucy, Benny, and I ignored Jaimes's mood and started watching a movie.

I looked up from the screen when I heard my parents finally come in. It was Mom's face I remember most. Something was wrong. And it wasn't the popcorn mess I'd made in the kitchen.

Her eyes were rimmed red. Her whole face looked swollen.

Lucy and Benny left quickly even though the movie wasn't over, and suddenly there was a family meeting.

"Are you okay, Daddy?" Roma asked.

"No, I'm not, honey." He spoke slowly, with a strange calm, his dark eyes slightly unfocused.

"What is it?" Jaimes asked. She was already crying, which really ticked me off.

"They think your father has what's called amyotrophic lateral sclerosis," Mom said, blinking her watery eyes.

"They think?" Jaimes asked hopefully. "So he might not?"

"I have it," Dad said. He wasn't crying. And it reassured me. I took my cue from him and stayed calm too.

"What's amyo-whatever?" Whitney asked.

"ALS," Jaimes said. "I've heard of it."

"It means that over time, I'm going to lose the ability

to move my muscles," Dad said. Roma inched closer and climbed into his lap.

There was a long silence as he hugged her to him.

"This is a progressive disease," Dad said finally. "Remember when we played soccer a few weeks ago, Golden, and I just thought I was really out of shape? And you know how I keep dropping things?"

Everyone nodded but me.

"It's my muscles. It's the disease."

"For some reason," Mom said, her voice becoming steelier, "Dad's neurons—the cells in his brain and spinal cord—are atrophying. They're dying, so the muscles aren't getting the signals they need to work."

"It's really handy to have a biologist as a wife," Dad said, smiling slightly as he reached over and took Mom's hand.

"Why are they dying?" Whitney asked.

"No one knows," Mom said. "There are really no known causes. But you won't catch it or anything."

"So what now?" Jaimes asked.

"It's a little different for everyone," Dad said. "But your muscles control your ability to walk and move and talk and breathe, so eventually I will probably not be able to do those things . . . but that's eventually. Not now."

Not now.

That's what he said. *Not now.*

I took a visual inventory. Dad was really strong. Big hands, big arms, and defined shoulders. He was walking and talking and definitely breathing.

Dad was just fine. This couldn't be right.

"You said it was probably tendonitis," I said.

Dad's eyes met mine. "It's not, and I'm so sorry, buddy. I wish it were."

"Maybe it's Lyme disease," I said. "Probably Curtis Meowfield brought a tick in the house."

"He tested negative," Mom said, shaking her head.

"It could be wrong."

"They're sure," Dad said.

I could feel my body threatening to blow up right then and there.

"The important thing is that we love you all very much, and no matter what happens we will always be a family," Mom said, like she was quoting a brochure.

"So . . . ," Jaimes said slowly. "Is there a cure?"

Mom blinked several times.

"At this moment, no," Dad said.

"But no one's stronger than your dad," Mom said. "So we're going to fight as hard as we can fight for as long as we can."

We nodded because this is the language of my parents. In the kitchen there's a big sign that says MARONI FAMILY, overlaid with cursive writing, *We Do Hard Things*.

That's what we do. Work hard. Bounce. Pivot. Find the possible. *At this moment.* That didn't mean *never.*

But Jaimes kept pressing in the wrong direction.

"Did the doctors give you a timeline?"

"Three to five years is the average length of the disease," Dad said. His voice broke slightly and he cleared his throat. "Sometimes less, sometimes more. I've likely had it for a while now."

"So you'll only have it for three to five years?" Whitney asked.

"Yes," Mom answered. "But . . . he won't get better."

Jaimes leaned back into the couch, her arms folded across her chest, her mouth set in a very straight line.

"And then what?" Whitney asked, confused. "After three to five years?"

"Well," Mom said, her voice getting very quiet. "He will probably . . . pass away."

"Pass away," Roma echoed, looking around the room for more explanation. But no one could say it. No one could say "die."

But they thought it.

There was this noise, like all the air being sucked out of the room. Followed by a commotion. There were sobbing sounds. There was hugging. There were tears coming down faces. Except for mine.

I sat on the couch, alone. Like a stone.

Because you know what I heard Mom say?

He will probably *pass away.*

Probably.

So . . . there was a chance. A chance he could live.

I would make sure he got that chance.

Ninja Tongue-Twister Champ of the Three Worst Words

I'm not gonna be most people.
—GOLDEN

All these months later we're still working on it, but every month it seems to get just a little bit harder.

Amyotrophic lateral sclerosis.

It's three long words, and I can say it faster than anyone in the family, like a ninja tongue-twister champ. I didn't mean to get so good at it, but it goes through my head over and over and over like a soccer move I can't shake. It's a super-frustrating disease to fight. One day a muscle moves—the next day? Nope.

But then other days he *can* move what he thought he lost, and I think that's because we started lifting weights together.

I've been working hard with the weights to bulk up my shrimpy arms, and it must be helping Dad, too, because he's been steady for weeks with no serious backsliding.

I figure Dad just needs to keep practicing so those neurons remember where to go and what to do. Last time I told Mom this she said we have to be careful not to get our hopes up too much.

"Why not?" I said. "Isn't that what hope is for?"

Since no one really understands this disease anyway, why not hope for the best?

"You're right," she said. But she doesn't seem to act like it much.

It's my unofficial job to keep reminding her.

This morning Dad's up early. Like me, he's always been an early riser, but these days it's *super* early. I'm beginning to suspect it's because he doesn't want us to see him taking the stairs, which he says is like watching a penguin flop down a flight. I don't tell him this—but it's kind of true.

"Hey, sleepyhead." He's sitting on a stool at the breakfast bar he built, watching the news on his computer.

"Hey, Dad."

I sit next to him as he switches to another window streaming professional soccer—Barcelona, of course, the team Messi signed with at age *thirteen*. I'm only like a *month* from that age!

"Watch how he controls the ball," Dad says.

"Sweet," I say, leaning closer. "Whoa! Look at that ball cross."

Dad gets up and walks to the fridge. The game is a rerun, but watching Messi never gets old. While Messi's feet fly across the field, Dad's feet stay close to the floor, and he moves slowly so he won't trip. Mom's even pulled up all the rugs in the house, so he won't. I notice that today, neither one of his arms moves back and forth when he walks. His right arm hangs totally limp and his left hand looks slightly clawed. Slowly, he raises the left to grasp the refrigerator door handle. It takes three pulls, but the door opens. I don't even realize I'm holding my breath until it releases with the door.

"Yogurt?"

I nod.

He shuts the refrigerator with his back and shuffles over to me, grasping the yogurt firmly in his hand. I reach out with both hands just in time.

He drops, I catch.

In return, I get the cereal, pour him a bowl with milk, and put his spoon in.

"Thanks. Teamwork." Dad smiles. His hand comes up like he wants to ruffle my hair the way he used to, but it falls back down.

"Teamwork," I echo. We watch as Messi brings the ball out of the air straight to his feet. He's in total and absolute control. "Whoa he's good."

Dad used to be able to do that. Today he awkwardly

raises his spoon. Milk dribbles from side to side, splattering onto the computer. "Speaking of messy. My brain's having a hard time telling hand to put spoon in mouth."

"You can do it, Dad!"

The spoon comes up a smidge, and I cheer him on. "Patrick Maroni is streaking toward the cereal goal!"

The spoon keeps going, and Dad leans forward. "Go, go, go!"

Dad lunges forward, his mouth covering the spoon.

"Yes! Goal!" I say, even though he probably spilled more than made it into his mouth.

He slowly chews and swallows as he looks at the screen. "I've never seen a player who can keep the ball so close to his feet—like it's glued there."

I nod fervently, scraping the bottom of my yogurt cup. I don't even like yogurt that much, but I couldn't say no after all the effort Dad went to to get it for me.

The game is tied and I turn up the volume.

"The rivalry is real," the commentator says. "It's anybody's game, but I'm making a prediction right here and now. Messi might be ranked number one in the world, but Brazil has had such a stellar season that I predict a win."

"What?! No way," I say dismissively. "No one can beat my soul brother."

Dad's eyes are shiny by the end of the game. I get it. No one loves soccer more, and Dad was *good*. Real good.

Watching film sometimes triggers the strange emotional side effect of ALS. Dad doesn't like it because then his nose runs. I don't like it because then I have to wipe his nose.

"I have something for you," Dad says, clearing his throat. "I should wait for your mom, but . . ." He walks to the coat closet but motions stiffly for me to open it. "In there."

I don't know what I'm supposed to be able to find in the closet. It has so many shoes we could open our own shoe store.

"It smells like feet!" I say, rummaging. "Dad, are you messing with . . . ?"

Then I see a shoe box. A *new* one. I can smell the newness—nothing like sweaty, smelly feet.

When I open the box, I almost have a literal heart attack.

Inside are the cleats I've wanted *forever:* Messi f50 World Cup limited-edition Battle Packs. They have spotted black-and-white sides, with three bright orange stripes from top to bottom. The tongue is spotted blue and white, the laces turquoise. Unlike professional basketball players, almost no soccer player gets their own model of soccer cleats. Messi is one of the few who has his own specifically designed cleats by Adidas.

"No way," I breathe. "How did you . . . ?"

Dad shrugs, grinning. But of course he knows. He always knows.

I lace up. A perfect fit.

They're like a rabbit's foot, a lucky charm, Superman's cape all in one—and I'm freakin' wearing them on my feet! I AM Messi!

Dad follows me as I sprint out to the backyard, jump off the deck, high-skip, and do a somersault.

"Pass," Dad says as I grab the soccer ball. He awkwardly steps down onto the grass with his bare feet.

I do, but instead of Dad receiving, the ball hits him hard in the ankles.

He makes an attempt to pass back, but Dragon-Ball P, who used to have the best touch, huge calves, and a shot so powerful it rivaled rockets, gets the ball maybe halfway across the grass. I run up and take it with my right foot, pull it back, and dribble toward him with my left. Just before reaching him I turn with the ball and blow past him. *Come get me!* I will him to do it.

Instead he loses his balance and sits down hard on the grass.

"Dad!" I say, rushing to him.

"Nice Maradona," he says, wincing. "Next time bend your knees and turn quicker."

I hold out both hands and pull up as hard as I can. He doesn't move.

"One more time. One, two, three, pull." He comes up slowly, and just when I think he's going to tip back over he steadies, breathing as heavily as if he's just all-out sprinted.

"You need a new passing partner," he says gruffly. "Where's Benny been?"

"Scholar Camp."

"All summer?"

"No," I admit.

"When's Lucy coming home?"

"In a week or so?" Eight days, to be exact.

When I'm sure Dad's not going to fall back over, I flick the ball up, this time bending forward, trying to land the ball between my shoulder blades, my arms out like wings. Instead the ball bounces off my back and rolls under the bush.

"So. Growth hormone?" Dad says, his good mood returning.

I roll back out from under the bush. "Yeah. Denied. Uncool."

"You don't need it," he says. "You've got your ten thousand hours chart. I bet no one else has worked as hard as you have this summer."

"Dad. Do you think I could be . . . captain?" It comes out so small and timid it's embarrassing. I drop down and do ten push-ups on the grass.

"Why not? You're Golden Messi Macaroni, right?"

"Yeah, but I'm not the best or the most popular—not like Benny. I'm not the biggest, strongest, or fastest."

"So? Wait—scratch my nose and get this grass off?" He wiggles his nose.

I jump up, wipe the grass off his face and hair, and scratch until he sighs happily.

"Thanks. As I was saying. You know, Messi's not the biggest and strongest."

I brighten. That's totally true.

"Even so, *why* do you want to be captain?"

"Why? Because I'm going to take my team all the way to the championship. We were good last year, right? But this year we'll be unstoppable! Dad, Mudbury has always been the underdog—even Jaimes's team only *almost* made it to the championship game. It's our destiny. I know it. I *feel* it."

Dad grins. He feels it too.

I start juggling the ball with my knees, feet, and head—just no hands. My all-time high is fifty-two touches in a row. Lucy has forty-nine. Jaimes did ninety-seven once. Benny can easily do a hundred.

But after only eight touches, the ball bounces off my knee and into the bush again.

Usually, Dad would take the ball and show me how to do it better. Not today. He stands still as I climb back under the bush.

Ten thousand freaking hours. Sometimes that number feels *so* far away. Heck. I wonder if I'm going to have to retrieve my soccer ball ten thousand times and get ten thousand scratches before I can juggle half as well as Messi—or even Benny.

But then again, you know what Messi says? *You have to fight to reach your dream. You have to sacrifice and work hard for it.*

Most ordinary people are capable of extraordinary things, but most aren't willing to do what it takes to get extraordinary results. Me? I'm willing!

"Hey, Golden," Dad says when I emerge.

"Yeah?"

He reaches out and takes my wrists with his hands. A light, feathery grip, but still a grip.

"It's a great game, isn't it?" His eyes are beginning to water. You see? *Nobody* loves soccer more than my dad.

It's then that it happens.

The whole season is laid out before me. I can see it so clearly.

Earn the starting forward position.

Get elected captain of the Mudbury Middle School soccer team.

Win the games. All the games.

Qualify for the championship game.

Under the lights.

Win the championship.

Dad walking onto the field.

Smiling.

Hugging me with strong arms.

Together, we hold the trophy up, high above our heads.

I see it so clearly, like the future has already been written. That's how it's going to go down. The impossible is going to be possible.

I see something else, a near-invisible thread connecting all of this to Dad.

The odds are stacked against him, too.

Everyone says he can't win.

They're wrong.

Dad and ALS? Ultimate underdog scenario of all time.

"Golden?" Dad says.

"Yeah?"

"Remember, in the end, it's just a game."

Huh?

"Since when?" *What a weird thing to say.*

Dad laughs at the look on my face.

"Help me inside? It's chilly."

"It's like a hundred degrees out."

"Says the boy who can move."

I drop the ball, hold on to his left arm, and lift his left foot onto the step.

"Come on, Dad. You got this."

I try to just steady his arm so he can practice lifting himself, but it takes twice as long as yesterday.

A bird squawks above us, and I look up to see it pass by Lucy's window, where our super-old Kermit the Frog lunch box hangs on a pulley rope connecting it to mine. When we were little we would send notes back and forth to each other.

Seeing Kermit suddenly makes me want to send a note and tell her everything that's happening. Lucy has been in Maine all summer with her mom. It's actually a miracle I've survived so long without her.

When she calls, I can't seem to say *Hey, Dad tipped over and can't ride a bike. How are you?*

Dad gives one more big push and we're up the two steps.

"Good job, Dad."

"Thanks for helping me," Dad says, with effort. "You help your teammates like you help me—and you're golden."

I nod, feeling my spirits lift even though he's been making that dad joke since I was born.

Most ordinary people are capable of extraordinary things, but most aren't willing to do what it takes to get extra-ordinary results.

Messi isn't most people.

Dad isn't most people.

My lucky Battle Packs sparkle from the ground, catching my attention.

I'm not gonna be most people either.

When the Season Really Begins: Hell Week

Slow makes smooth and smooth is fast.

—COACH

Soccer preseason is called Hell Week.

It's exactly what it sounds like—hot and really hard.

I'll complain with the rest of the team, but secretly I love it.

Hell Week is that magic space between summer and the start of school. No homework, no teachers, no bus drama. Just me, my teammates, and a soccer ball. And now—new f10 Battle Pack cleats.

The first morning, I put out food and fresh water for Curtis Meowfield. Instead of meowing politely like a nice cat, he chases me until I run inside and slam the front door shut.

My phone dings. Benny.

lucy back?

no

ready for preseason?

u know it!

swim to blueberry island
after?

can't w/out Lucy!

true. can i come over?

I don't text back because I don't know what to say
except that Dad's not ready.

Benny doesn't text back either, and I stare at his message,
feeling guilty. I push it away, though, because today is the
start of everything and I can't not be happy. I'll see Benny all
week on the field. It'll be fine. Today, the Mudbury Middle
School Magpies (a very smart bird, but worst mascot name
ever?) soccer team meets their very own Lionel Messi!

World champion.

World domination.

Extraordinary.

* * *

On the ride over to the school, I try to focus only on soccer and not on Lucy and how she should be in the car with us.

My hands are sweating, my preseason nerves a frayed jumble of knots twisting in my stomach. I've also never been so pumped.

As we pull out of the driveway, we pass the same silver car I saw the day before. It turns into the driveway as we go by.

"It's that weird lady again!" I crane my neck as her car slowly makes its way up the drive and stops. "What's she doing?"

Mom doesn't answer my question. She's got a distracted look on her face.

"I feel like I'm forgetting something," she says. "Soccer balls?"

"At the school."

"Right. Cones?"

"In the back."

"Pinnies?"

"Got 'em."

"What would I do without you?"

I push up my Messi hair. "I don't know, Coach. I really don't know."

That gets a smile out of her.

It's hot when we get there. The temperature is close

to ninety with what feels like a hundred percent humidity. The heavy wet makes the White Mountains appear hazy in the distance. It's the end of August in Mudbury and so hot that small animals will die without shade. The weak will stumble and fall. Only the strong will survive. That's me. I pound my chest, shin guards, and cleats.

I also sniff my armpits, and just in case, check to see if I'm getting pit hair.

Nothing yet.

But—upward trajectory! That's what Dr. Arun said about my growth chart.

I'm early to practice because I drive with Coach, who, like every soccer season, the second we arrive transforms into this thing where she's no longer my mother. She's harder, with a look in her eyes I don't dare cross, a look that says *LUNGES, SQUATS, AND SPRINTS UNTIL YOU DIE!* It's like having the Incredible Hulk for a mom.

While Coach goes inside to talk to the sickest dude around, our athletic director, Mr. Toomey (otherwise known as Mr. T, due not so much to his name but to his identical resemblance to the iconic "I pity the fool" professional wrestler), I step onto the field, green from so much summer rain. It's quiet, empty. I close my eyes, take my first step, feel the grass under my cleats. My second home.

I start to take a lap before the team arrives, something I'm sure a committed Messi would do. The only saving grace from the heat and intensity of the sun is a slight breeze whispering through my overgrown hair. As I run, I glance down, seeing the blur of blue and orange of my wicked cool cleats.

Coach says pricey shoes don't make the player, but I'm feeling pretty much invincible. I can't wait for my boys, especially Benny, to arrive so I can show them off. I have a sudden and sharp ache just to see Benny and Lucy. Usually we're hanging out at the lake all summer, pushing each other off the dock, skipping balls and rocks, catching and releasing tadpoles in buckets. I've hardly seen *anyone* for two months—except the Squirrels. Do I even know how to talk to normal humans anymore, not just oversized rodents?

The school doors bang open and out walk Coach and Mr. T. I'm comforted that he's exactly the same as the last time I saw him, complete with the shaved head. His biceps are huge, bigger than my whole body, and he walks like a bodybuilder, his arms out to his sides just slightly, the cotton of his shirts always stretched thin.

"Welcome back!" Mr. T booms, surveying the soccer field. He hands me zip ties. "Nets?"

We start with the farthest goalie net. I feel like even more of a shrimp next to his hulking presence. Uncool.

"Dang, Golden. You've gained some weight this summer! You pumpin' some iron?"

I puff out my chest, thrilled. "Working on it. Still too small."

"Small can be an advantage on a soccer field, though," Mr. T says. "Lower center of gravity, quicker turns. But I bet you're gonna hit your growth spurt any day now."

"Today would be good!"

He starts stringing the first goal. "Where's your dad today?"

"Oh, you know, pumpin' some iron."

Mr. T glances at me. I blush at my obvious lie, but he doesn't call me on it.

"He still coaching at the high school this year?"

"Of course!"

"Don't know anyone who loves soccer more than your mom and dad. You let me know if you need anything— anything at all—even if it's just to talk, okay?"

"Sure."

He gives me a second look that I busily ignore, getting out another zip tie. Adults always want to talk so much. Today's about soccer.

We cinch the last zip tie before turning to walk back across the field. You might not think it's much to look at, not like the big green field and stands across the street at the high school. We don't have a huge electronic score-board or big bright lights that come on at dusk. We don't even have bleachers. The team benches are old planks sitting atop tree stumps and fit like five players. The grass is a little long, with a few dirt patches, the middle a bit bumpy, and Mr. T still hasn't painted lines.

But I love this field. I've spent basically my whole life here.

Mr. T heads back inside, and I drop to the ground to do as many push-ups as I can before my arms and shoulders and back are burning with fatigue. *Bigger stronger faster!*

I hear voices now, car doors slamming, cleats hitting the pavement. I get up and take a deep breath. I can hear them laughing, pushing each other, unzipping their duffel bags, digging for their water bottles, the sound of cleats stomping on the ground. One by one, they start to take the field.

My teammates have arrived.

During Hell Week, Coach packs a three-a-day into one two-hour practice.

Practice starts at 3:00 p.m. sharp, and Coach is serious about that "sharp" part. We do push-ups for every minute someone is late. "In soccer," Coach says, "you live and die as a team."

Mudbury is a K-8 school, and because of our small class size, we're coed. We have boys AND we have girls—which sometimes makes other teams underestimate us. Suckers!

"Yo Ho Ho," I say when I see Benny.

"Goldie-Locks," Benny says right back. If he's annoyed about me ghosting before, he doesn't show it.

We automatically do our handshake: palm, palm, backhand, backhand, slide, elbow, finger lock, pull away.

"Hey," Brady says, giving me a friendly shank in the stomach. Shanking is when you curl your pointer finger and come up real close, put one hand on a shoulder like you're giving a hug, then shank! Right in the gut or side with your curled finger. Last year, you couldn't walk down the hall without someone getting you. I haven't been shanked in so long, it's surprisingly comforting—even though it hurts.

"Sweet shoes," Brady says as I jump away, rubbing my side.

"Thanks," I say, ready to show them off, but I nearly drop to the ground when I see what Benny and Brady are both wearing on *their* feet: brand-new Nike Mercurials. Price tag: $200. "Fly knit?" I whisper.

"Benny and I got 'em yesterday," Brady says. "After swimming to Blueberry Island." Matching shoes. *Blueberry Island?* Without me and Lucy?

The instant betrayal must show on my face because Benny says, "It was so hot and I didn't want to wait forever, you know?"

"*I* would wait forever," I say, but I regret it immediately. It comes out all whiny and uncool.

Brady snickers.

"I'll still totally go with you and Lucy," Benny says. "Whatever."

Doesn't matter. I shrug it off. I'm wearing my Messi Battle Pack cleats. *Unstoppable.*

I juggle the soccer ball, trying to keep it from touching the ground. But on the fifth touch it bounces off my knee and into my nose. Hard. It hurts so bad I turn around so Benny and Brady won't see how my eyes smart.

Brady laughs again, making my eyes water even more. Middle School Boy Rule #1:

YOU CANNOT, UNDER ANY CIRCUMSTANCES, CRY.

"Are you okay?" Sunny asks me, coming over.

"I'm totally fine." I shake her off. *Be a man! Be* the *man! Be Messi!*

The thing is, I would probably think it was funny if a ball hit Brady in the face. I'd probably laugh—I don't know why.

I try to juggle again, but I'm rattled. No one votes for a crybaby for captain. Looking around, I feel panicky. I don't know who else saw, and everyone is here. Except Lucy. I wish she were here.

"Hey, Moldy Goldy!" Slick calls. Goldie-Locks. Goldfinger. Golden Doodle. Goldfish. I've heard them all, but everything is worse coming from Slick.

My birth certificate officially reads Golden Patrick Maroni. My parents say they loved me when I was a baby, but I sometimes wonder.

Not that the name Slick is, like, normal or anything. But it's actually his last name, and kind of cool. "Golden" is so weird I might as well be named Fish Stick.

I try to ignore Slick like the unflappable Messi would.

"Golden, can you get the balls out of the equipment shed?" Coach asks.

Game time! I run toward the shed, thankful to get away, and also thinking about the question Dad asked me. Why do I want to be captain?

Why? To lead this team to the championship.

The real question is—how am I going to get everyone to vote for me so I can?

I've come up with a few answers, but they mostly come back to: I need people to like me. I need to only say nice, positive things this week. I need to show them that I'm the guy who steps up.

"Hi, Goldie," someone says too close to my ear.

I turn, annoyed to hear another nickname, but it's just Ziggy. Ziggy with the dirty-blond, shaggy hair and big teeth that are constantly stained blue from the amount of Mountain Berry Blast he chugs.

"I'll help you get the balls. Get it, *balls*?"

"I get it," I say, opening the shed and hauling out the

two bags. Last year? I couldn't have picked up two bags at the same time, so what Dr. Arun said about my growth chart must be true. Wicked.

"How're you doing?" Ziggy asks, following me back to the field. "How was your summer? I was wondering if you wanted to go to that new Marvel movie next week?"

"Maybe." I try to sound friendly, but not too friendly, while flinging the bags onto the field. The thing about Ziggy is you can't just be friends with him. As soon as you're nice he becomes an overenthusiastic octopus that tries to slowly smother you to death. On the other hand, he will be voting for a captain.

"Thanks, Goldie," Coach says before Ziggy can respond again. I move out of her way so she can't ruffle my hair. Sometimes Coach forgets the need for clear boundaries in public.

Benny jogs over to me. I see his overpriced shoes, which he doesn't even need because he has this crazy natural ability. I know everyone's going to vote for him for captain because of it, when he doesn't even care. Ten thousand hours? I've put in way closer to that and he's still way better.

But when I look down at my own shoes I instantly chill. I'm *literally* in Messi's shoes. Besides, Benny's my best friend. He shows it, too, when he rescues me from Ziggy's tentacles.

Coach blows the whistle, and Benny and I join our teammates on the end line. C.J., Benny, Mario, Brady, Chase, Ziggy, Moses the Goat Boy, Dobbs, and Archie are all in the first row. The girls are banded together tighter than a wad of gum, but I still see Sunny, Sissy, Hannah, Sam, Ava, Savannah, Paige, and Mari.

There are nineteen of us because Coach doesn't make cuts like I would. With this many players, you have to fight for a starting position. *Fight*. Exactly.

Preseason starts with her next whistle.

We stand arm's length apart on the field facing Coach, each with a soccer ball at our feet. Coach paces in front, whistle around her neck, wearing old indoor cleats, hair in a ponytail.

"Tell me, team, what happens when I blow this whistle?"

"STOP!" Dobbs blurts out.

Coach ignores him and points at Benny.

"We freeze."

"Correct. And if you don't freeze?"

"Ten push-ups," we chorus.

"How you follow the rules and help each other will naturally allow our captains to emerge. We'll vote in one week."

This statement changes the energy immediately. We are teammates this week, but also competitors.

Benny, C.J., and Brady are the most popular boys in our class, but Benny has the edge because he's really funny, totally chill, and seriously the most athletic person in our entire school at any sport.

Middle School Boy Rule #2:

THE MORE ATHLETIC, THE MORE POPULAR.

Even if you're a complete jerk.

Luckily, Benny Ho is not a jerk.

"Warm up!" Coach says. "Dribble, right foot only. Go."

I take off.

"Keep the ball close. This isn't a race. Slow makes smooth and smooth is fast."

As we dribble, Slick kicks my ball away so that it looks like I've lost control of it.

"Hey!" I say loudly, chasing it down.

"No toes," Coach says on our way back, like nothing happened. "Left foot!"

I pass Moses. He trips and falls over the ball. Goat smell wafts up into my nose. Moses and his family really do breed goats—and the smell is where Slick's nickname for him, Goat Boy, came from. When we were little, Moses and I used to be friends. I loved petting those goats until one day, when middle school started, we just weren't friends anymore. I don't really know what happened. Moses is alone most of the time and doesn't actually seem to like soccer. When I asked Mom why he even played, she said, "Everyone wants to belong to a team." Maybe she's right.

"Good work, Moses," I say, trying for captain-level

encouraging, but my compliment sounds awkward to us both, and he looks up, surprised, as I dribble past him. Left foot, no toes.

I refocus and push myself to go harder, feeling the burn in my quads, finishing the drill in a tie with Benny for the first time ever.

Very cool.

By Friday morning, after four full days of Hell Week, I'm so sore I can hardly walk.

"Just wait until high school," Jaimes says, pouring herself a bowl of cereal. "In the real world—"

"The *real world*," I interrupt. "Oh, never mind. I'm just in unreal middle school, unlike the gritty real world of high school."

"So touchy."

"So annoying."

Jaimes looks at me like I've stabbed her in the heart. One minute she's insulting me and the next she's offended. Girls are so weird.

"Whatever, I literally played soccer all summer and I can hardly feel my butt cheeks."

"Ew. Please don't put that image in my head."

"Butt cheeks, butt cheeks, butt cheeks!" I say, running circles around her because no one is more fun to annoy than Jaimes.

She gets even by driving our entire family to preseason camp, which is literally the scariest thing I've ever experienced.

"It's like driving a huge boat," Jaimes says, clutching the steering wheel, her knuckles dead white.

"I like the new car!" Roma says.

"It's actually a van," Whitney says. "It's so big we could live in it!"

"That'd be so fun with you guys," I deadpan.

Whitney and Roma clap their hands.

"I miss Dad's truck," I grumble.

"I miss Dad's truck too," Dad says.

The truck is still sitting in the driveway until Dad can recoordinate his legs and feet.

He's sitting next to me in the middle seat. There is a space next to him where Mom said his wheelchair will eventually go. Or not. I'm betting on the truck's comeback first.

Jaimes pulls into the parking lot. I exhale an exaggerated breath.

"Whew! We've lived another day."

"Your witty little comments aren't cool."

I ignore her and push up my hair—at this rate I almost need a headband.

Whitney and Roma jump out and run to the playground.

"Need help?" Mom asks Dad, poking her head into the backseat.

"Yep."

Mom grasps both of Dad's hands with hers. At the count of three she pulls as Dad steps out of the van, which is more of a slow slide, until both feet are on the ground. I look away and accidentally let out a sigh.

"Go ahead, Golden," Dad says. "Go warm up."

So I do. I leave them in the parking lot and jog to the field, feeling like a jerk for abandoning Dad and also that I can move and feel every one of my very-much-working sore muscles. I take deep breaths. For the first time in my life I don't want Dad here. I don't want Benny and my whole team to see him shuffling instead of sprinting like he was still capable of doing last season. I want them to see Dad like he was, in his triumphant comeback, not like this. But I couldn't tell him not to come.

Benny sees him first.

"Dragon-Ball P!" he shouts, running over.

The team turns. There's a second of hesitation before they bound over after Benny as Dad and Coach step onto the field.

Thankfully, Dad is able to slightly lift his right hand to high-five. *That's right, Dad. Show 'em what you got.*

During the warm-up, Dad sits on the sidelines under the shade of Roma's giant My Little Pony beach umbrella because Mom forgot the regular-sized one. Great.

"Hey," Benny says next to me. "Dragon-Ball P is here!"

"You like his umbrella?"

"Dude, it's awesome."

I seriously love Benny for this comment.

"He said we should hang out before school starts."

I nod slowly. Seeing Dad on the field is one thing. But Dad at home dropping stuff? Or having a nurse visit? All the meds on the windowsill, the accumulated clutter, piles of dirty laundry, lack of good food in the fridge because Mom and Dad can't seem to find time to grocery shop? Oh, and let's not forget the horror of all horrors: that I now share a room with Jaimes, who has recently been suggesting we paint the room a pastel yellow to match the whole "cool beach vibe" she has going on? Yeah, not on my life.

"I need to get out. With my brother at school I'm practically an only child living with Grandma and the parents," Benny continues. "Totally outnumbered."

"Grandma Ho!" I say. "Who's she hangin' with these days?"

He hesitates. "Grandma is slowing waaaaay down. She's old, you know?"

"Not that old!"

"Well, not too old to tell me the ancestors want me to work harder in school."

"School hasn't even started yet."

"That's what I said!"

This is what Grandma Ho does: brings the dead to the living. She says our ancestors are all around us—we're just too busy to notice. Lucy is particularly enchanted with the idea.

"I miss Grandma's food." I pat my stomach. "I've been starving all summer."

"I'd know that if you'd hang out with me." Benny doesn't look at me, but I can hear a change in his voice. My guilt springs back up.

"I . . . it's been kind of crazy lately, you know?"

"I'm cool with crazy," Benny says. "You know what's even crazier? I kind of miss the Squirrels!" He looks so shocked that I laugh out loud.

Coach interrupts. "Boys, should you be talking when I'm talking? No? Correct. Thank you very much."

"Sorry, Coach," we say together.

"Why is ball handling so important?" Coach asks. Ah, she's rusty. Coach knows better than to say "ball handling" in front of middle school boys.

Mario laughs so hard he trips over the ball and lands on his face, which makes most of the team erupt.

"Grow up," Sunny says, glaring at us. She probably wants to be captain too.

We start short passes, while every now and then Dad says things like "Nice move!" and "Good turn!"

My teammates beam with every compliment, and my own confidence soars with Dad on the sidelines.

"High knees!" Coach yells.

I bring my knees up high like my life depends on it so Dad will see this, too. And also because I know that if you want to be the best you have to train like the best. You can't slack off—not ever. And I need to show the team my effort. Brady and Benny are working hard. C.J.'s goofing off, which will work in my favor.

"Dude, chill," says Slick. "You look like a kangaroo on crack."

Slick, on the other hand, has a way of making you feel like crap no matter how hard you try.

I wipe my forehead and inhale a lungful of hot, thick air, but I keep going just as hard. The sun and humidity are double-teaming us today, and unfortunately, our field has no shade.

"Is Coach like this all season?" Hannah, a new seventh grader with a pink stripe in her hair, nervously whispers while we hold a low lunge.

"You haven't seen anything yet."

Hannah whimpers.

"Backward lunges!"

That's cruel, even for Coach. My quads are burning so bad I want to roll over and die. I clench my hands together, nails piercing the beds of my palms as I lunge.

I glance over at Dad, see that his eyes look misty. He wants to play again, I know it. He wants to move and sprint and pass. I know because it's exactly what I want. We're the same like that. Our eyes lock, and at that moment we make an unspoken deal: *You don't give up on me and I don't give up on you.* The energy shifts around me once more, adrenaline filling my whole body.

"I think I'm going to be sick," Hannah whispers, her knee dipping toward the grass.

"You can do it!" I whisper back, and she manages to hold the position a second longer.

"Water," Coach finally says, pointing to the bleachers. "One minute. Go."

Water. I'm desperately thirsty but realize I didn't bring any. There was a time Mom used to pack water and snacks for me. Now I'm like her wilted, forgotten house plants. *Pff.*

I walk to the water pump just as Slick pulls it up. The warm water shoots out, drenching my legs and socks and soaking my new Battle Packs.

He laughs and splashes me again, hoping I'll come after him. Instead I just stick my face under the water, letting it wash away the salty sweat even though it stings my eyes. The water is warm, but I gulp it down anyway because I'm going to need it for the only thing left: sprints.

I might not be the best ball handler, might not score the most goals, might be the team shrimp, but there is one thing I can do: RUN. When Coach calls us back, we get set to sprint to the six-yard line, the eighteen, the midline and back, and then—a full-field sprint to the end.

We take off, and Messi's words come to me: *You've got to fight! You have to work hard, sacrifice.*

My Battle Packs push me forward, the universe on my side.

Fight.

I run harder and faster.

I won't give up, Dad.

I pass Moses over and over. His cleats look about two sizes too big, forcing an awkward running gait that further slows him down. I feel bad, but I have to maintain my focus. I run until I'm in the lead, until I cross the finish line, until I see the look of pride on Dad's face. I keel over, fighting nausea and breathing harder than I have in my life.

From the ground I watch the rest of the team finish, the sun beating down mercilessly. As we try to recover, we watch uncomfortably as Archie, Ziggy, Moses, and Hannah slog it out to the finish line. Step after agonizing step. Slow. Painful. Coach glances at me. Her eyes go from me to my teammates and back to me again, hands on her hips.

"Yo, we could be here forever," Slick says under his breath.

In the periphery my eyes catch Dad. He looks

uncomfortably hot, and he has to sit in that stupid chair under that stupid umbrella until we rescue him. But all of a sudden I notice Dad is wiggling a little bit, like he's struggling to stand up on his own.

I sit up.

Come on, Dad! Do it.

I stand, staggering slightly from heat and fatigue, all my focus on him.

Dad fights harder, scooting forward in his chair.

I'm not sure how long it takes, but somehow Dad does it. He stands. He teeters forward, then back, before righting himself in a standing position. Sheer willpower.

"YES!" I say. "YES!"

I whirl back around to face the field, to face the last lone runners.

"Come on!" I yell. "Run! You can do it. Give it everything you've got!"

I keep on cheering until the last one, Archie, barrels over the white line. I stick my hand out to give him a high five and he grasps it, pulling me to the ground with his weight and falling on top of me. The wind gets knocked out of me. Can't. Breathe. I'm like a squashed bug under a tree.

"Thanks, Golden," Archie says above me, his face bright reddish purple.

I manage to squeak "No problem" from underneath him.

I Share a Room with My Sister

I am a member of a team, and I rely on the
team, I defer to it and sacrifice for it,
because the team, not the individual,
is the ultimate champion.
—SOCCER GREAT MIA HAMM

On the ride home Dad and I scheme about the best field combinations to win games.

Actually I scheme and he nods, eyes closed, head pressed against the headrest as he breathes in and out, deliberately filling and emptying his chest.

"You okay, Dad?"

"Hot."

"At least you weren't cold," I say helpfully.

"True. But that Mom. Tough coach."

I use my shirtsleeve to wipe the beads of sweat rolling down his face.

"Thanks," he says as Mom cranks the AC.

Is it my imagination or does his voice sound more robotic than a few hours ago?

"Spoke with Benny," Dad says, eyes still closed. "Invite him over. And Lucy. Friends are important. Right now especially."

Mom makes a tired noise, and I'm both annoyed and relieved. But maybe Dad's right. Benny saw him and didn't freak out. Maybe I can have him over, and Lucy, too, once she's back.

"I'll help . . . ," Dad says. "It's important to keep trying to . . . normal."

"I know," Mom says shortly, and he doesn't press it further.

When we get home I help Dad slowly make his way to the couch.

"Go shower, Mini-Messi," he says. "Stink."

So I do, then head to my room. Correction. What *used* to be my room.

Jaimes is sitting on *my* bed, writing in a notebook.

She has the nerve to say, "Can't you wear more than a towel when you walk in here?"

"Uh, this is *my* room and you're on *my* bed."

She puts in her earbuds and flops over so she can't hear or see me.

I loved having my own room.

I loved the quiet place where there were no flowery

bras hanging from the door handle, no long loud phone calls, no fussing over what time I wake up or go to bed.

Dad started building Jaimes her own room in the basement two years ago, when it became obvious she wasn't going to be able to last with the Squirrels, so it's supposedly temporary, but here she is, acting like she's never moving out.

The walls are up and the ceiling and flooring are in. Dad was going to hire an electrician to do all the wiring and then put on the finishing touches like baseboards and door handles this summer. Now he can barely lift a hammer. In fact, when's the last time I saw him carry anything heavier than a yogurt? But he's got to finish because my survival *depends* upon it.

The only good thing is that Jaimes gives me advice about girls and tells me what to wear. Which is kind of good, but also annoying. Like now.

"Not that," she says, unplugging her earbuds when I try on a pair of soccer shorts and a T-shirt for the first day of school. "It's eighth grade, not gym class!"

"It looks good!" I protest.

Then again, maybe Jaimes knows what she's talking about. All the girls in my class think Jaimes is super pretty and cool, though I don't get it. We both have Dad's wavy brown hair and brown eyes, but she rings hers in eyeliner. The very thought makes my eyes water and itch.

"Fine," I say. "Pick an outfit—but I get final veto power."

She jumps off the bed, glances out the window at Lucy's, and gives me a smug smile. "Got to dress to impress."

"Stop it."

She rummages through my drawer, finding some khaki pants I only wear to formal stuff.

"No."

"Yes. Think about what Dad would wear."

"A collared shirt every day?"

Jaimes smiles. "Exactly. And *all* the girls love Dad. My soccer team—dying." She tosses her hair as she leaves the room.

1. Gross.

2. I hate that she said "Dad" and "dying" in the same sentence.

She returns with one of Dad's shirts.

"No."

"Just try it on."

When I do, she insists we go show Dad. He's playing checkers with Whitney when I appear wearing his blue-checked-and-three-sizes-too-big-for-me shirt.

"Dad," I say in my bored, I-don't-care voice. "Jaimes said I should raid your closet and wear your shirt tomorrow."

"He should also wear a tie," she says unhelpfully.

"Yeah, so I can look like a complete dork."

Dad looks at Whitney. "Move the checker on your

right, diagonal one spot." This is how Dad plays most games recently—he does the mental work and we do the physical moving of the game piece. Another thing we need to work on.

He sizes me up. "It's true. You should dress more like me—but you have a few more years until you wear that particular shirt."

"Told ya," I tell Jaimes.

"I'm just saying that if you looked more like a gentleman maybe you'd *act* more like one and Lucy Littlehouse would love you." She folds her arms in her very annoying, superior way. "Oh, get wrecked, Goldie-Pants."

I feel my face turning red even though Jaimes is totally wrong.

I chase her around the room until Mom comes in and pulls me into a bear hug.

"You know," Jaimes continues, "some people say guys and girls can't be friends."

"Well, they're stupid."

"Stop teasing Golden, Jaimes," Mom says, hugging me tighter. "It would be a shame for you to ruin their friendship."

"As if she could!" I say, wriggling out of her grasp.

"Aha!" Dad says, eyes on the checkerboard. "Crown me, Whit!" He looks triumphant. "The muscles aren't working as well, but the mind is as sharp as ever."

Mom crosses the room and kisses Dad.

"Ew," we say.

"What?" Mom asks. "Someday you'll be glad your parents loved each other so much."

I take note of her mistaken use of the past tense and kick a couch cushion.

"Stephen Hawking lived with ALS for like fifty years," I say.

Everyone stops and turns to me.

"Uh, that was a non sequitur," Jaimes says.

"Stephen Hawking died," Whitney says.

Before I can retort, Mom smooths everything over with a "We'll take what we can get, won't we?"

Take what we can get? She's the one constantly telling us to *follow your dreams!* and *dream big!* And then when I do, I'm told to settle?

I go to *my* room, take off the ridiculous shirt, and juggle the soccer ball, working out the frustration. My family needs to try harder. Like fifty years harder.

And you know what? I get fifty-three juggles in a row! All-time high!

See, Mom, I say in my head, making a mark on my ten thousand hours chart.

Hard work and dreaming big give you all-time highs.

* * *

That night, before bed, Benny texts me.

Lucy back from Maine
yet?

Not yet

I peer out the window. There's a sign stuck in the grass out by the mailboxes, but I can't read it. I wonder if that strange woman with the deep voice who completely misjudged Curtis Meowfield's inner qualities put it there. Maybe she's a politician.

As soon as she's back then, Benny texts. Blueberry Island—don't forget!

How could I forget???

ur forgetting a lot of
things dude

huh???

He doesn't text back. What's he talking about? I'd never forget our back-to-school tradition. One night in August before school starts we always swim out to Blueberry Island just before the sun sets because once Lucy said the sun was setting on our summer and it was time to jump forward into fall.

So of course we can't go without Lucy.

I drift off to sleep dreaming of headlights pulling in next door, the sound of roller skates—and loud meowing.

Or maybe it isn't a dream, because in the morning? Lucy Littlehouse's car is in the driveway.

Roma Tries to Poison Me on the First Day of School

Have a good day, darlin' girl. Be kind, be brave,
and remember who loves you!

—GOLDEN (THE MORTIFYING THINGS I NOW HAVE TO SAY TO ROMA)

In the morning I gulp down a huge smoothie so quickly I almost don't notice it's a very strange blue.

When it hits my taste buds, I shudder. Gag. My stomach roils strangely. "Ack! That's . . ."

"I made it!" Roma says proudly. "Because I'm a helper like Mom said."

"What's in it?"

Her eyes light up. "Leftovers."

If this is Roma's way of helping out, I'm doomed to shrimp status forever—because I won't be eating.

Roma covers her mouth, giggling. "And it turned your teeth blue."

I look in the bathroom mirror. My eyes bug out. "Roma!"

I put my mouth under the sink and scrub my teeth with my finger.

"Lucy!" I hear Roma squeal. My heart beats faster and I scrub my teeth even harder.

"Hi, Roma! Is Golden here?"

"Yes, but his teeth are blue."

Lucy laughs. "An epic start to the year. Tell him I'll see him at school?"

"Aren't you going to school with us?" Roma asks.

"I'll take the bus with Benny."

I run out of the bathroom just in time to see her blond hair flying behind her as she skates outside, jumps off the stairs, and skates away.

I want to catch up to her and ride the bus, but I can't start eighth grade with blue teeth.

No, after years of being the minions, we are finally the Big Bad Bosses. Kings of the Castle. First graders will look at us in awe. Seventh graders will bow. We own the sole athletic field at recess. We make the morning announcements and generally know that finally, we're the coolest.

So I scrub my teeth, then grab my stuff quickly because I have to get to school.

And Jaimes is driving. So yeah, nothing is for certain.

"STOP," she says when I give her the *I'm terrified!* face as we get in the car.

"What?" I say innocently. "I said nothing!"

"Golden," Mom warns, stomping on her imaginary brake pedal in the passenger seat as Jaimes reverses. I could tell her: it doesn't work.

Roma grips my arm from the backseat until it goes numb.

With Jaimes at the wheel, it's probably a good thing Lucy didn't jump into the car pool like she always has before. She took the bus to school. I would know: I watched her roller-skate down the driveway before I could even say hi. And what else? She pulled out that sign in her yard and tossed it aside on the way. That politician lady must be bad news. I knew it!

Dad makes a weird swallowing sound.

I turn to him, buckled beside me in the backseat. "You okay?"

He swallows again. "Yep."

For the first day of school we woke extra early to pack snacks, to drink Roma's horrid smoothie, to make sure Dad's shirt was buttoned, tucked in, shoes tied. He doesn't say he's nervous, but I can tell by his eyes—he is. And it's the first time he hasn't driven us to the first day of school in his truck.

Dad uses his left arm to lift his right arm onto his lap, pinching the fingers on his left hand together, as if to make sure they're still working. I do the same. They are.

"Are you going to be able to hold the whiteboard markers, Dad? Or pass out papers?" Jaimes asks.

"Of course," I answer for him. Honestly, Jaimes's lack of confidence is super annoying.

When Jaimes rounds Cemetery Corner, the Squirrels and I hold our breath, as is the tradition.

There are A LOT of cemeteries all over Mudbury, but the one on Cemetery Corner, with Raymond Von Mousetrap's headstone, is the most visible from the road. Many others are hidden. Sometimes you'll be walking in the woods and come across a completely forgotten grave-yard and have to hold your breath extra quick.

"Breathe!" Jaimes says impatiently, looking in the rear-view mirror.

"Everyone knows what happens if you don't hold your breath when you pass a cemetery," Whitney says.

Roma loudly exhales. "The ghosts want to steal our souls! Lucy said."

It's true. And very Lucy.

Suddenly the breath is knocked out of me for another reason as our van swerves into the opposite lane, the back end of the big white boat fishtailing as we now face down another car. Jaimes screams. Mom screams. Roma and Whitney scream and dramatically crash into each other.

Then thankfully Jaimes quickly pulls us back into our lane.

"Jaimes!" Mom says, her voice rising. "You don't ever *ever* swerve into traffic like that—not for *anything*!"

"There was a squirrel!"

"I DON'T CARE! KILL THE SQUIRREL! DRIVE OVER IT! SMASH ITS GUTS ALL OVER THE ROAD, BUT YOU NEVER SWERVE! That's how teenagers die, and I cannot have you die. Do you understand me?"

"Rayna," Dad says quietly. "Let's . . ."

She silences him with a death glare.

Mom carefully composes herself by taking deep breaths and assuming what she calls her warrior pose. Chin up, shoulders back. When she speaks again her voice is lower. "You don't swerve into traffic for squirrels. You slow down and try to go around it if you can. *Never* swerve."

Jaimes clutches the steering wheel with white-knuck-led hands like she can't let go.

"We're supposed to hit the squirrel?" Roma whispers from the back.

"My butt is so sore," I announce, to change the subject.

"It's the lunges," Mom says, still forcing a calm voice.

"Seriously, though," Jaimes says. "Did I hit a squirrel?"

"Best lower-body exercise there is," Mom says. "Quads, hamstrings, glutes, and calves!"

"Is the squirrel dead?" Roma asks me, her eyes big with worry.

Whitney looks behind us. "I don't see any guts."

"My butt is so sore I probably won't be able to shoot the ball," I say louder.

"Dead!" Roma begins to cry. "Please don't be dead!"

"It's not dead," Dad says, breathing slowly in and out. "Roma, it's just fine."

We drive so slowly the rest of the way to school, I could have run faster.

But when we get to the school, Jaimes turns abruptly into the parking lot without signaling.

The Squirrels scream again.

"Jaimes!" Mom says.

"I'm doing my best!"

"I can't play soccer if *I'm* dead!" I yell.

My whole family glares at me.

Finally, our big white boat of a van comes to an abrupt halt in front of the main doors, and we all sag with relief.

"Thanks, Jaimes!" I say. "For barely letting us live another day."

"You're welcome, Blue Teeth Boy."

I resume scrubbing as Whitney, Roma, and I get out of the death car.

"You remember your cleats, shin guards, and clothes for practice?" Mom calls after me. I'm surprised she remembered to even ask. Of course, what she didn't remember is that . . .

"No practice today—remember? Dad's appointment?"

"Right!" She closes her eyes and touches her temple.

"Which is a bad idea the day before we vote on captain," I say.

"What do you want me to do?" she snaps.

"Golden?" Dad says quietly, interrupting. "Watch out for your sisters."

I look ahead to see Whitney being scooped up by her fifth-grade friends.

But Roma.

She's standing in the parking lot by herself. She smiles widely, showing her missing front teeth. Her hair is kind of a mess. I wonder if I should learn to, like, brush Roma's hair? *What am I saying? Why isn't Mom doing this? Why do I even have to think about it when I'm already the one helping Dad so much?*

"Say hi to Lucy," Jaimes loudly singsongs out the window, before honking the horn and peeling out. I hope she gets busted. I turn toward school, and Roma reaches for my hand.

"This was Daddy's job and now it's yours!"

"It's still Dad's job," I say. "He's just late to school."

"No. Now it's yours."

I decide not to argue with an irrational six-year-old.

Holding my hand with a python grip, Roma leads me past the yellow middle school buses loaded with my classmates, through the front doors, and all the way down the hallway.

But apparently I don't have to worry about my reputation.

I swear, every single girl who witnesses the two of us skipping down the halls starts smiling, hands to heart. For real. Roma is either really cute, or Jaimes was right about the collared shirt thing.

Roma's classroom walls have giant dinosaurs painted on them. For a brief moment I forget how awesome eighth grade is going to be. I want to be back in first grade, when worries were reading chapter books and getting a turn petting the class hedgehog.

"Now," Roma says. "Say what Daddy says."

"Um, bye, Squirrel."

"No! Say 'Have a good day, darlin' girl. Be kind, be brave, and remember who loves you!'"

"No." The mortification never ends.

"YES!"

Roma's face reminds me of Mom's on the soccer field. She's not letting this one go.

"*Fine.* Have a good day, darlin' girl," I say in my bored voice. "Be kind, be brave, and don't forget how stinky you are."

Roma puts her hands on her hips.

"Remember who loves you," I whisper.

"You do!" she yells. "Boy with blue teeth!"

When I turn around, Sunny and Sam are standing in the hallway, living heart-eye emojis.

"Soooooo cute!" Sunny says.

I close my eyes and groan. Of course my teammates were there.

But on the plus side, when I open my eyes, I finally see her: Lucy Littlehouse.

After a whole summer without her, she looks both exactly the same and totally different. The morning sunlight hits her blond braids, making them shine. She's wearing a longish blue jumper thing that makes her eyes even more blue, green sneakers, tinkling bracelets on her arm, and a huge smile on her face.

My whole entire body, including my brain, freezes.

What if we don't have anything to say to each other anymore?

What if she's forgotten that I'm her best friend? What if . . . ?

I'm completely immobile.

Be Messi cool! Speak! Move!

I wonder if this is how Dad feels. Your brain tells your muscles to work and they simply WILL NOT. She gets closer and closer. I manage a smile but, remembering my blue teeth, clamp my lips together.

Lucy ignores my awkwardness and throws her arms

around me as she whispers, "I have so much to tell you!"

"About what?" I say eagerly, relieved my vocal cords have started working again.

"The Dark Lord is rising," she whispers before Sunny and Sam whisk her down the middle school wing.

My eyes go wide, my insides shrink. The Dark Lord.

That can't be good.

I look after her, not even feeling the shank Mario gives me on the way to homeroom.

Mr. T is also wearing a collared shirt, but his looks like all the seams are going to burst at any minute to reveal a superhero suit. Around his neck is a multicolored scarf that only Mr. T can pull off—and get this: he crochets them himself with his six-year-old daughter! The man contains multitudes.

"Eighth graders," he booms. "This is the moment you've been waiting for. The bigwigs on campus. I'm looking at each one of you to step up."

I smile. Exactly. Mr. T gets it.

"Expectations," Mr. T continues. "No goofing around in the hallways, no slacking off in class. Also: no physicals and permission slips this week? No soccer, cross-country, or club participation. Got it?"

When Mr. T walks by, I can't help but hold out my

hand to high-five and say, "Yo, we got this, big-time bro, my T-man!"

Mr. T stops walking and does not give me a high five.

The whole class stops talking.

I slowly lift my eyes to Mr. T's.

Mr. T is not laughing.

Not smiling.

"Outside."

I follow him into the hallway. Slick pretends to slit his throat, and C.J. faux-chokes himself.

"Golden," Mr. T says. "Do you want to survive?"

"Uh . . . yes?"

"Am I your best buddy?"

"Uh . . . no?"

"Correct. I am your teacher. I am most definitely *not* 'big-time bro' or 'T-man' in the classroom."

His voice is so low and foreboding I'm pretty certain I'm about to be expelled, but then he sighs.

"You're going through some tough stuff right now."

I absently scratch my head.

"But I'm also guessing you don't want to be treated any differently than I've always treated you, which has always been pretty good. Correct?"

I nod.

"Right. So I'm going to suggest that you be respectful in the classroom."

"Sorry, Mr. T. I didn't mean . . ."

"I know."

We walk back into the classroom, my classmates pretending they didn't hear every single word.

I do the only thing I can: remember Rule #1. No tears. Play it cool. Pretend everything's chill. Like I don't care at all.

Lucy turns around and gives me a sympathetic look as I take my seat. I smile back.

"Golden," she whispers. "Your teeth are blue."

Perfect.

The Second-Worst News of My Life

It's not who starts the match; it's who finishes.
—THE ORIGINAL DRAGON-BALL G

It's unfortunate we don't have soccer practice, as I feel a great need to run a few miles and score a few hundred goals to get over the not-so-awesome start to the year. But this does mean I get to take the bus home with Lucy and Benny—and the legendary Mrs. Gagne, otherwise known as Gag Me.

Gag Me is our bus driver and lunch lady rolled into one terrifying curmudgeon. We've been scared of her since kindergarten, when she told us vacuum cleaners were invented for adults to vacuum up their misbehaving children. I've only recently gotten over this childhood phobia.

At four-eleven, she's tiny, and looks older than a shriveled apricot. She has really short wispy white hair that looks more like fur, and she keeps her nose scrunched up to keep her extra-thick glasses on and her snarl in place.

"Good afternoon, Mrs. Gagne!" Lucy says. She's never had any Gag Me fear.

"Ms. Littlehouse."

Benny and I just run to the back.

The three of us sit next to each other, all crammed into one bench like we always have. When Lucy moves, her earrings and bracelets remind me of wind chimes, and for the first time I notice she smells like lemons. Since when do I notice how Lucy *smells*?

"Goldie," Lucy says. "Are you going to talk to me or what?"

I turn to Benny. "Are my teeth still blue?"

"Yep."

Back to Lucy, I explain. "Roma poisoned me with an unknown-blue-ingredient smoothie this morning."

"Plant fertilizer is blue," Lucy offers far too cheerfully.

"Dude," Benny says, elbowing me. "Is that what's been making you so weird?"

"How was Maine, really?" I ask, changing the subject. I don't need to focus any more on how weird I am.

"Oh, it was glorious!" Lucy says, her eyes lighting up. "You should see the ocean—and the sand was so soft I could have slept on it. I already told Benny all about it this morning on the bus but I have shells for both of you and I'll take you swimming there someday because I swear you can see every sea creature imaginable."

I frown. It actually sounds like Lucy was happy to be away.

"But enough about that. How's Dragon-Ball P?" Lucy asks.

"Great!" I say. "Just at an appointment today. But wait, you said you had something to tell me—about the Dark Lord!"

Lucy twists her mouth around. "Oh, I don't want to talk about it right now. I want to talk about our swim. Did you go without me?"

"Golden said we couldn't," Benny says.

Lucy looks very pleased.

"And preseason!" Lucy says. "How was it?"

"Awesome."

"Hard," Benny moans, looking at me like I'm unhinged. "Coach is killer."

"Tomorrow's the captain's vote," I say, rubbing my hands together. My heart pounds hard.

"Who's going to be the boy captain?" Lucy asks.

Benny and I both pause before we each say the other's name.

"Competition!" Lucy says.

I flex my arm. "Whose bicep is bigger?"

"Oh, that's how it is?" Benny asks. He flexes his own arm as the bus comes to a jolting stop.

"Off!" Gag Me shouts.

"Want to . . . come over?" I ask before I can think too hard about it. The house *is* messy, but oh well.

"Duh." Benny smiles as we jump off the bus, and we do our handshake.

"I've been waiting all summer!" Lucy says, skipping ahead.

At the top of the hill, we're greeted by meowing.

"Oh, my sweet Curtis Meowfield!" Lucy says, scooping him up. Curtis stares at me, his paws protectively around Lucy's shoulder. "Thank you for feeding him when I was gone," she says. "Curtis tells me he enjoyed his time with you."

I pretend I want to pet him, but Curtis isn't falling for it and hisses at me. I jerk my hand back.

That's when a car passes us, honks, and turns into the driveway.

Lucy suddenly stops and frowns. "Oh."

"The Dark Lord has arrived," I joke. "During the *day*time!"

Benny elbows me, but he's trying not to laugh. The Dark Lord is what we call Lucy's mom's boyfriend because the only time we ever see him is when he comes over after work, in the dark.

Usually Lucy thinks the nickname is funny, but today she mumbles, "I'll be right back," before hurrying down the driveway and into the house.

At home I manage to find some not-too-old baby

carrots and crackers for Benny and me before we practice goals in my net outside. When Lucy still hasn't come out a half hour later, I jump quietly onto her front porch, tiptoeing to the window.

"What are you doing?" Benny whispers.

"The Dark Lord is never here at this time of day," I whisper back. "Something's up."

I peer in as Benny joins me. The three of them, Lucy, her mom, and the Dark Lord, are gathered around a computer.

"They're looking at . . . houses," I whisper. Though I can't see why, unless Lucy has developed some random new interest in real estate. Not that that would really surprise me when it comes to Lucy.

They scroll through images, and the adults talk in excited voices. I press my ear against the windowpane. I can hardly hear a word, until I finally make out "You'll love it."

Whatever Lucy says back, her voice sounds flat. Like she doesn't agree at all.

Then the Dark Lord says something that ends with "the Realtor."

I back away, confused.

"A Realtor *sells* houses," I say. "Lucy loves this house."

Benny keeps peering into the window. "The pictures of houses are in Maine," he says.

An entirely different state. Like, over a hundred miles away. Where that *glorious* ocean water and sand are.

It suddenly dawns on me that I might be an idiot.

"What?" Benny says, seeing my face.

"I don't think Lucy was on vacation this summer."

"Huh?"

"I think she might be . . . moving."

"What!" Benny says. "There's no way."

I run down the driveway as fast as I can, finding the sign that Lucy threw down this morning. It's not a campaign sign at all.

It's a FOR SALE sign.

I feel so sucker-punched that my eyes water. I swallow it down and march along the driveway, holding the sign up for Benny.

"Look!"

Benny's mouth drops open.

I chuck it as hard and as far as I can, into the woods.

I avoid Benny's eyes while I get mine under control and kick the soccer ball hard against the house.

Lucy moving is not actually a possibility. Like, at all.

She just got back! I barely survived without her.

The ball bounces off the house and hits me in the chest.

I fall to the ground, and this time I can't hide the tears that spring to my eyes.

I let Benny think it's the soccer hit that's hurt me so much.

Ten Thousand Touches

Ten thousand hours is the magic
number of greatness.

—MALCOLM GLADWELL

That night, I'm lying awake and thinking of last winter,
when Benny, Lucy, and I set up this elaborate soccer game
in Benny's house, rigging up some sweet goals out of
white plastic laundry baskets. Grandma Ho sat in her big
chair, drinking her tea, and refereed. She's totally biased,
but on that day, she correctly predicted that Lucy would
win the last three games we played.

Our soccer field was a really fancy flowery living room
rug. Benny's mom likes flowers and nice things and keeping her living room super clean. Shockingly, she doesn't
like soccer balls in the house hitting her nice things, but
Grandma Ho is more chill.

Mom used to be more like Benny's mom. Now she'd

hardly notice if we broke half the living room. I shouldn't mind, but I do.

Anyway, for our indoor soccer game, we only had a few rules: The ball had to stay on the ground. It could hit the couch as a bounce-back pass, but no walls, television, or windows. I was up by one point and was just pulling my leg back to kick another goal when Mrs. Ho appeared in the doorway. She shrieked, and I fell right in front of the goal without even scoring.

Benny, Lucy, and I laughed about that for a long time. So did Grandma Ho. Lucy and I walked home together, our shoulders touching until we were racing each other up the hill.

If Lucy moves, we won't ever race up that hill again. It's funny how you can miss someone who's still here. Kind of like Dad.

Stop it. Dad's not going anywhere.

My thoughts are interrupted by the now-usual sound of Mom helping Dad to the bathroom.

I look at the clock: 5:32 a.m.

I slept terribly, dark dreams swirling, memories cycling every time I woke. My head hurts.

Lucy can't leave.

The Dark Lord is trying to ruin our lives.

My arm is hurting from being slung over my Argentina

World Cup soccer ball, now slightly wet from my drool. I wipe my mouth and sit up.

The whole house is quiet again. I look to the window, to where the sun is coming up, slowly lighting up my whole room. Minus Jaimes's nasal snoring sounds, it's a super-cool way to wake up. If I pause to watch them, I can see the puffy white clouds move quickly across blue sky. Lucy used to say the cloud dragons will send us secret messages if we watch carefully enough. But now the world is spinning and I can't even focus on the clouds.

Dude, why don't we just ask her? Benny said yesterday.

But I brushed him off. Lucy would have told us if she was moving.

Wouldn't she?

I turn my head toward Lucy's window. Her shades are still drawn. The Kermit the Frog lunch box hangs on the pulley. Very carefully and quietly, I write a note and put it in Kermit, then pull the rope until the lunch box is just outside Lucy's window. I pull hard three times so Kermit hits her window, hoping she'll wake up and see it.

My thoughts are interrupted by heavy breathing. I look down.

Dad.

He's standing next to an old Adirondack chair, his hand pressing down for support. At his feet is a soccer ball. He brings his right foot up, trying to tap the ball. He tries over and over, breathing deep breaths, but mostly missing. This small movement is something he taught me before kindergarten. It's a basic ball touch. Something he mastered when *he* was in kindergarten. Something that's now getting harder.

Come on, Dad.

You don't give up on me and I don't give up on you.

He lifts his foot once more, but it falls to the ground without even touching the ball and doesn't come back up. My heart sinks with it.

He stops to breathe, tired.

I turn away, tripping over my soccer ball, and fall on the Sleeping Beast.

Jaimes opens one eye and aggressively bares her teeth. "Golden, *STOP!*"

I have this uncontrollable urge to laugh. Which of course makes Jaimes even angrier. She covers her head with her pillow and says something I can't repeat. I ignore her and retrieve the ball, juggling with my knees to muffle the sound of Dad losing control of the thing he most loves to do.

"Golden, the sun is barely up!"

"Ten thousand touches," I tell Jaimes. "Just wait. Soon I'm going to eclipse even you." She opens her eyes to glare at me.

"Get wrecked," I say.

Just as I knew she would, Jaimes flings off the covers, grabs her blue Adidas World Cup ball from under the bed, and begins juggling beside me.

We have soccer balls rolling around every room of the house. Everyone plays—even Roma's on a team. Playing soccer is practically our family's mission statement. And every soccer touch counts for something. It's hard to say how many touches, seconds, minutes, or hours I've really logged touching the soccer ball in my life, maybe closer to ten thousand than I think.

I'm only on touch seven when the ball bounces too hard off my left ankle, hits the window frame, and falls to the ground.

"I win," Jaimes says. "*You* get wrecked, Goldie. I'm taking a shower. A long one."

I examine the window frame. Only a tiny chip of paint is missing from my most recent hit. But hey, if you value boring, unchipped doorframes and sloppy ball control, by all means, keep the soccer ball outside or sitting neglected in the garage for nine months out of the year. From first-hand experience I know that until you master the ball, it has to roll across kitchen floors, hit walls, windows, cupboards, your little Squirrel sisters—and your snarling older one, too. The ball flies off your knees and hits telephones, breaks dishes, and busts windowpanes until you can control it from ever hitting anything you don't want it to again.

That's the price you pay for greatness.

I start getting ready for school and glance out the window again. Dad's slowly making his way into the house. But he's no longer alone.

"Hi, Lucy Goose!"

"Hi, Coach Maroni!" Dad and Mom traded off coaching us before we got to the middle school team, so most of my friends still call him Coach too. Lucy's wearing her roller skates with her pajamas, hair still in braids. Lucy greeted him with her normal, super-cheerful voice. But did she notice how hard it was for him to move? To get up the stairs?

She must have because I watch her hold out her arm, like it doesn't freak her out at all, and Dad leans on her to get back inside.

What's really unfair is that Dad put in his ten thousand hours. I've seen the footage from his pro days, studied him as Coach. He had mastered it. Now, as I watch him shuffling inside, I wonder what it feels like to have put in your ten thousand hours only to go backward in time and have to start all over.

But . . . even the greatest of all time have temporary setbacks. I mean, Messi *retired* after that devastating 2016 World Cup elimination. Of course he couldn't stay away—not when he loved the game so much. So look who's back on the field dominating? That's right! Our man Messi!

You know what he says? *You can overcome anything, if and only if you love something enough.* I love soccer that much. Dad does too. That love and determination are going to save both of us.

Running downstairs, I wait until Lucy skates in to pull a Maradona move on Mom, who is standing in front of the microwave, wearing her bathrobe. I accidentally bump into her while turning.

"Bend your knees," she says irritably. Mom is so not a morning person.

"Push-up contest," I say to Lucy, dropping to the ground. "Bigger stronger faster," I say between breaths.

"You're lucky I've got to catch the bus or you'd be losing right now," Lucy says. "I'll take you on at practice— see you there—for the captain's vote!"

A thrill goes through my body. *Captain. The armband.*

"That's right . . . today!"

"You didn't forget *that*, did you?"

Now she sounds like Benny. What exactly do they think I'm forgetting?

Lucy skates out of the kitchen and across our porch and jumps smoothly onto the driveway before I can ask.

"Check Kermit!" I yell after her.

"Honey?" Mom says, putting her hand on my shoulder. "Even if today doesn't go the way—"

"Mom! You don't have to protect me. I'm fine."

"Golden?" Dad calls from the bathroom, distracting us. "I really need a shave."

I wriggle away from Mom and walk in to see Dad's left hand slightly raised, holding his razor.

"Me?"

"I'll show you how. Good for you to learn anyway. Get my face wet?"

"Dad . . ." I really don't want to do this, not after the toenails. I want to just sit here and tell him about my Lucy suspicions, but instead I say, "I saw you practicing this morning."

"Golden, shave."

"Dad . . . I don't think . . ."

"It's very simple."

"If it's that simple, then how come you don't do it?"

"Five minutes!" Mom calls. "Where's my purse?"

"Get my face wet. Put on shaving cream," he says impatiently. "We don't have much time."

I do, but tentatively.

"Yep. Now razor."

"Dad—"

"Put the razor on my face. Swipe down slowly . . . slowly! You don't need to go against the grain. Go *with* the hair. Good."

Pretty soon I'm doing it—shaving him. "So, Dad. Your touch is looking . . . okay," I begin again. "Let's play after practice—and we can lift weights, too."

Dad sighs like I'm not listening, even though I am. "Son, let's focus on this. Me and you. Right now."

I accidentally nick his chin.

"Let's go," Mom calls.

"Sorry!" I wipe the little bead of blood off and finish quickly. Then I pat down our hair, pushing it up in front. A little water. A little gel.

"Very Messi-like," he says, grinning.

I want to race Dad to the car like we used to, but instead we walk super slowly. It gives me time to think about all the jumbled-up stuff going on in my brain.

I want to think about soccer, but instead it's Maine and stupid new houses and razors and *right now*.

All the things that *almost* made me forget that today is a very important day.

Step one in my master plan—the captain's vote.

A Hero Will Rise

There's no one I believe in
more than you, Golden.

—LUCY LITTLEHOUSE

A few hours later Mr. Mann smiles widely while introducing the first science unit: Human Reproduction.

Mortifying.

I duck my head, pretending to take very detailed notes, but that's even worse.

"That's right, my young friends, by the end of the term you'll know exactly where babies come from. No longer will you have to rely on the knowledge of your friends and bus mates to incorrectly educate you," Mr. Mann says.

Oscar falls out of his chair, laughing.

"Let's show some maturity," Mr. Mann says.

"Sorry," Oscar says. "My mom says I'm impulsive because of my undeveloped frontal lobe. I'll eventually grow into it."

"Let us hope," Mr. Mann says wryly.

Lucy, Benny, and I are sitting in a row like we always do. "The Three Musketeers" is what Mr. Mann said when we came to class together. *But for how long?* When the bell finally rings and we're able to pack up, Lucy tries to talk to me about the captain's vote, but it sounds like gibberish and my eyes won't focus. All I can think of is *not* talking about moving and *wanting* to talk about not moving at the same time.

I walk through the lunch line in a daze as Gag Me doles out a spoonful of overcooked beets.

"No thanks."

"You take it, you eat it!"

"But—"

"Next!"

Grimacing, I sit down next to Benny, saving a place for Lucy.

"What's wrong?" Benny asks.

"Look at my lunch."

"Peanut butter and jelly?" he offers, handing me half of his sandwich. I'm grateful but I can hardly take a bite.

"What else is up?"

I shake my head.

"Fine, then. Keep your secrets to yourself like you have all summer."

"I did not!"

"Tell me, then!"

I open my mouth and close it.

"Whatever," Benny says. "I'll just go hang with Brady then, if we're not gonna talk."

"Okay, fine," I burst out. "Today is the captain's vote and I'm trying to focus on soccer, but I can't stop thinking of how the Dark Lord is planning an evil takeover."

"So let's just ask her," Benny says.

"Tell her we were spying through her window? Uh, super creepy."

"True," Benny says. "Still. It's not like Lucy wouldn't tell us." He pauses. "Let's say you're right and she is moving. What are we going to do?"

Lucy and Ziggy arrive at the table at the same time, and Ziggy quickly squeezes next to me in the space I was saving for her.

"Hi, Golden," Ziggy says. "Who are you voting for today?"

"Benny," I say. "You?"

"You or Benny." I swallow soft boiled beets, feeling slightly hopeful.

Lucy and Sunny start talking about summer and how Lucy got such a great tan.

"Maine was amazing," Lucy says. "We were at the beach almost every day."

"*We?*" I interrupt. "As in you and *the Dark Lord*?!"

Lucy laughs. "He's actually not that bad."

"Do you hear this? We gotta keep her from going to the dark side," I whisper to Benny.

"But, dude," Benny breathes. "The Dark Lord is almost like her *dad*."

"He's not!" I say just a little too loudly.

"Lovers' quarrel?" Slick cackles, flicking my ear as he passes.

"Shut up, Slick," Benny says, halfway rising in his chair.

The lunchroom pauses. Slick glances at Benny and shrinks away.

See that? That's the power Benny has that I don't.

The aroma of warm, soggy beets rises as the chatter resumes, offending my sense of smell.

I take a bite of the peanut butter sandwich.

"So what do we do?"

"I don't know yet. But something," I say, determined.

Even though we're dealing with a seriously ginormous problem, I'm feeling slightly calmer. Benny and I are on the same side.

We just have to make sure Lucy is too.

When the final bell rings, we're out the door and on the field in about five seconds.

"Hi, Coach," Benny says when she arrives. "We voting today?"

"Today is the day!"

I start clapping my hands, get out the ball bags for the drills, lay down cones with C.J. and Sunny, move the benches with Benny and Paige, find the pinnies and hand them out for the scrimmage. Today, because it's the captain's vote, everyone is being a little nicer, a little more helpful.

I try not to think about it, about the fact that my entire season plan rests on the outcome of this vote. I try to never stop moving even though Slick calls me a tryhard about five times and I can hear Brady asking Chase to vote for him and Sunny telling Hannah and Savannah that Lucy would be the best captain even though she missed preseason. I keep moving, and with each movement, the worry melts away a little more until I'm in the zone. Me and soccer, just like it's always been meant to be.

At the end of practice, when we run sprints, I run hard, leaving worry behind. I run so hard and so fast, I'm in my own personal pain cave by the end.

"That's right!" Coach is saying as we near the end. "A championship season starts right here and right now."

Chase and I run neck and neck, neither one willing to be second, reaching the end line at the same time, collapsing on the sideline.

It's all good until Chase starts wheezing.

"Where's your inhaler?" I ask quickly.

He shakes his head.

"You forgot it? How can you forget something that makes you *breathe*?"

Benny crosses the finish line next.

"Dude, help!" I say. "Asthma attack!"

"Inhaler?"

"He forgot it."

Chase puts his hands on his knees, inhaling like he can't get enough air, his lungs desperate for oxygen.

"He's fine," Benny says, but his voice is way less certain than his words. "He's always fine."

"He doesn't sound fine. He sounds like he's . . . suffocating." I choke out the word.

Suffocation. That's how most ALS patients die. I looked it up once and I wish I hadn't. It's a fact I never allow myself to think of, but suddenly it's right in front of my face. You slowly suffocate to death because the diaphragm is a muscle. And the neurons that tell the phrenic nerve, which tells the diaphragm to rise and fall, will suddenly stop working. The diaphragm is what lets the lungs fill with oxygen and push out carbon dioxide. If the lungs don't do this, you don't breathe. If you don't breathe, oxygen can't circulate to the cells in your muscles. You will gasp for air until—

It's a good thing Chase starts breathing again because I'm about to hyperventilate myself. He suddenly stands upright again and pounds on his chest, willing his lungs to work.

"See?" Benny says, shaking me back to life.

Chase claps me on the shoulder. "See?" Like I'm the one who was just about to die.

We face the field, and I feel my heart continuing to race. I focus on the grass and breathe in, breathe out. The diaphragm, the lungs, the heart. Still working. I have to chill. Captains can't freak out over stuff like that. I look up just as Moses trips.

Ziggy looks like he's dragging his feet behind him, not even trying. Archie is trying so hard he's sweating through his shirt, breathing practically as hard as Chase was, like he wants to go faster, he just can't. His face is bright red from effort and the blistering heat.

They're the last three on the field.

"Sucks to be last," I mumble.

"That's 'cause *they* suck," Slick says, laughing.

"No . . . ," I say. "It's like their feet or their ankles or their body or something—they just can't run as fast. At least they're trying."

"What did you say?" Slick asks.

"I said . . . they're trying!"

Anger prompts me to do something I've never done before: I step off the white sideline.

I take another step, my Battle Packs propelling me forward even though my legs are toast.

I start jogging. At first I don't even know where I'm going. I just have to get off the line.

"What's Tiny Tot doing?" I hear Slick say.

"He's . . . running," Lucy says.

I jog until I reach Moses, Ziggy, and Archie.

"Finish!" I say to the guys. "Come on!"

I turn and face the team as I jog with them, wanting to shrink into the grass and disappear. I hate being last. Like really, really hate being last. But I don't shrink. I raise my chin and face the line.

You know what happens next?

Benny steps off the line.

Followed by Lucy. She starts skipping, then running.

It's a domino effect. One by one, the whole team begins running too. Even Slick.

As we run I get another idea: I start a slow clap.

It too has a domino effect. Suddenly everyone is clapping with me, gradually getting faster and faster.

We don't stop clapping until every single one of us is all the way back to the sideline.

Coach blows her whistle. It drops from her mouth.

Her eyes meet mine.

"That," she says, "was . . . very cool."

* * *

After one last water break, Coach hands out little slips of white paper that I tore in half last night, along with every pen I could find. Everyone writes two names: one boy and one girl. My hand is so shaky and clammy I can hardly spell or think.

I hesitate. Would it be so bad to vote for myself? I decide it would, so I hastily write, *Benny*. And *Lucy*, of course.

After, we sit on the grass, fidgeting, waiting while Coach counts the votes. I grab handfuls of grass to hold still.

Parents are starting to arrive. I see Mrs. Ho pull into the parking lot, followed by . . . the Dark Lord. He's *never* picked Lucy up. Why's he always around now? My eyes narrow. Benny elbows me.

"Subtlety," he says, "is the way of the spy."

"Bring it in!" Coach says.

I clench my hands. The anticipation makes my toes curl up like Dad's left hand.

Slick taps the ground impatiently. Even Benny looks nervous.

"Team," Coach says. "You have voted for your two cocaptains."

I brace myself to hear "Benny" and "Sunny."

Or "Lucy."

"Congratulations . . . ," Coach says, "Lucy Littlehouse."

Lucy looks surprised as we clap—and super happy. I whoop.

"And your second captain is . . . Golden Maroni."

For a half second the world stops spinning. I look around. Is this really happening?

I'm not the only one who's shocked.

Slick raises his eyebrows sky-high.

But then Archie lets out a war cry that kind of sounds like "Macaroni!"

Ziggy plays air guitar.

Benny lifts me off the ground and shakes me.

And I can tell Mom's excited but trying to be professional.

It feels unreal, even as the team claps and gathers around.

Captain. The armband.

My eyes find Lucy's. *Cocaptains.*

We grin and high-five like ten times.

Dad. I can't wait to tell Dad.

It's like the universe is responding to everything I've ever wanted. Telling me my plan is going to work. That anything is possible.

You don't give up on me and I don't give up on you.

It's, like, the greatest moment of my life.

I'm Your Captain Now

Everyone sit down. I run this show.

—MESSI DIDN'T SAY THIS. BUT THERE'S A GREAT MEME OF HIM SAYING IT.

The next day, in the boys' bathroom at Mudbury Middle, I push up my hair all Messi-like, but it's so long it falls back in my eyes.

I grin at myself in the mirror anyway, reliving the greatest moment ever, over and over.

Benny was a shoo-in. Then again, this summer I spent more time with my soccer ball than I did with humans. Compared to Benny, it feels like I've always had to work so much harder to be almost as good, but maybe those ten thousand touches are finally starting to pay off. And deep down inside, I kind of feel like I deserve it. Yeah, life has thrown some suckiness at me, but I didn't give up. And look what happened? A dream came true.

A Messiquake has exploded into my heart.

I can't ever be unhappy again.

I flex my bicep, where the captain's band will live.

Brady comes into the bathroom, and I put my arm down and hastily clear my throat.

"Hey," I say with as deep a voice as possible.

"What's up." He nods.

I escape the bathroom and walk down the middle school wing, so busy living my best life I almost don't see Lucy standing next to my locker until I'm right in front of her.

"Hey, Captain," she says.

"Hey, Captain," I say back.

We fist-bump, and her eyes light up with excitement.

"Golden, we're going to be the best team in the world. And the best captains."

"For real."

My heart beats a little faster. If Lucy is excited to be captain, she can't be moving, right?

"What's the matter?"

"Nothing, let's get to class!" I say, taking off in that direction.

"Dude, congratulations," Mario says, fist-bumping us when we walk in.

Benny and I do our handshake before sitting down. I can't tell if he's disappointed he wasn't elected captain or not, but he acts happy for me anyway, and that's what makes him such a good friend.

I've never been the most popular kid in school before, though I have enjoyed some notoriety. Like, my mom and dad have made our town a soccer hub. They're the former soccer stars who settled down to live out their dreams in the super-small town of Mudbury (personally I don't get it—Mudbury versus pro soccer? It's not even close). They're credited with producing some of the best high school and college soccer players in the state. It's cool to be the kid of parents like that, but even that became over-shadowed with "the diagnosis." Now, for the first time in over a year, I'm "captain" instead of "that poor kid whose dad has ALS."

Being captain? It's what life is *supposed* to be like.

"And now, class," Mr. Mann says, "let's talk about ovaries and sperm."

Unfortunately, middle school has a way of bringing you back down to earth.

"Hey, Captain!" C.J. tackles me on the soccer field that afternoon. After the enlightening egg-and-sperm lesson, I bolted out of the classroom, beyond ready for my first practice as captain.

And now I'm eating dirt, sandwiched by C.J., Chase, and Brady.

"Get off," I say, struggling beneath them. I definitely need to add more push-ups to my workout. More bench-pressing, too.

"Well, isn't this sweet," a voice above us says.

One inch from my nose is a familiar pair of worn-out cleats.

"Hey, Coach!" C.J. says loudly in my ear as the boys scramble off me.

"You aren't hurting my baby boy, are you?"

"No way, Coach!" Chase holds out his hand and hauls me up, patting me too hard on the back. "Love this guy. Captain."

"I'm too jacked to get hurt," I say, flashing my abs. "Punch me right here."

"Or you could warm up," Coach says.

"Yes, Coach!"

C.J. puts on his gloves and heads to the net while the rest of the team gets ready to take shots.

I scowl.

"Baby boy?" I say to Coach. "A captain doesn't need *his mom* to rescue him."

"Well then, he doesn't need his mom to lead warm-up, either, right?"

"What? Oh! What should I do?"

"Figure it out—*Captain.*"

Lucy and I stand in the middle of the field, while our

team is in complete chaos. Few of us are actually ready to go. Some of our teammates are still on the bleachers, slowly lacing up their cleats. Others are taking wild shots on goal, while most mill around doing nothing. Mario kicks Brady's soccer ball over the fence. Coach looks at Lucy and me like *Get this under control.*

"Okay, team," I say.

"Golden, you gotta command their attention," Lucy says, standing on her tiptoes and holding out her arms. "Ladies and gentlemen, lend me your ears!" The team quiets and stares at us.

"See?" Lucy says. "Your turn."

My mind is blank. Warm up. Warm up. How do we warm up?

Coach taps her foot on the ball.

"Oh yeah," I say. "Dribble, right foot."

"What did he say?" half the team asks as the other half starts dribbling.

"DRIBBLE!" I yell to the rest of them.

Dribbling is followed by dynamic stretches, followed by lunges. It's something I've seen Coach instruct a hundred times—because Coach loves all forms of torture.

"Nice, Ava!" Lucy says.

I try to remember coaching tips I've heard Mom and Dad say.

"Uh, get your knee down," I yell at Mari.

"I *am*, Goldie!"

"Nice effort, Moses!" Lucy calls out.

"Don't put your knee on the *ground*," I tell Slick. He rolls his eyes at me.

"Fine. Everyone hold the lunge until Slick does it right," I say.

The team holds the position and yells at Slick. He sends me hate daggers with his eyes.

"I'm dying," C.J. says. "Seriously, hurry up, Golden." My quads are burning too, but I'm the captain. I can't show pain. Also, why does he say *I'm dying*? I want to say, Dude, no you're *not*.

That's usually the end of our warm-up, but I decide to add leg lifts and crunches.

"I think that's good, Golden," Lucy says, but we can't just be good. I want us to be great.

"Plank challenge!" I yell. After a solid three minutes, the entire team is practically crying, and Coach taps her watch.

"Get a drink," I pant.

"That was the worst," Brady mutters.

Once we've rehydrated, Coach takes over. How does she get everyone to listen without raising her voice? Each drill reveals our talent and skill, but also our weak spots. We have a *lot* of work to do.

At the end, Lucy and I divide the team up for the

scrimmage, which is hard because everyone fights about who they want on their side. We argue until we hardly have any time to scrimmage at all. After just a few minutes, Coach wearily calls out, "Golden Goal time!"

With one minute left, we're tied. I see my opportunity to be *the man.*

The Golden Goal is the last goal, the best one, the shot everyone wants. I've always secretly thought that was why I was named Golden—because my parents love soccer *that* much.

"Ball!" I yell. Hannah passes to me. Instead of passing it to Benny up the field, though, I keep dribbling.

Mario comes at me.

"Pass!" Benny yells. I hear other voices shouting the same thing.

But I don't. I keep the ball ready to score. I've GOT this. To make it look really good, I flick the ball up for a header. The ball goes up, but instead of heading the ball in, I collide with Mario right in front of the net. My hair is so long in front that I can't see for a second, which allows Mario to intercept the ball and pass to Lucy.

Lucy dribbles and passes the ball to Sunny, who scores on C.J.

Ugh.

"Golden! Pass!" Coach calls, frustrated. And she's not the only one.

"Geez, Captain," someone says. This time it's sarcastic. "Show-off."

"Dude, I was open," Benny says, looking hurt.

"I thought I had it," I say. But everyone just shakes their head. Except Lucy and Sunny, who are high-fiving their team's victory.

Thankfully Coach has us run sprints to finish the day, so I don't have to keep talking about this. I run my heart out, making sure I finish first or second, to make up for my mistake.

"Don't forget your fat little friend and Goat Boy out there, suck-up," Slick says, crossing the finish line and falling to the ground.

I look at Moses and Ziggy, who, as usual, will finish almost last.

Except for Archie. Once they cross, he's totally alone on the field, huffing and puffing. Not giving up.

Wearily, I step off the line.

"Don't even think about it," Slick says. "If you keep running back that means we all have to run too."

I hesitate and take a step back until Lucy looks at me.

"We go back for those left behind—*don't we*, Golden?"

"Yeah," I say. "Of course."

"*Don't we, Golden?*" Slick mimics.

"Be quiet, Slick."

"*Be quiet, Slick.*"

We run until Archie crosses the line. "Thanks, you guys," he says. "I'm sorry I'm so slow."

"Don't be sorry, Archie," Lucy says, but she's looking directly at me.

When we get to the huddle Coach raises her hand in the air, holding a pack of gum.

"MVP of the day. Awarded at the end of each practice for the best effort and hustle."

"Archie!" C.J. says, patting him on the shoulders.

"Archie!" the team yells, applauding.

Archie's whole face beams like he's won the World Cup.

"Listen up," Coach says. "In a week we have our first game against Merrimack Middle School."

Merrimack!

I realize that's only four practices before we take on our biggest rival and toughest team in the league. In game one.

"Come back tomorrow ready to work hard again," Coach says. "Sleep, vegetables, and positive self-talk. And . . . I hereby decree the no-sugar challenge! I want you all to steer clear of sugar until the end of the season, but especially before practices and games."

There is an audible gasp.

"Does Powerade count?" Ziggy asks.

"Archie?" Coach says over the objections. "Final cheer?"

"One, two, three, Magpies!"

After the cheer everyone starts to disperse, including me.

"Captains?" Coach says. Lucy and I stop and turn. Coach nods toward the field, at all the scattered cones and loose balls.

Oh. Right. You'd think the captains would be the ones who *wouldn't* have to clean up.

"Guys, come help!" Lucy yells.

But it's too late—everyone has wandered away. They're all getting in cars to go home.

Lucy and I look at each other, then spend the next fifteen minutes cleaning up and hauling the ball bags into the shed.

Besides the armband, which I don't even wear in practices, why did I even want this job? What's so great about it? Picking up cones and balls and getting yelled at for not doing it right? No one's even listening to me. I realize I have no idea what a captain is really supposed to act like.

I look down at my Battle Packs, wondering what the great Messi wants me to do now.

Lucy and I Make a Plan

Where there's a will, there's a freakin' way.
Am I right?
—GOLDEN MARONI

"Can I catch a ride?" Lucy asks after practice. She looks uncertain. She used to ride home with us every day, but this year she's been going home with Benny. She probably doesn't want to ride in a big white whale.

"Lucy!" Roma screams when she gets in the van. Roma and Whitney hang out on the sidelines during our practices, since Dad has either physical therapy or his own practice to run.

"Can you ride home with us every day?" Whitney asks, snuggling up to Lucy in the backseat.

Lucy shrugs. "I'm not supposed . . . to bother you guys."

"Lucy!" Coach-who's-slowly-de-Hulking-back-into-Mom says. "You're never bothering us. In fact, I'll be insulted if you don't ride with us every day from now on—and that includes going to school."

"I'll be insulted too," I say. Lucy grins.

"What about when we have a wheelchair?" Whitney says.

"*Pfff*," I say. "*If* we have a wheelchair."

"We'll make room!" Mom says, like I didn't say anything. "It's going to arrive soon—just so we can get used to the idea."

I look out the window.

"You're sweaty," Whitney says to Lucy.

"Duh," I say. "Athletes sweat."

"I probably smell, too," Lucy says.

"We still like you," Whitney says.

"Did you do better than Golden?" Roma asks, looking up at Lucy adoringly.

"Of course," Lucy says. "He can't get past my mad skills."

"What!" I say.

"You should ride home with us more often," Mom says. "Keep Golden humble."

"Can you eat dinner with us?" Roma asks.

"Yes!" Mom says. "Golden's my sous-chef tonight."

"Again?" I groan.

"Read the chore chart," Whitney says.

"I'll help," Lucy says. "My mom isn't home until late anyway."

"What about the Dark Lord?" I ask.

"Golden," Mom says. "I want you to stop calling him that. His name is George."

Georgie Porgie I don't really care what his name is.

Mom smiles at Lucy. "You have to stay for dinner. It's been too long without Lucy Littlehouse in the Maroni house."

"It's my favorite house in the whole world," Lucy says. "Like, for real."

I try to imagine dinner. She's seen Dad a little, but not much since June. He can barely raise his fork now. What if I have to help feed him? We pull into the driveway, and now my palms start to sweat.

Lucy elbows me. "What's wrong?"

"Maybe you don't want to eat with us," I say before Lucy comes into the house. "I mean . . ."

"Don't be an idiot," she says, walking right past me into the kitchen.

Mom says she's just supervising, so Lucy and I decide on tuna fish casserole for dinner, since the only other thing I'm good at is cereal. But Mom hasn't had time to go to the store for a while.

"Can we borrow a can of tuna fish from your house?" I ask.

"Race ya!" Lucy calls, taking off, and I jump up and race her to her front porch, crashing into the front door.

A new wreath falls off and onto the ground.

"Oh, shoot!" Lucy quickly hangs it back up, patting it nervously like it's fragile. "Stay here. I'll grab the tuna fish."

"Now I'm not allowed inside?" I joke as she opens the door.

But by the look on Lucy's face, I wonder if it's not a joke. "Wait, for real?"

"No, it's just . . ." Lucy sighs. "Come in, but take off your shoes and don't touch anything or they'll freak."

I stop abruptly as soon as we enter. "Whoa. It's like super clean—like museum clean."

"Yeah . . . we've been purging."

"You purged the cool elephant lamp?"

"Mom did."

Lucy tiptoes across the kitchen floor in her bright pink soccer socks and opens the cupboard.

I look around, my eyes settling on a business card and brochure on the counter. I pick them up and slowly read a name out loud: "Myra Martin, Realtor." The lady with the silver hair and car. Of course. I knew it, but my stomach still sinks.

Lucy slaps them both back down on the counter, covering a smiling Myra's face.

We stare at each other in a terrible silence.

Lucy twists her mouth around as if thinking carefully. "I got your note in Kermit," she finally says. "'Which is better: Mudbury or Maine? Circle your answer.' Seriously, Golden?"

"I was just wondering."

"You could have just asked me."

"You can just tell me."

"I like them both in different ways."

"Okay . . . are you moving to Maine?"

It comes out as an accusation.

A look crosses her face, like she's going to either laugh or cry. What if she cries? Please don't cry. I take a tiny step back.

"I saw you looking at houses," I say. "Through the window. I've even met *Myra*—and I *saw* you pull up the For Sale sign."

"We can't find that sign anymore," Lucy says, getting out the tuna fish. "Do you think *that's* a sign? That we're not really going to move?"

"I threw it really far into the woods," I say.

A smile spreads across her whole face and she begins laughing.

"Lucy, it's not for real, right?"

She waves her hand, grabbing the tuna with the other, but there's worry in her eyes. "My mom is just . . . Love makes you crazy. And Maine was amazing. That's over now. At least for me."

I follow her out the door.

"Lucy, there was an actual sign in your yard. . . ."

"Yeah." She sighs breezily. "But now there's not."

"Lucy, we're Mudbury lifers—at least until we're recruited for the US National Team. Why didn't you tell me?"

"Because it doesn't matter what they decide. I'm not going," she says. "They can go without me. I can . . . share a room with Jaimes."

"Jaimes shares a room with *me*," I blurt out before I can stop myself. I blush all the way up to my hairline. "Don't tell anyone!"

"Like I didn't already know—my room is right across from yours."

"Oh."

"And who would I tell?"

"Slick. The boys."

Lucy rolls her eyes. "As if I'd do that. Come on," she says, handing me the tuna, followed by three cartwheels across the grass.

I feel a surge of hope.

Could she really *not* go? Could she stay and be my real twin sister even if her mom and *George* moved? I start to feel lit up inside at the possibilities. She could sleep in a really cool tent. Or we could build a tree house and live out there, or we could actually finish the basement and Jaimes and Lucy could share. Lucy could FaceTime her mom and maybe . . . But in the back of my mind I have a nagging worry that most parents take their children with them when they move.

Details.

I focus on the tree house option instead. We'll hang Christmas lights for sure.

A Haircut That Tries to Ruin My Life

ANYONE can be negative.
Being positive is the real discipline.

—COACH

"You're weirdly quiet," Jaimes says while we do the dishes after Lucy goes back home.

I shrug.

Dinner was fine. Everything was fine. Jaimes talked about the highlight tape she needs to make for soccer recruitment, and Whitney said she wanted to try field hockey next year (the *betrayal*). Dad ate and chewed more slowly, but Lucy didn't seem to notice. Or maybe she was pretending not to? But then Mom got out her laptop and started reading about you-know-what again.

"Golden?" Jaimes says.

"Do you think it would be cool if I got a tattoo?" I ask loudly.

"Mom," Jaimes hollers. "Your son's demented!"

Mom's sitting at the kitchen table. She doesn't even look away from the computer. "Sure," she mumbles.

"Sweet," I say. "When?"

She looks up, eyes still glazed over. "What?"

"You just said I could get a tattoo," I say.

"Actually, she agreed that you're demented," Jaimes says.

"Tattoo?" Mom says. "Did you know Messi has his mother's face tattooed on his back?"

"I'm the one who told you that."

"Well, anytime you want to get me tattooed on your body, go for it."

"Seriously?"

"Dare you."

"Could I get a haircut instead?" It's getting so long I'm looking more like a dog than Messi.

Mom hesitates. Dad is the one who always cuts my hair.

"I'll try."

She closes the laptop and we head upstairs.

"Have Dad show you," I tell Mom, trying to explain what the Messi cut looks like. Dad appears in the doorway and explains numbers and the blades.

"Got it," Mom says. She turns the clippers on and jumps.

"Mom . . . ?" I lean away from her. Dad looks from the clippers to my head.

"I can do it!" she says. The clippers buzz terrifyingly in front of my face.

"Tell me about Lucy," she says, starting on the back of my head.

"Well . . . I think the Dark Lord is trying to kidnap her. . . ."

"It's *George.*"

"He wants to take Lucy away!"

"What's that supposed to mean?" Jaimes asks, suddenly appearing in the doorway.

"Sell their house and move."

Jaimes looks as struck as I feel saying it out loud.

Mom hesitates, and I feel something harden inside me.

"You *knew.*" Betrayed by my own mother. Again.

"I met the Realtor a few weeks ago," she admits. "I was actually hoping it wouldn't happen. She came by to suggest ways we can help the sale."

"Like what?" Jaimes asks.

"Like cleaning up our yard, mowing, weeding, and painting. All of which I have no time for at the moment."

"That's why we have children," Dad says. None of us laugh.

"I thought you were on my side." I can't believe she knew this and didn't tell me.

"We're all on the same side, Golden," says Mom. "But the Littlehouse family moving is pretty much out of our control."

"No it's not. Besides, *George* isn't a Littlehouse."

"Golden."

"What? You have to fight for the things you love. . . ." I realize I've just said the word "love" while talking about Lucy.

"You can get a tattoo of Lucy's face so you'll never forget what she looks like!" Jaimes says, smirking at me.

"Shut up, Jaimes."

"Golden," Dad says. "Don't say thaa-aat."

The slow slurring is new. It makes us all freeze for a moment. Even Dad.

That is, until Mom wobbles the clippers and a large piece of hair falls into my lap. I hold it up, confused.

I can tell by the way Dad and Jaimes go TOTALLY AND UTTERLY RADIO SILENT and the way Mom inhales with the clippers still buzzing above my head that something is very, very wrong. Besides all the other already totally wrong things.

I run to the mirror and scream. The front where my Messi bangs used to live? Totally gone.

I'm officially living a nightmare.

Mom and Dad are going back and forth about blade clipper size. I can barely hear them. The world shrinks, becomes black around the edges. I suddenly have tunnel vision where all I can see is a buzzed stripe down the middle of my head. Like a skunk stripe. Or like Mr. T's Mohawk, except the exact opposite.

Was this Mom's diabolical way of distracting me from Lucy moving?

"I'm so sorry, Golden," Mom says. "I've never cut—"

"You're not even trying!"

I end up banished in my bedroom. Alone. Again.

Totally not cool.

"Whoa, dude," Benny says as we walk into class. "What happened?"

"Mom got ahold of the clippers."

"Ohhhh," he says. "It doesn't look . . . that bad."

"Lies. I'm hideous."

Mom tried to fix my haircut by giving me a buzz cut.

We kind of made up. I felt bad that she felt bad, and that was making Dad feel bad, which doesn't help keep him motivated.

But I look nothing like Messi anymore. I rub my practically bald head and slam my locker door shut. *It will grow, it will grow, it will grow.* I do ten push-ups in my head.

"Today," Mr. Mann says a few minutes later, once class starts, "we're going to talk about the miracle of life."

He's the only teacher I know who ever says things like "Class, we're going to talk about your poop." Which is what he said the first day of school last year, when we were studying the digestive system and nutrition. Go ahead, ask me. I'm a sinkers versus floaters expert.

"The miracle of life?" Willow asks. "With these guys?" She looks over at the boys and rolls her eyes while Mr. Mann starts the film.

"Are we going to see a baby born?" Ziggy asks. "'Cause I've seen that stuff on YouTube."

"That's what you watch on YouTube?" Willow asks.

"No, I mean . . . !" The whole class starts laughing and I join in, relieved it's not me this time. Mr. Mann pauses the film until we are silent again.

"May we resume?"

We nod, stifling the rest of our laughs as the video starts.

The cheesy couple on the screen keep looking at each other in a way that makes me so uncomfortable I want to run far, far away. I'm glad the lights are out so no one can see my face.

The big egg and sperm come to the screen. But then twenty minutes later we're watching the birth scene, and I want to bury my head in my arms, except I can't stop watching in horror as a slippery baby is proudly held up. The cheesy couple beam. I pretend to scratch my ear so I can glance over at Lucy and Benny. Lucy looks enthralled, like she's never seen anything so amazing. Benny is pretending not to look at me, too.

I wonder if my parents were that happy when I was born. There's a lot of pictures of Mom holding me as a newborn. There's also this picture of Dad holding me wrapped tightly in a blanket. On my head is a small knit cap, a soccer ball pattern all over it. Dad is wearing a short-sleeve shirt; his arms are strong and muscular. Mom said he held me up like Mufasa held up Simba to the lion pride, exclaiming, "Look at him—my Golden Boy!"

Judging by this video, though, they must have cleaned me up a LOT first.

Ew.

The Night I Make My Dad Fly

You don't give up on me and
I don't give up on you.
—DAD

We spend the whole week preparing for our big matchup against Merrimack Middle School. Me and Lucy take turns leading the warm-up, and with everyone so focused on the first big game, we're surprisingly effective.

On Thursday it's Lucy's and my birthday. In the morning, Roma brings me a "surprise smoothie" I pretend to drink, and then at practice everyone on the team sings "Happy Birthday." The boys team up and shank me, and after the scrimmage Coach says, "Lucy and Golden can be our birthday MVPs." We split the pack of gum. Cinnamon, my favorite flavor. Things must be on the upswing.

"Blueberry Island tonight?" I ask Benny. With all the

Lucy moving stuff, we still haven't gone. My birthday seems like the perfect time.

"Uh . . . it's getting kind of cold. But hey—happy birthday, dude!"

He doesn't want to go? He loves Blueberry Island. Still, he leaves me holding the ball bag, confused, as he catches a ride with his dad, and Lucy jumps in with him. Mom and I are going to pick up Whitney and Roma from their soccer practices and then catch the second half of Jaimes's first game.

I'm still thinking about what's up with Benny when we get there—until I see Dad, head coach, on the side-lines. He's not holding a clipboard or a piece of paper like he used to. He stays in one spot, his left arm hanging, hand slightly clawed. His right hand is wound around . . . a cane. A *cane*? Since when?

When Jaimes scores a goal in the last five minutes I see him smile but not clap his hands. He wears a hat, but never once does he adjust it. Who put it on his head? What if it's too hot or itchy? And at the end of the game, when the whistle blows, the entire Mudbury High team runs to Jaimes and their goalie, jumping up and down, but Dad stands all by himself. He doesn't even *try*. Not even on my birthday.

When they're done celebrating her winning goal, Jaimes links arms with him as he congratulates the girls, then helps him walk to the van super slowly, using the cane for support. Her team watches them the way I do: like we're witnessing something we're afraid of seeing.

Once we make it home, I walk straight past a cake Mom actually made, go to my room, and glumly make two marks for two hours on my ten thousand hours chart. I should be happy—it's my birthday, and I'm two hours closer to my dream. Except for the first time in my life, I don't want time to pass by so quickly.

Ten thousand. Sometimes that number looks so impossible.

I look out the window. No sign of life next door. Did Lucy forget about our birthday potluck tradition? Is she at Benny's house eating dinner? Having fun without me even though she hasn't moved anywhere yet?

Ten thousand hours of Lucy and Benny friendship? That's a number we've already achieved. Easily. It can't end just because the Dark Lord says so—or because Benny won't go swimming.

I rub my practically bald head and watch as a truck pulls into the driveway. Slick's dad. Slick is in the passenger seat. Great.

Downstairs, Roma calls, "Golden! Look!"

"What's going on?" I say, trudging down the stairs.

"They're measuring, to build your dad a ramp," Mom says. "We've talked about this."

"Yeah, but . . . on my birthday?"

"Why does Dad need a ramp?" Roma asks, giving Mom an out from the guilty look that passes over her face.

"Better Rollerblading," I say. "Duh."

"Yes, that," Mom says evenly. "But remember when we told you, honey, that Dad will eventually be in a wheelchair?"

Dad is standing by the window when she says this, and I see his left hand, holding the windowsill for support, tighten. His right hand holds the cane. My nose goes all tingly like it thinks it might need to cry. *Stop!* I command.

"Cool," Jaimes says, still high from her win. "We still building a covered bridge?"

"Yeah, real cool," I say. "Dad won't be able to walk, but hey, we'll have our very own covered bridge."

My family turns to look at me.

"You're such a jerk sometimes," Jaimes says.

"I was kidding. . . ."

"Jaimes," Mom says.

"It's so like you," Jaimes practically spits at me. "To make everything a joke like nothing matters. No wonder Lucy wants to move."

"She does not!" I yell.

Instead of physically tackling my sister and being grounded for life, I stomp outside, but I see Slick's dad holding a tape measure and a hammer. There's something hammering on my insides, too. Why is Slick's dad so nice and Slick such a jerk? Why did I say that about Dad? Why is my head bald? How can Lucy move? Are we still the Three Musketeers? Why is all of this *happening*? I'm supposed to be the captain, but I've never felt less in control. I hate it.

I hear a door open, but I don't want to "talk about it" so I sneak in the back door and duck into the bathroom before anyone can see my face. Of course, as soon as I lock the door, there's a knock.

I splash some water on my face so that it doesn't look like I've been crying. Inhale one-two-three and hold and exhale one-two-three. Mom's "warrior pose." Shoulders back.

More persistent knocking.

"What!" I say, swinging the door open.

It's Roma, looking small and impossibly hopeful.

"Want to play soccer?" she asks.

"Heck yeah I do."

We play in the backyard, using Roma's new pink f50 ball. It's pretty sweet—even if it's pink. After a Maradona move, I look up and spy Lucy in her bedroom window, watching.

"Lucy!" Roma yells. "Come play!"

Please.

I wave for her to come outside.

She disappears from the window, and I wilt like an underinflated soccer ball.

But a minute later her front door opens. She's got her orange cleats on, a cool turquoise bandana on her head. We're both red-eyed, blotchy-faced birthday babies.

We don't have to talk about it.

I pass her the ball.

She passes it back.

And for the first time all afternoon, I smile.

We play soccer until Lucy's mom pulls in with balloons, takeout, and another cake.

"Sorry I'm late, birthday twins!" She kisses both me and Lucy on the cheek before going into our house.

Dad comes out onto the porch, leaning on the cane.

"Birthday . . . dinner?"

I wipe my sweaty face, not wanting to go inside yet, not wanting to see Dad get birthday cake frosting all over himself.

"Wait. Last week you said you'd fix my bike."

"Gold . . . ," he says wearily.

"It's good practice for your hands. And it is my birthday."

Lucy shoots me a look. It's a low blow, but I can't help it.

Dad gives a long exhale before stepping awkwardly down the stairs where his ramp will go. He heads toward the shed. The cane makes a strong whack on the ground with each step. I don't look at Lucy's face.

"It needs a new tube," Dad says, after he's instructed me on pumping the tire, to no avail.

"Let's go in the truck to get one. I'll help!"

"Golden, it's getting late. Plus there's dinner. Tomorrow we'll buy a new tire tube."

"We have to go to the lake now! Benny's waiting," I fib. "For a birthday swim! We never got to go this summer."

Lucy looks at me, raising her eyebrows.

I can't explain the urgency, but who knows if we'll ever get the chance again?

Another exhale from Dad. "Blueberry Island is pr-pretty special. Use Jaimes's bike?"

"The chain is off."

"Use my bike."

"It's too big."

Dad uses the cane to pull on Whitney's bike handle.

It's bright yellow with a retro banana seat and sparkly yellow and pink streamers that fly off the back when you're bookin' it down the road.

"Heck no."

"Beggars can't be choosers," Dad says.

True. I jump on the bike and look at Dad. "Well? You're coming, right?"

Dad looks at his bike and then at me. "I don't think . . ."

I pat the seat behind me firmly. "Beggars can't be choosers."

It's a monumental effort to even get Dad on the seat. First we have to lean the bike against the wall. Next, Lucy and I have to hold Dad and lift his right foot over the bike without him falling over. Lucy swallows hard. I want to tell her I know exactly how she feels.

Dad feels her hesitation too. "I'm okay, Lucy," he says. "Just can't make my . . ." His voice trails off as he tries to get on the seat.

"I got you," she says, stepping forward and holding us steady. She helps Dad put his arms around my waist. His clawed left hand grasps his right one and he clenches as tight as he can.

"Okay," he says uneasily.

"Text Benny?" I ask Lucy. There's no way he won't go if Dad's with me.

Lucy texts—then grabs her roller skates.

I start to pedal down the long driveway. Dad is heavy weight on the bike, and we wobble precariously. Fear grips me, knowing I can't stop or Dad will fall off. My calves strain against the pedals as I lean forward and push harder, feeling my quads burn with exertion that feels both good and terrible. My hands grip the yellow handles.

"You can do it," Dad says, arms around me, both of us praying they'll stay there.

His voice helps me pedal harder until I'm at the end of the driveway, the orange glare of the sunset still bright enough to light the way down. I pray there are no cars coming because once I start I won't be able to stop.

"Hold on, Dad!"

Lucy soars past me, straight down the hill. "Wheeeeee!" she yells, her braids flying behind her.

Dad makes a sound like he's both terrified and excited as we start down the hill too. We go faster and faster until suddenly Dad's hands come off my waist.

"Dad!"

My bike wobbles when I glance back, but Dad is still there. His eyes are closed. His face is turned to the last rays of sun, his arms dangling out behind him, body buoyed by the wind.

"Pedal, Golden! I'm flying!"

My face hurts from smiling so widely.

When we finally coast to the bottom of the hill, Benny's waiting for us in his driveway.

"Nice bike!" he yells, turning out to join us.

"Banana seat!" I yell, pedaling hard to keep our momentum.

Mr. Ho is standing on the porch. Surprising me, he gives me a thumbs-up.

"Next time you're taking me, Golden! Happy birthday!"

"Blueberry Island in the dark?" Benny says excitedly, pulling up next to me. "Wicked."

Finally, the road evens out, and Dad collapses against my back, his left hand pinching my shirt. Light snakes through leaves, lighting our way to the beachfront.

Whitney's bike tires hit the rocky gravel, spitting small rocks out of the spokes. I take Dad's left hand, keeping him tight around my body. *I won't let you fall, Dad.*

When we make it to the water's edge, Lucy and Benny immediately rush to our side to steady us.

"Dad? You okay?"

"That was . . . something," he breathes.

We look out to the water and back to Dad. I didn't really think this part through.

"You swim," he says. "I'll wait here."

Benny was right. The water is shockingly cold as I glide underwater like a seal. But underneath the surface, my world is silent, calm, and uncomplicated. Every worry floats away. I exhale until I have no more air in my lungs. When I come up, my lungs fill with cool September air. I glance back and see that Dad's sitting in the sand, head tilted up at the stars. I don't know how we're going to get him back home, but I focus on the look on his face instead. The memory of him flying.

The three of us stay together, changing strokes when our arms become tired. Swimming to Blueberry Island has been a rite of passage since we were little. Dad taught us to swim by telling us stories of its hidden forest with fresh blueberries and the elusive loon and heron birds. It seemed epically far back then, but it's not really. I'm so out of practice, though, that my muscles tire quickly.

"Remember when we used to think there were crocodiles in the lake?" Benny says as I keep pushing.

"*Don't* say it, Benny!" Lucy says.

My imagination spins off in dangerous directions. Who knows what's really under our feet? Who knows how deep the lake really is or what lives under the dark mud?

"I don't like not being able to see," I say.

"But sometimes it's more fun to not know, right?" Lucy says. "Surprises are fun."

Something about the way she says it makes me uneasy, but I don't know why. I know how much Lucy loves surprises.

We reach the island, breathless, putting our feet down on the slimy rock-bottom shoreline of the island.

But when I scour the bushes for our precious prize of hundreds and hundreds of tiny sweet-tasting blueberries, I come up empty-handed.

"I knew it. We're too late," Benny says, frustrated. "They were here in July and August."

"Keep trying!" I say.

"We can't make our friendship pact without them," Lucy says.

"Friendship pact?" I say, blindly feeling more bushes for blueberries. Even with the moonlight, I can barely see the bushes, let alone berries.

"From fourth grade," Lucy says. "We said we'd renew it when we were eighth graders."

"I remember," Benny says. "Golden wanted to do a blood pact, but none of us wanted to prick a finger. So we mashed blueberries between our fingers and pretended it was blood."

I pause in my search, smiling at the memory.

"They're gone, Golden," Lucy says, pulling me up. I look over at her, struck by how the water slides off her golden hair and drops off her nose, how the moonlight beams right off her. "But it doesn't matter," she says, holding her hand up in the air. "We can still make the pact."

Benny and I touch our fingertips to hers.

"Under the full moon that rises over Highland Lake on this night," Lucy says, "the day of our birth, September eighth, the day Golden and I arrived on this earth and immediately journeyed to find Benny at preschool . . ."

Benny and I laugh as Lucy continues. "As blood brothers and sister . . ."

"Blueberry blood," Benny amends.

"Yes," Lucy says seriously. "We solemnly promise to be friends forever and always."

"And our friendship shall always consist of epic adventures, night swims, and championship games," I say.

"And Curtis Meowfield." Lucy smiles.

"And we will always tell each other the truth," says Benny.

"And we will never let anything or anyone come between us," Lucy says.

The Dark Lord comes to mind, but I shake it off quickly.

"And we will always share our food," I say. "Right, Benny?"

"Golden!" Lucy says, laughing.

"You've seen my fridge."

Lucy finishes solemnly. "No matter what our future holds."

"No matter what," we say in unison.

We squish into a hug that breaks only when Benny swats at a mosquito and I remember Dad's got to be fighting the bloodsuckers on land, without the ability to swat.

"Come on," I say. "Let's get Dad."

We dive in, blueberry blood pact renewed. Halfway

back to the beach, the clouds swim across the sky and cover the moon. I swim faster in the inky black water, trying not to think about the deep dark depths under me, trying in vain to scan for Dad on the shore.

"What was that?" Lucy whispers, stopping midstroke.

"What?"

"Something touched my foot."

We start swimming like it's an Olympic sprint.

But when we reach the shore we find something much worse than a sea creature slithering over a foot in the deep.

Dad is nowhere to be found.

"I don't see him in the water," Lucy says, splashing along the shoreline.

"Dragon-Ball P can swim!" Benny says. "He wouldn't just drown . . . right, Golden?"

"No . . ." I try to sound confident, but I frantically scan the water.

"Maybe he started walking home," Benny says, wildly swatting. "The mosquitoes are wicked bad tonight!" We jump on our bikes, Lucy laces up her roller skates, and we head toward the road.

"What if he was kidnapped?" Lucy asks.

"Dude, of course he's not kidnapped," Benny says, pedaling. "He's a grown *man*."

"He wouldn't really be able to fight back, though. Dad!" I yell, cursing myself that we didn't do more strength training this summer.

"Maybe if he really *had* to fight, he could," Lucy says. "I saw this show once where a man was in a wheelchair and his baby fell into the pool and he *made* himself fall in, swim, *and* save the baby."

"There he is!" I yell, my lungs filling with relief. I make out his silhouette only a few feet ahead of us, inching down the road, arms not swinging.

"Dad!" I say, catching up to him on my bike. "You were supposed to wait."

"Mosquitoes," he says. "Eating me alive. Sorry to worry you." He shakes his head irritably at a mosquito buzzing close to his ear. I smack it, but the blood splatters grossly on Dad's face.

"Sorry."

The bike ride home is torturous. We're wet, tired, and cold, and Dad is heavier on the seat behind me.

Mom's probably looking for us by now. The Squirrels are probably hysterical. I consider calling for a ride home, but Jaimes would probably run us over before we even got in the van.

When we finally make it back to Benny's, I'm thrilled for a short break. Benny's dad runs out with a Tupperware of noodles, like he's been waiting.

"Mmm, Dad's favorite," I say as the incredible smell drifts over us.

"We'll bring you more," he says, tying the bag onto my handlebars. "Now you better get home. Your mother called."

Uh-oh.

He pats Dad on the back, looking concerned. "You want a ride up the hill?"

"I got it!" I say, stubbornly tightening Dad's arms around my waist. "Thank you!"

"You should have said yes," Lucy says. "How in the world . . . ?"

"I can do it!" I say. "Right, Dad?"

When he hesitates, I pedal even faster.

I push ahead, Lucy skating beside me, both of us trying to gain momentum for the uphill ride.

"You got it," Dad says. "Come on."

We make it halfway up, my calves straining, lungs about to explode. I try to keep pushing but can't make the pedals move another inch. I hop off and catch Dad before he falls over.

"I've got your noodles, Coach!" Lucy proclaims, swooping in to grab them from me.

We abandon the bike on the side of the road, Dad's energy as flat as a dead balloon. Of course that's when the mosquitoes descend again, attacking with a vengeance.

"Go ahead!" I call to Lucy, swatting furiously as she skates. "Save yourself!"

But one look at Dad and she skates back. Together we support him on either side and attempt to climb the hill, all the while fighting the swarming mosquitoes and trying to save the noodles.

Dad is breathing hard, and I think of the cane. The one I purposefully left behind so he could practice walking.

Now without it, Dad's barely moving.

"Keep going," I say. "Please, Dad."

We're only a couple hundred feet from the driveway, but Dad falters, barely able to take another step. We grasp him, but my hands slide on his skin from the exertion and sweat. I push away the sinking feelings threatening to rise. *No, Dad can do this. Like the dad saving the baby in the pool Lucy was talking about. He can do it for himself.*

"Call . . . Mom," Dad says, panting.

"You can do it!" I say, coaching him like he'd coach me.

Just then, I hear a sound coming from the bottom of the hill. I turn my head to see a dark figure running at us, pulling something loud and clunky.

"Yo," a voice says. "I got you, Dragon-Ball P!"

"Benny!"

He's pulling his old red Radio Flyer wagon. I almost cry out of relief. We carefully lower Dad into it, his back resting on the wooden slabs, and then the three of us, me and my best friends in the whole world, push and pull Dragon-Ball P up the gravelly road. It's at that moment that I know I was foolish to keep Benny away all summer, to think for even a moment that he and Lucy would be embarrassed to be my friend or too sad to stay to watch what's happening. I know now that they'll never abandon me, because that's what friends never do.

Dad's a good sport, keeping calm as he tries to stay upright while the wagon jostles and bangs him around with every tiny bump and rock in the road.

When we make it, panting, to the top of the driveway, someone is waiting. But it's not Mom.

It's the Dark Lord.

He springs forward and grabs the wagon from us like he's some sort of hero, and wheels it down to the house.

Mom is waiting. Her lips are in a Coach tight line.

"Happy birthday, Golden," Lucy whispers.

"Happy birthday, Lucy."

The Dark Lord takes Benny home as we get Dad inside.

My cold birthday dinner and birthday cake are still on the table, but Mom doesn't mention either. With Jaimes's help, they get Dad into the shower. He sits on a stool in his boxers and Mom uses the showerhead to wash the sweat and mosquito blood off him.

Given our harrowing trip home, I peek through the

door crack with dread. But instead of doom and gloom, Dad seems . . . transformed. He has a smile on his face, eyes closed. Water is pouring out of the shower spigot, down his face, over his eyes, nose, and mouth.

"Did you actually ride a bike?" Mom asks.

"No," he says, triumphant, water splashing out of his mouth. "I was *flying*."

And no matter how mad Mom is, I'm suddenly triumphant too, that I could make him feel that way.

Like we really can do anything together.

Even if it takes ten thousand tries.

Squirrel Hair and Other Tasks a Mini-Messi Shouldn't Have to Do

Sometimes there are no second chances, no next time. Sometimes it's now or never.

—SOCCER GREAT ABBY WAMBACH

The next morning I oversleep.

These days, that's really not good.

When I bounce downstairs, Jaimes is rushing around the kitchen and pouring four cups of milk. "Hurry up."

"Yes, Mother Gothel," I say, trying to do a pull-up on the doorframe.

"You're not funny!"

"Kind of funny." The molding above the door suddenly gives way, and I find myself on the floor holding a broken piece of door trim.

"Golden!" Jaimes shrieks. "Dad can't even fix that anymore!"

"Yes he can!"

"And we *really* don't have time for you to work out while I get everyone ready for school. Especially on game day."

"It's not game day."

"For me and Dad! Not everything's about you. And it's an important game for me," Jaimes says, setting out my multivitamin like she's the boss.

"You shouldn't wear that to school," she continues, getting huffier by the minute.

I look down at my perfectly normal basketball shorts and T-shirt. "What's the problem?"

"You wore it *swimming* last night!"

"Actually," I say, "it's none of your business." I don't tell her that none of my clothes are any cleaner right now.

"Actually, it *is* my business, since we're related."

"Great. I'll go to school naked."

Whitney walks into the kitchen and screams, making me jump a foot.

"WHAT?" I say.

"You're going to school *naked*?"

"Yes! And stop screaming, you DEMENTED SQUIRREL!"

I look in the fridge for something to eat. Big surprise, nothing there. "We need food!" I yell.

On cue, Jaimes hands me something small and shriveled. "Apple."

"It's a million years old—and stop trying to be Mom."

"Fine, go hungry," she retorts, very Mom-like.

I spy the birthday cake on the counter. Using my hand, I take a big scoop and shove it into my mouth.

Jaimes's mouth drops open as steam nearly comes out of her ears.

"See how mad you can get!" I say, cake crumbs accidentally spitting out of my mouth and onto her face.

Admittedly, her self-control is impressive. When she speaks, her voice is dangerously low. "Well, now you definitely have to change."

I look down and see a big smear of icing and crumbs down my front. Ugh.

I run upstairs and pass the bathroom, where Mom is combing Dad's hair. Mom's also shaved his face.

"That's my job," I protest, stepping closer. My eyes widen. "What did she do to your face?"

"Mosquito bites," Mom says tersely.

Instant guilt floods through me. His head is covered with angry red welts. His right eye is partially swollen shut.

"Do they . . . itch?"

"I'm experimenting," Dad says. "If I tell my brain they don't, they won't."

"Well, that's great," Mom says, sounding snappish. "Because you won't be able to scratch them."

"Sorry," I say weakly.

"Hurry up, Golden," Mom says. "School."

I run to my room and throw on a pair of mostly clean jeans.

"Where's my belt?" I holler, kicking over piles looking for it.

"I don't wear your belts. Did you get Roma up?" Mom yells back.

"No time! I have no belt, no clean clothes, no food except one rotten apple, and I'm already a shrimp so I can't afford to lose any more weight!"

I hear her footsteps coming down the hall. I hide behind my bedroom door. Mom appears in the doorframe looking like she's making the Hulk-Coach transformation. She eyeballs me right through the crack of the doorframe.

"First, you're being very rude."

"Sorry, Mom," I say automatically.

"Second, it looks like you're wearing clothes and your pants aren't falling down."

"Sorry, Mom."

"And third, you're not starving just because you have to eat a piece of fruit for one meal until I can go grocery shopping today."

"Sorry, Mom."

"Golden?" Her voice sounds like roiling water about

to boil, spill out, and scald me. I've been waiting for this since I got home last night, and now she lets me have it. "Your dad CANNOT swat at mosquitoes anymore, so when you take him on a bike ride without telling me—"

"I know, I know. I said I was sorry! But you know what Lucy said? She saw this show where this completely paralyzed man saved a baby from drowning because he had to, so maybe—"

"Golden, enough!" She turns and walks back to Dad.

"Just sayin'!" I say defensively, but she never listens to my ideas, so I shouldn't be surprised.

I swap dirty shirts, then go down the hall to find Roma still in bed, even though Whitney's probably been up for hours. I poke her shoulder, jiggle her, but when none of that works, I eventually resort to tickling her awake.

"NOOOOO!" she shrieks. Success.

"Get up—we're late." I look at her snarly hair. "Roma, you've got to start using a brush and looking presentable." I look around to make sure Jaimes didn't hear me.

I hand Roma a brush. "Put it in a ponytail."

"You do it." Roma thrusts the brush back at me.

"No. I'm not doing your hair."

"Dad would!" Roma howls.

"We're late!" Mom yells.

"Let's go," I say to Roma, trying to hurry her up.

Her face scrunches up and she throws the brush at me, then herself onto her bed.

This is getting us nowhere fast.

"Fine!" I say to Roma. "Where's the iPad?"

There are 10,593 choices of How to Make a Perfect Ponytail on YouTube. Including How to Make a Perfect Ponytail, How to Have a Volumized Ponytail, How to Do a High Ponytail, Poofy Ponytail, Basic Ponytail, Invisible Ponytail . . .

"It's really not that hard," Roma says.

"Easy for you to say—you've got hair!"

I make my best attempt, and by the end, Roma looks like a disheveled rocker with a slight side ponytail, but hey, it's effort, man.

She snuggles up to me. "Golden, I love you."

I totally melt. "Thanks, Squirrel. Can we get dressed now?"

She looks up at me and whispers, "I don't want to die."

"You're not going to die."

"How do you know?"

"Because I do."

This death-obsessed sister thing is exhausting.

"Clothes?"

Roma points to the piles of clothing all over her and Whitney's floor.

"Clean?"

Shrug.

I realize that unless *I* do it, no one's going to.

When Roma is dressed (semimatching, clean-questionable) I pull her to the stairs, a pile of her laundry in my arms too.

But we get stuck behind Dad, who is super slow today. Like snail slow. Like sloth slow. So slow I feel like I'm itching out of my skin. "Beep beep, coming through, slowpokes." I squeeze Roma, then me and the big pile of laundry, between Mom and Dad. Mom looks like she wants to knock my block off, but I'm too mad at her to care.

"Sorry to hold the train up," Dad says, right eye looking even puffier as he tries to rub it with his right shoulder.

"Dad! Tell your brain!"

Mom scratches his head to spite me.

I face her from the bottom of the stairs, the laundry higher than my head.

"Roma has no clean clothes."

Mom just blinks at me.

"Laundry's my job, remember?" Dad says.

"Yeah, but . . ."

Dad leans forward and speaks more softly. "And I could r-really use your help."

I find myself even more mad at Mom when she swallows and looks away.

I shove the laundry into the washing machine, and five minutes later we're out the door and on the way to school.

"Whit, Roma, did you pack your snack?" Mom asks.

"I'll just ask my friends," Whitney says.

"No one got me anything," Roma says.

Mom turns around, like it's just occurring to her that Whitney's mooching and her youngest child needs food.

"Oh, Roma," she says. "You've got to get up earlier—and pack a snack."

"Usually mothers do that," I whisper.

Mom looks at me a full five seconds before turning back around in her seat. She stares straight ahead without a word. Dad is eyeing me. I clench my teeth and refuse to feel guilty even though it's starting to creep up my legs and into my ice-cold heart.

"Listen, Roma," I say, my voice cracking. "In this family it's every kid for himself." I point my finger at her. "No one is going to do anything for you."

"Spoken like a true captain, a real team player," Jaimes says sarcastically.

I finally make eye contact with Dad, who is frowning at me.

"Here, Roma," I grumble, opening my overstuffed backpack, which triples as my book-soccer-lunch bag. "Popcorn and an apple. Eat the apple first." The last apple.

The old shriveled apple from the fridge, the last coveted piece of fruit.

"Good leaders eat last," Dad says approvingly.

Good mothers buy food. They take care of their kids. They don't give up on dads and accept that it's all over before it's over!

I manage to keep my mouth shut and glance at my watch instead. We are so late.

Dad taps his foot lightly on the ground. He's late too, and now he walks twice as slow as me. How long will it take for him to get to his classroom? Mom works from home, researching and stuff, so she has time to walk Dad into the classroom, right? Or does Jaimes do it? Does Dad's class wait while their teacher, aka Dragon-Ball P, strongest man alive, penguin-shuffles down the hallway?

I look over to see Dad aggressively wiggling his nose but not touching it.

"Want me to scratch, Dad . . . just a little?"

"Nah!" He exhales and grits his teeth. "We got this! We got it!"

I feel calmer just hearing him say it, even if no one else seems to.

Friday night, the last night before our first game, I finally do my own laundry properly. Jaimes showed me how to work the machine and pour in detergent correctly—since

I forgot to even add soap with Roma's.

While my clothes dry, I ask Dad to "help me" do a workout in the garage before the big game. But my plan is really to help him.

"Here," I say, handing Dad a ten-pound hand weight.

"Yeah, that's not happening," he says. He's already breathing hard from just walking down the stairs and into the garage.

"Start light," I say, putting a five-pound weight in his hand.

I use the tens myself for alternate bicep curls. "I'm the man!" I say, even though I can feel them getting heavy.

"Huh," he says. "Is that what makes you a man? Lifting weights?"

I think about this. I mean it's a thing, right?

"Golden, when I can't even lift this five-pounder, will I still be a man?" His eyes bore into mine.

"That's why we're practicing!" I protest.

"Golden, I'm losing my strength even with the practicing. I can't run, can't shoot, can hardly walk. It's not that I . . . don't want to. You know I *love* soccer. But you know what I love most?" He swallows hard.

"Us?"

He nods. "My dream team. Hard seeing you being unkind and angry with Mom—"

"I'm not—"

"Mom," he interrupts, "is doing what two parents used to. House, work, kids, soccer, bills, groceries, laundry . . . taking care of me."

"Oh," I say, sullen.

"Sit by me."

I sit.

"Sh-she didn't make this happen to me. I wonder if I've set a good enough example of how to really b-be a man if you d-don't see th-that." He stops talking and breathes heavily.

I uncurl his clawed left hand and take the weight.

He continues to breathe in and out for several long minutes.

"You're captain *on* the field. How about off the field too? We need a . . . leader."

I look up at Dad. Isn't that what I've been trying to do? But I think of Roma and the reluctant ponytail, and the piles of dirty laundry and dishes and clutter that someone needs to take care of. I guess I can do more.

"If you remember anything I've taught you, I hope it's to treat . . . people well, especially your family. *That* will make you a man."

"I'm sorry, Dad."

"Give Mom a big hug. The kind I can't any . . . more."

Dad's hand on mine is how I notice his forearm. It looks like a small mouse is jumping under his skin. I flinch.

"What's that, Dad?"

"Muscle spasm. I'm getting more of them. All over my body."

"How long will it last?"

"A few minutes? Sometimes a few hours."

I place my fingers on his arm. I can feel the twitching, like electricity trying to run down a broken circuit. Moving, stopping, starting, jumping.

"Does it hurt?"

"No."

"It feels weird."

"I'm actually grateful to feel it. It shows my muscles are still working."

"Do you feel my hand on your arm?" I ask.

"Yes."

"This?" I lightly pinch.

"Yes."

"How about this?" I scratch the mosquito bites on his head and arms and neck.

"Yes," he says contentedly. "I feel everything. Funny that doesn't go away. There's s-something wrong with the signal, the neurons, coming from my brain—but not the other way around."

I lean my head against his shoulder, hoping he can feel that, too.

* * *

Later that night, I lay out my shorts, socks, and Battle Pack cleats. Tomorrow Coach will hand me the captain's armband and Mr. T will hand out uniforms; I'll for sure be wearing jersey #10: Messi's number. I scrounge around the house for white athletic tape to tape around my soccer socks. One, to keep them up, and two, it looks wicked cool. Very carefully I write my hero's name on the white tape, with a black Sharpie: Messi #10.

I touch my left bicep where the armband will live and feel the muscle flex beneath my touch. I remember the twitching of Dad's muscle spasm and wonder what it must feel like.

I kneel by the side of my bed to pray, something I've only ever done because Mom and Dad told me to. But today I decide on my own. After all, Messi's a believer too. I've seen him do it a hundred times—pointing at the sky when he scores, like he's acknowledging something or someone up there who holds pieces of his destiny.

Destiny.

It does seem like "destiny" flies in the face of ten thousand hours and actually *earning* a starting position. But even I have to admit—after all the fighting, after all the hard work—there's a piece of me that's looking for a miracle.

So I look up and put my hands together.

My mind wanders to my field, to Dad on the sidelines,

watching. The very thought makes my heart pound nervously. Our conversation runs back through my mind. *You know*, I reason with God, *if the disease was to stop right now and Dad wouldn't get any better but he wouldn't get any worse, I could be happy with that. For real! Even if he couldn't ride a bike or kick the ball or run with me on the front lawn— I'd never complain or ask for anything ever again.*

You can overcome anything, if and only if you love something enough.

And I do. I love Dad that much. I love him even more than that.

That's our destiny. *Please.*

Game Day

There's no doubt. It's certain that
I'll be one hundred percent.
—LIONEL MESSI

Buzz!

There's a noise that's trying to pull me out of my sleep, out of dreams. . . .

Buzz!

Ignore it.

Buzzzzz!

I jolt awake, realizing the buzzing is my phone.

Jaimes puts a pillow over her head.

Someone is texting. A lot.

I reach for my phone, expecting Lucy or Benny, but when I rub my eyes, I see it's only 5:46 a.m.

It's Dad: help pls

I sprint to his bedroom, afraid he's suffocating under his covers.

Mom is the only one in the bed, though, sound asleep.

I stumble down the stairs and hear him in the bathroom.

"Dad?"

"Here."

He's sitting on the toilet.

"Sorry to wake you," he says. "Can you pull me up?"

"Yeah, sure."

"Already wiped."

I laugh self-consciously. *Thank goodness.*

"Two hands," Dad says, grasping my right hand with his clawed one. His right hand is completely limp. I have to grab it with my left hand and hold on tight.

"One-two-three-UP," Dad says. His speech sounds thicker—but that's normal for the mornings. I pull at the same time he tries to stand. He only comes up an inch.

"Again."

I pull and ask, "Why are you down here?"

"Woke early. Wanted to make . . . breakfast for game . . . day."

It takes three more times, and eventually I end up grabbing him underneath his armpits, wrapping both arms around his entire upper torso. When he's up, we both fall backward into the sink. Using all my strength, I manage to steady us back upright.

"Thank . . . you," he says, breathing hard. "Sorry to ask. . . ." He exhales.

"Sure, Dad. It's fine." No big deal. Dad needs help and I can help him, like when Messi assists a goal. Kinda like that. I pull up Dad's boxers and pants, which now both have a simple elastic band.

"Dad, who will you ask if you have to go at school?" I ask, washing his hands.

"Call Mom. And hope she picks up. I mostly hope I don't have to go."

I think of Nurse Verity being surprised Dad is still working. The way she keeps hinting at his retirement. I shake the thought away. I'm getting so good at doing that, it's practically my superpower.

"Well, this is one way to start my season opener," I joke.

Dad laughs. "I've always loved your optimism, boy."

One of the best parts of an away game is an early dismissal. At 1:45 the principal's voice announces over the loudspeaker: "For all our seventh- and eighth-grade soccer players—you may go get dressed. Good luck!"

As we file into the tiny, smelly bathroom that doubles as our locker room, Mr. T walks around and hands each of us a soccer jersey.

I reach out my hands for Messi's #10, of course.

Mr. T hands me #5.

"Um, there's been a mistake," I say.

Mr. T looks at his list.

"Nope."

"Uh, Mr. T? I *have* to be number ten."

"Someone else asked for it first," he says. "You'll have to deal."

Someone else asked for it? *Everyone* knows that's my number.

"Who has number ten?" I ask. "I'll trade you."

Slick holds up his uniform. "I got it." *Oh no.*

"Trade?" I ask hopefully.

"I'm number ten and you're number five—for half the size of me!"

Slick gleefully puts on the jersey. I take a step closer to him, annoyed that he's kind of right. He's a solid foot taller than me, so I'm looking straight up into his nose hairs. Ew.

"You know I want it and that's why you won't give it to me."

"Twenty bucks, shrimp."

"Don't be a . . ."

"Take it or leave it."

I kick his bag across the bathroom.

"Golden, chill!" Benny says as Slick laughs.

"Let's go!" Mr. T booms through the doorway.

"Get it together," Benny whispers as we walk. "You're the captain."

I snap back to attention. Benny's right. Captain. Focus. That's what Messi would do. That's what Dad would say. If Mom hasn't forgotten them after my fifty reminders, I'll be wearing a captain's armband on my arm today.

"Captains!" Mr. T's voice booms. "Med kit, ice, soccer balls?"

I completely forgot about all these details, so I sprint back down the hallway to find Lucy.

By the time we have the med kit and the ball bags, everyone else is on the bus, Gag Me at the wheel.

Slick smiles his smarmy smile and adjusts the jersey so the number ten is more visible as I walk by. I pretend he's invisible.

I end up being squished in between Ziggy, who is chomping on a candy bar, and Benny, who saved me a seat. Lucy and Sunny sit across the aisle.

"I don't think you should be eating that," I say to Ziggy, at the risk of sounding like Jaimes. "It's game day."

"Ziggy," Lucy says, "Golden's right." She's wearing feathery earrings and this cool red-and-yellow bandana over her braids today.

Ziggy holds the chocolate in his mouth and pulls up his shirt. Attached to his abdomen is a small square machine that has a tube coming out of it to control his diabetes sugar numbers.

"It's not beeping," Ziggy says, chocolate drool running down his chin. "So I'm fine."

"Doesn't that hurt?" Benny asks.

"Nope."

"Coach really hopes she doesn't have to stab you with a needle," I say, referring to the syringe filled with glucagon she keeps on her for Ziggy, just in case.

"You can trust Coach," Lucy says. "She can totally stab you with a needle if she has to. If she can't, I will."

"Thanks, Lucy!" Ziggy says, sounding genuinely pleased. "Coach has medical training, right? Because of your dad?"

I shrug.

"Will he be at the game?"

"Yeah. Jaimes is driving him over as soon as their practice ends."

"I wish I'd moved here sooner," Ziggy says. "I heard he's like *the man*. Like no one can get past him and that he's so strong that *nobody* messes with Dragon-Ball P!" I see Dad in my mind. *The man.* I'm on his shoulders at the top of Mount Kearsarge and I swear, I can see the whole world from up there—including Barcelona.

"What's wrong with him?"

"Nothing," I say. There's nothing *wrong*. Just some things that don't work right.

"Nothing except ALS," Lucy says from across the aisle. "And what you've heard about him is true. He *is* a legend."

"No," Moses says, looking up from drawing. "You have to die to be a legend."

"No one's dying! It's game day!" I yell, louder than I mean to. "Can we all focus?!"

Everyone looks at me like I said something weird, but have I mentioned? It's really hard to focus with the Mudbury Magpies.

Raindrops begin hitting the bus. And when I look outside, more.

Great.

Gag Me turns erratically on the dirt road and slams the brakes so hard we hit Merrimack's school curb. From outside, I can hear Merrimack students laughing at us.

While we file off the bus, Coach starts talking.

"Don't ask me about the weather. Here's the way it works: we plan to play. If there's a change due to weather or an asteroid strike or anything else, we'll hear about it. Focus on your warm-up and plan to play!"

Slick does his best to throw me off, flaunting his jersey while we warm up in the rain.

"Do you see something?" I say. "'Cause I see *nothing*."

"Let it go, Golden," Benny says. We dribble side by side. I try to focus, copy Benny. Like Messi, his focus is his superpower. I shake out my hands, stretch out my neck.

"Forget everything like Coach said," Benny says. "Leave it outside the white line. We're inside the lines now. Here to play and that's it."

"Okay," I say, but I'm kind of annoyed. I'm supposed to be the captain, the one giving the pep talks. Why is Benny telling me what to do too?

Five elementary schools feed into Merrimack Middle School. It's a huge school—and the sports are big too. They have tryouts. They make cuts. I bet they have pit hair. They only take the best, the top eighteen. Versus us, Mudbury Middle. We take everyone: good, bad, and in between. It's a noble position, but there's no doubt: we're always the underdog. But ever since my parents became coaches of Mudbury? We're also their biggest rival.

I pound on my shin guards, feel the white athletic tape with Messi's name on it, getting smudged from rain. I try not to take it as a bad sign, even though nothing else has gone right today and Dad still isn't here.

Luckily, things look up because Coach pulls Lucy and me aside and delivers the moment I've been waiting for: the beloved armbands.

"You are our elected captains. Serve your team well."

Lucy claps her hands and proceeds to do a cartwheel.

I try to feel humble, but as I slide the armband up my

arm, I'm inwardly fist-pumping like a World Cup champ.

"We're going to play a four-four-two today," Coach says.

Four defenders, four midfielders, and two strikers.

Coach starts to pace around our circle. The rain continues to fall. "Merrimack is strong and fast and has excellent ball-handling skills. We have to play a defensive game."

"Yes, Coach!"

I hold my breath when she gets out her starting lineup.

"Golden. Center striker with Benny."

"Yes!" High five.

"Listen, boys. Today is not about you scoring goals and being the hero. Play wide and defensively. Got it?"

"Yes, Coach."

"Circle up!" I say when the rest of the lineup is announced. "Archie?"

"What time is it?" Archie yells.

"GAME TIME!"

"I *said*—what time is it?"

"GAME TIME!"

Archie throws the soccer ball into the air, and we yell, "AhhhhhhHHHHHHHHHHHHHH," getting louder and louder until the ball hits the ground at the same time we do.

"Go get 'em!" Coach yells.

As we run across the field, Lucy yells, "Psych 'em out! Do some burpees in the rain! Nothing can hurt us today!"

We do it, sliding across wet grass, doing a couple of up-downs until we're completely soaked. Merrimack looks at us like we're nuts. I feel my leg muscles, my calves working. I feel a rising within me, that feeling of happiness that I'm about to run. I reach up to squeeze my captain armband. *Captain.*

We start strong, all of our preseason energy coming to a head at once. When Lucy passes me the ball from the middle, I can hear Coach in my head. *Slow makes smooth and smooth is fast.* Nothing can stop us now.

I keep looking for Dad on the sideline in between plays. Still not here. I dribble past a defender, who is so big he could step on me and no one would notice, but I do a quick fake to the right before going left and I'm past him.

"Golden, pass!" Slick yells. Yeah, right. Slick has my shirt. He's not getting *my* shot.

Benny gives me a warning look, but he's not captain.

I let it rip and the goalie reaches, lunging left, but not in time. The ball sails past the tips of his fingers, right into the back of the net. GOAL!

Merrimack's defensive player #4 is so mad, he chirps in Benny's ear, "Hey, Chopsticks."

"Don't be lame!" I yell at #4.

Benny doesn't outwardly flinch, not like he used to.

Unfortunately, racist dumb stuff like that happens some-times. Instead he just does what he can do: this sweet fake-out past the defense, and getting a corner kick for us.

Chase gets a head on it, but Merrimack retaliates too quickly. They pass really well, and we have to play just like Coach said: defensively.

We hardly make it out of our half of the field again, but we defend well enough to keep our lead into halftime. When I jog to the sidelines, I notice Dad still isn't here. I want to ask Mom where he is, but she immediately starts talking strategy.

When the game resumes, our defense stays strong until the second half, when Merrimack scores on a pen-alty kick because Ziggy touched the ball in the box. We're tied.

"Ziggy!" I yell in frustration. "Come on!"

"Hey!" Lucy says. "Stop!" She talks to Ziggy quietly while Coach subs me out and tells me to chill.

"Let's recover!" C.J. calls from the box. "One more, team!"

We don't score again for the rest of the game, but we also don't let in any more goals.

We end with a 1–1 tie, something we've never been able to pull off against Merrimack before. We'll take it.

My team walks off the field soaking wet, muddy, and grass-stained. Smiling ear to ear.

I already can't wait for the rematch. In the championship. Winning—and that time will definitely be in front of Dad. I'm going to make sure we have NO penalties. We just have to work harder.

When we pull into our driveway, wet and chilled, the Dark Lord is by the mailbox, actually outside in daylight. The rain has stopped, and a huge rainbow hangs suspended in the sky.

"What's he doing?" I ask.

"Putting new numbers on the mailbox," Lucy says, biting her lip. "So it looks better for the Realtor."

I stop breathing.

George walks up the driveway, kisses Lucy's mom (ew), and asks how the game went.

I ignore him completely but let Lucy dance me around the driveway yelling, "We are awesome!"

"Sorry I couldn't be there," he says. "Definitely next time."

I run into the house to look for Dad.

He's lying on the couch looking wiped out.

"Dad's fine," Jaimes says, wrapping a blanket around him. "Sorry we didn't get to your game. It was too wet."

"Who coached your practice?"

"Kelly, Dad's assistant."

"Was he outside in the rain?" Mom asks.

"He waited in the car," Jaimes says, shaking her head.

"I'm fine. Tell me about the game," Dad says, shivering. I pull the blanket up around his neck and start going through the game highlights. His eyes light up, like he could get off the couch and start running down the field with me again.

"We would have won, too, if Ziggy hadn't had a hand ball in the box! I was so mad."

"Remember you win and lose as a whole team, right?"

"Yeah."

"Everyone messes up."

"I guess. We'll get them next time. But the real downer is I didn't get Messi's number."

"Make your own number mean something."

"Did you know 'fan' is short for 'fanatic'?" Jaimes says.

"Who wants pizza?" Mom interrupts. "To celebrate?"

"Go without me," Dad says, closing his eyes. "Hard to eat today."

She comes to sit down next to him, puts her hand on his cheek.

"He's okay," I say quickly. "Right, Dad?"

"Just tired."

Mom scratches his mosquito bites. He sighs happily.

"We're bringing the pizza here," Mom says. "Lucy and her mom are bringing a salad. And George."

My eyes widen. "The Dark Lord is coming *here*?"

Mom gives me a withering look. "It's *George*."

"Slow down, Golden. There are others who'd like to eat."

I stop mid–pizza shove and glance at Dad, who is looking at me pointedly from one of the barstools he managed to seat himself on. I wonder if "Good Leaders Eat Last" is just a saying or if I'm literally supposed to eat last forever. Mom puts a piece of pizza in front of Dad. He looks down but doesn't touch it.

Roma shields Dad's plate before Lucy's mom can put salad on it.

"The croutons can kill him," she says solemnly.

"Roma," I scoff, "don't be dramatic."

I reach over and put Dad's left hand on the table so he can eat, but he still doesn't touch the pizza.

Lucy's mom and *George* laugh and talk with everyone . . . until they get to the serious part.

"As you may have heard," Lucy's mom says, "we've talked about moving."

The room goes quiet.

Lucy looks up at me, and her entire face crumples.

"We've gotten a really great job offer," the Dark Lord says. "In Maine."

"You have or *they* have?" I ask.

"Golden," Mom says.

"Fair question," he says, putting his hands up. "I'm the newcomer here. You've been neighbors a long, long time."

"Our whole entire lives," I add.

"Yes, I, uh, realize this must be very hard for you."

Would it be very hard for him if I threw an entire pizza at his face?

"It's hard for all of us," Lucy's mom says, taking my parents' hands in hers. "We've been together for so long. You've helped raise my little girl."

"It's for sure?" Jaimes asks.

"We've got a showing for the house tomorrow," Lucy's mom says.

I feel my whole body get hot. Lucy gulps and her eyes get teary—which makes Dad's eyes get teary. I have to do something.

"Well, we've actually decided that Lucy will stay here," I announce.

The adults laugh like I've made a joke.

Mom cuts Dad's pizza into teeny tiny little pieces, and Dad finally opens his mouth. I can feel my face burn. I know he can't raise his left arm to his mouth very well, but he could at least try. He sticks out his tongue. Mom puts a tiny pizza piece in his mouth and carries on the conversation like nothing is amiss.

"What's the timeline?" Mom asks Lucy's mom.

What's the timeline?

185

Three to five years.

And then what?

And then he'll die.

I don't hear what Lucy's mom says. I don't want to. I watch Dad chew and chew and chew. He swallows, smiles, and opens his mouth for more, reminding me of a baby bird.

"Can I feed Daddy?" Roma asks.

"Small," he says.

She puts a crumb on his tongue.

"Maybe-uh-little-bigger."

She puts a bigger piece in. He closes his eyes, chews.

Dad's arm swings out softly, brushing across my arm, resting there. At first I think it's to comfort me. Then I realize he's in trouble.

"Daddy?" Roma asks.

Dad is turning a strange reddish purple. He makes a gagging sound.

"Patrick!" Mom screams. She jumps up, pulls Dad forward, and gives abdominal thrusts. I freeze, not knowing what to do. Roma and Whitney start to cry.

"What do I do!" Jaimes yells.

"Hold your dad, Golden," Mom instructs.

I grab Dad and hold his shoulders while Mom tries to get him to cough up the pizza. She pulls up his shirt, her hands under his ribs. His midsection, always so hard and rock-solid, is loose, flabby white, and weak. He's like a rag doll being pushed up and down, his limp arms hanging down by his sides. He makes another gagging noise, a curdling sound like he's trying to cough and can't. His eyes are turning glassy and his face is an unnatural blue.

"Hang on, Dad," I say, pounding on his back. "Cough!"

Dad is beginning to lose consciousness. It's then that the Dark Lord springs into action. He whacks Dad on the back directly between the shoulder blades and gives another abdominal thrust. Dad coughs, making a gagging sound.

"Got it," George says, hooking his finger in Dad's mouth and fishing out a saliva-drenched pizza bite. "Everything is fine. He's okay."

They lay Dad down on the floor now, legs splayed out in an undignified way, but he's breathing. Taking big gulps of air. Breathing.

"Here he comes. He's coming around. Everything's going to be just fine. Patrick, can you hear me?"

There's a gasping sound.

"Patrick?"

We hear his voice before we see his face.

"I'm here. Good . . . pizza." Our eyes meet. "Gold . . . en?"

"The pizza's not *that* good," I say, forcing a smile for the Squirrels' benefit.

"Dragon-Ball P?" Lucy says, squatting down by Dad.

She reaches down and holds his hand like she used to do when she was little and she didn't have her own dad's hand to hold.

"Lucy Goose," he says. She wipes her eyes with her jersey.

Dad doesn't eat anything else. When he's ready, we get him back on the barstool and then slowly we resume the conversation like what just happened is a small blip in any normal person's day.

"What were you saying?" Mom asks.

"Well . . . it will likely take months to sell," Lucy's mom says, clearly shaken. She keeps glancing at Dad, with that look I hate, even though I keep looking at him too. "Ideally we'll finish the school year. We made a deal with Lucy that we'd definitely finish the soccer season. Can't miss that!"

I look at Lucy, who hasn't mentioned this detail. Is she giving *in*? How can they still be thinking of leaving with what just happened? With everything going on with Dad? He's practically Lucy's dad too. Not *George*.

"We'll definitely stay until it sells," the Dark Lord says.

Definitely stay until it sells.

And there it is. My in.

I accidentally smile. The Dark Lord watches me with curiosity.

I resume a neutral face like I didn't just have the best idea ever.

I know exactly how to keep Lucy here.

They said it themselves.

They'll stay until the house sells.

So the house can't sell.

And Lucy will stay.

The Day She Actually Crashes the Big White Whale

The best decisions aren't made with your mind,
but with your instinct.

—LIONEL MESSI

One week later and it's another game day!

Today we travel an entire hour away to play Franconia Middle School near the White Mountains. I can't wait for the bus ride and Secret Circle. Coach is dreading both.

I'm wearing my jersey to school like I told the rest of the team to do.

Jaimes and I walk to the big white boat, loaded down with our backpacks and soccer gear, but instead of getting in, I drop my stuff and run to the mailbox.

Curtis Meowfield is on a mission too, and meows insistently at me.

At first I think he's trying to bite me until I realize he's meowing in approval.

We've never done anything together, but here we are looking left and then right. Curtis plays the lookout as I very carefully peel the brand-new numbers off Lucy's mailbox.

The impossible, Dad said, *is always possible.*

Curtis walks so close to me his tail flicks my leg. Like a high five. Maybe we aren't friends exactly, but we both need Lucy.

And now we have a common enemy.

"What the heck are you doing?" Jaimes asks when I get into the van.

I smile, making room for Whitney and Roma. Roma's wavy hair looks like a giant beehive had a fight in it.

When I wrestle with her hair, she cries. When I suggest we buzz it like mine, she cries. When I say she can go to school with it like it is, she cries.

"I'm never going to have kids," I say, finally getting her hair into the rubber band.

Roma looks in the mirror and stops crying. "I love it, brother!"

I flex. Maybe I'll have ten kids.

"I can do my own hair," Whitney says.

Eventually Dad comes out of the house.

"Does he look like he's shuffling more?" Jaimes asks, starting the van.

"Nope."

"You didn't even look. You live in denial."

"Dad's just tired today," I say. "Don't let him work too hard at practice."

"Golden . . . Dad's energy has nothing to do with me or the team."

Dad's followed by Mom, who is carrying jackets, her purse, and a frazzled expression.

"Ew," Jaimes says, looking in the mirror. "Is that a pimple?"

"Can you please not say 'pimple'?"

"Don't worry," she says. "If you ever hit puberty you'll get pimples too."

"If Jaimes was a pimple I would pop her," I say for Roma and Whitney's benefit. They collapse into their seats, laughing.

It takes an excruciatingly long time for Dad to shuffle to the van.

"Yur moh needs mo help," he says. We stare at him, his speech so thick and garbled this morning I can barely make out the meaning.

Jaimes and I take Dad's arms. We pull while Mom pushes from behind. Dad waddles up the small van ramp. Roma grabs on to his left arm, while Whitney pulls the right.

"Than yooo," Dad says.

I want to tell him to enunciate but keep my mouth shut.

"Golden," Mom says as Jaimes begins backing out.

"Don't freak out when I tell you something, okay?"

"Since when do I freak out?"

"I just got a phone call. The wheelchair is arriving this afternoon."

I shrug like I'm not totally freaking out on the inside.

"It's really going to help Dad—especially at school. You see how long it takes for him to walk from one place to another."

Dad glances over at me and down at his seat belt buckle, tapping it with his left hand. I pull down his seat belt and buckle him in.

"Thankssss, bud." He swallows thickly.

"What's happening?" Whitney asks.

"Tongue," Dad says. "The muthles . . ."

"The tongue is a muscle," I say to her, sticking my tongue out to make her laugh. "Dad needs some time to warm it up. We can do some tongue exercises!"

I can see Jaimes shaking her head. "Mom, you've got to talk to him."

"Uh, I'm right here."

"Golden, did you know that lifting weights just tires Dad out and doesn't actually help him? The only reason he does it is because you—"

"That's not true!" I yell. "It *has* helped. I know because I've seen it, right, Dad?"

"J . . . aimes!" Dad says sharply. "Don't. P-please."

"Not here, Jaimes," Mom says. "Just drive."

Not *here*? I'm so rattled I'm shaking, but Jaimes distracts me by slamming on the brakes. We all fall forward, including Dad, whose head snaps forward and back, hitting the headrest, hard. He winces in pain. He glances at me. . . . *You're totally right about her killing us with this driving thing.*

"That was fun!" Roma yells.

I reach over and steady Dad's head, scratching his mosquito bites while I'm at it.

Mom closes her eyes and loudly inhales. I get the feeling it's preventing her from killing her offspring.

My stomach growls as we turn into the road.

I swivel and stare at Lucy's mailbox, to where the address numbers should be, the ones now rolled up in my pocket. Jaimes follows my gaze and is so distracted that something awesome happens—she *hits* the mailbox with the van. There's a crunch and the entire mailbox smashes into the street.

My family goes nuts.

"OPERATION MAILBOX DOWN!" I say.

I can't say what Jaimes says back to me.

Ten minutes later, with Mom sending a flurry of apologies to Lucy's mom via text, we're driving again. A mere thirty-five minutes late for school.

"Stop sign!" Mom says as Jaimes slams her foot down on the brakes, coming to a full stop in the middle of the intersection next to our school. Why Mom continues to let Jaimes drive is a complete mystery.

"I think we should definitely start praying more," Whitney says. "Like other families do."

"I think we should get out of the intersection," I say.

Jaimes looks at me with utter contempt.

"Dear God," Whitney announces. I glance at the clock. Thirty-six minutes late. "We're thankful we're still alive and that Jaimes didn't murder any real squirrels trying to cross the road, as is their right, and please help us today to . . . be brave and to do our best and love our fellow beings. Amen."

"That's very nice, Whitney," Mom says.

"Did Lucy teach you that?" I ask.

"I learned how on YouTube."

Mom turns around. "You learned to pray from You-Tube?"

I open the door and jump out. "Bye!"

"Bye, lovessss," Dad calls to Roma and Whitney as they follow me out. Roma stops and stares at Dad.

"Are you ever going to be able to walk me inside again?"

"God is the God of miracles," Whitney says sagely.

Dad opens his mouth and nothing comes out.

"Come on," I say, grabbing Roma's hand and starting to run into school.

"Whit, let's go!" I say.

"I believe—you can't make me not!"

"I wasn't . . ."

"The only thing you believe in is yourself and Messi and becoming a professional soccer player. Why don't you try believing in something important?" Whitney bursts into tears and runs up the stairs.

"Whitney!" I yell. "I was going to say I'm glad you believe. . . ."

But she's gone.

After I drop Roma off, going through the kind-brave-darlin'-girl-I-love-you thing, I walk alone, down the middle school wing.

I wave at Whitney when I pass her classroom. Her face is red and worried as she scrambles to open a note-book and get to the assignment everyone else has already started. When she finally sees me, I wave until she comes out—teachers let us do that now. Pity perk.

"I'm sorry, Whit," I say. "I didn't mean to make you sad. We both want Dad to get better, right?"

She nods.

"So let's keep doing what we're doing and make it happen. Deal?"

She holds out her hand and we shake.

Whitney walks back into class with a smile, and I continue my walk down the hall with a little less angst. I guess

I need to help Whitney and Roma know that everything I do is for Dad. Maybe Whitney is spending too much time on YouTube and everyone's too busy to notice. Dad's right. The Squirrels are annoying, but they're part of my team off the field. They need a captain too.

The thought comes before I can stop it: *What would our family be like without Dad? What if his neurons keep dying? Will I have to become, like, Roma and Whitney's new dad? Will I be doing Roma's hair every day? Is that my destiny? HAIR?*

No.

I'm supposed to be Messi!

Overcoming the odds, being a champion, THAT is my destiny!

I literally stand in his shoes.

Whatever Jaimes was saying, she's wrong. The game isn't over until we stop fighting.

Like my ten thousand hours chart.

Ten thousand touches.

Ten thousand tries.

Ten thousand spectacular fails until you finally get it.

I'm trying so hard to stay positive. Just because I'm failing right now doesn't mean I'll stop.

Believe me, if I could, I'd never doubt again. I'd believe every single second and never ever stop.

* * *

I think about all of this through the rest of the school day, on the bus, until the second I finally step on the field. We play Franconia in the shadow of the mighty White Mountains. We demolish them with a 6–0 win, with five different players scoring and assisting. During the second half, Coach pulls out all us starters and tells everyone we're not allowed to score anymore. But then on a fluke shot, Paige gets her first goal and, well, we have to go wild. I feel a little bad, a little awkward, shaking hands with the opposing team after, because no one likes to lose like that—but we've all lost like that.

We do Secret Circle in the back of the bus, out of Gag Me and Coach's earshot. We ask all the most secret questions, like who we like, who our first crushes were, and who we think is coolest. Usually I love it.

But nobody is going to ask me the questions I'm still trying to answer—

Were we destined to have a dad with ALS or is it all just random? Is this a test? To see how much we love him?

This is how I'd answer:

Ten thousand tries until we've mastered the impossible thing? That's nothing. Nothing compared to how much I love Dad.

We create our own destiny.

ALS doesn't stand a chance against the Maroni dream team.

The Day I Meet Sugar Ray—
and Start a War

Some people think football is a matter of life
and death. I assure you, it's much more serious
than that.
—BILL SHANKLY, SCOTTISH FOOTBALL (SOCCER) PLAYER

"Today we're going to talk about the care and keeping of babies," Mr. Mann says. "You're about to experience how much time and energy a child requires."

As if I need more practice taking care of a child. Roma's hair and laundry alone are seriously cutting into my ten thousand hours.

Mr. Mann points to the five-pound bags of sugar on the counter. "Welcome to parenthood."

"Isn't it a little ironic that babies need healthy food and our babies are made of sugar?" Sunny asks.

"Indeed," Mr. Mann says. "Budget constraints."

He holds up a bowl where everyone's name is printed

on a small slip of paper. "I will do a random drawing. You will pair up as parents for the next two weeks."

I cross my fingers. *Lucy or Benny, Lucy or Benny.*

"Sam and C.J.," Mr. Mann says. "Congratulations." He picks up the five-pound bag of sugar and hands it to Sam.

The class erupts.

"Lucy and . . . Benny!" Mr. Mann says, holding up two more slips of paper. *Of course.*

"Sorry," Benny whispers to me.

"Whatevs." I shrug like I don't care.

"Golden and Slick," Mr. Mann says.

I collapse on my desk.

Anyone else would have been better. Slick? Totally uncool.

"This five pounds of sugar is now your baby," Mr. Mann says. "Print a face—and no, it can't be my face or anyone else's in this class—and after, diaper your child." He holds up the smallest preemie diapers I've ever seen.

I sprint to the computer and print off my idea.

"Messi!" Benny says, pulling it out of the printer. "What a surprise."

"He makes a cute, and determined, baby," I say. "Can't you tell? He was born for greatness."

Lucy has printed out a baby girl face. "My darling Estelle!"

"A word of caution," Mr. Mann says. "In the past I've noticed questionable parenting techniques. For instance, would a responsible parent leave their baby in a locker while eating lunch? Or unattended during soccer practice?"

Slick breathes down my neck like he wants to *eat* our sugar baby.

"Remember, if your baby is neglected in any way—left on the counter in the bathroom, accidentally rolls into a pond, or is left alone while you play at recess—I will take the baby and you will fail this assignment," Mr. Mann says. "I'm going to give you five minutes to discuss your custody arrangement."

I pull the baby Messi closer.

"It's not like I want *you* as a partner either," Slick says, pulling Messi out of my arms and taking out a Sharpie.

"Give him back—and don't write on him!"

"You can't have him all the time," Slick says. "Anyway, I'm going to be a great dad."

"Don't you have a dog?" I ask.

"And a gecko."

The lunch bell rings, and Mr. Mann holds up his hands. "Go to lunch. And think about what you are putting in your mouth and what you feed your little ones. There is a link between the amount of processed food and sugar we consume and disease. Obesity, diabetes, cancer, Alzheimer's . . ." I wait keenly, to see if he says ALS. He doesn't.

"Come on," Benny says. "Let's get lunch."

"Thank goodness. I'm literally starving." I pat my growling stomach. The grocery situation has not gotten any better.

"Catch," Slick says, throwing the sugar bag into my arms before running down the hallway. "I wrote his name on the back!"

"Wait a minute," I say, looking at the name. "*Sugar Ray* isn't his name!"

Slick's annoying cackle echoes down the hallway.

After school and soccer practice, we pull into the driveway to see the Dark Lord installing a brand-new black mailbox.

I try to scoot into the house before I have to talk to him, but Lucy excitedly introduces our babies when he comes walking up the driveway.

"I've always wanted to be a mother," Lucy coos, rocking Estelle.

"I'll babysit anytime!" Whitney says.

"They're adorable creatures!" says Roma.

"I quite agree," George says, smiling. I avoid eye contact.

"Want to play soccer?" I ask Lucy.

"Maybe later. Estelle has just sat through two hours of practice and needs some attention."

"Golden," Mom says, "can you give George a hand with the mailbox? We did run it over, after all."

"I'll help!" Roma announces, taking Sugar Ray out of my hands.

"That would be great!" the Dark Lord says. "I'm almost finished."

"Uh, I believe it was Jaimes who ran over the mailbox?"

"And you would be happy to help," Mom says, giving me *the look*.

We walk in awkward silence all the way down the driveway, which feels like a hundred-mile death march.

I hold the wood stand steady while he anchors the mailbox on.

"Nice and sturdy!" George says, shaking it. "Should hold up against sisters behind wheels."

I stifle a laugh when I remember I *do not* like the Dark Lord. Or *George*.

He pulls out new number stickers from his pocket. I look my most innocent.

"This looks even better than before. I should probably *thank* your sister." My mood darkens. We've actually *helped* him?

"Weird thing is, when I picked up the old mailbox, I noticed the numbers were gone. Like, vanished! Poof!"

I stay silent.

"Listen, bud, I get it."

"Get what?"

"See, I don't really think you hate me. I think you just need someone to be angry at. I mean, what's going on with your dad must be so tough."

I am not having this conversation.

"I'm sorry, I'm saying the wrong thing. I know you and Lucy are really going to miss each other. . . ."

I stare at him. He has no right to talk about *anything*. He's the reason that's happening in the first place.

It's lucky for him that looks can't kill. I turn and walk up the driveway.

"Golden," he calls. "Just because we move doesn't mean you and Lucy won't still be friends! Just like removing the numbers won't stop people from finding the house."

I don't stop. I keep walking, spying a newly flowering plant right under Lucy's window. Lucy is right above me. She leans out and waves. Like she's giving me permission for what I'm about to do. I look back at the Dark Lord and am seized with inspiration.

He wants to fight with me? I'll fight.

With my eyes fixed on his, I reach down and grab the plant by the roots. And I yank! It comes out of the earth easily.

"Golden!" I hear Lucy gasp.

I raise my eyebrows at *George* and drop the plant on the driveway before running into the house.

He's going to murder me. Or tell Mom. Which is worse?

Yo, brother, I text Benny, running into my room.

What's up?

> The Dark Lord. Epic battle
> begun. Come asap.

The battle lines are drawn. And I need my friends.

Benny arrives ten minutes later—with food.

"You didn't ask for that, did you?" Mom asks me. "We're fine and don't need anything."

"I didn't, I swear—Benny just knows I'm underfed."

"Golden," Mom says irritably, "stop being dramatic—but, Benny, we are very thankful."

Sugar Ray sits next to me as I melt into dumplings and homemade chicken soup.

"I love Grandma Ho's food!" I say.

"This was Mom. Grandma's hardly cooking anymore," Benny says, looking down. Mom pats his shoulder, but I don't know why.

"Well?" Benny asks when my family has gotten up from the table. "What's up?"

Taking one last slurp, I walk to the window and spill everything. I can't believe the Dark Lord hasn't been over to talk to my parents yet.

When I come to the part about pulling out their plant by the root, Benny looks more appalled than awe-inspired.

"For real? You know how Lucy feels about . . . living things."

"I did it *for* her. She'll be thanking me later. Anyway. Look—it's . . ." I peer closer out the window. The plant is already back in the ground like I never pulled it up in the first place.

My eyes narrow. "What should we do next?"

Benny shakes his head and walks back to the table.

We're interrupted by Mom using the blender.

"Have some of these, Dragon-Ball P," Benny says over the roar, pushing some *shumai* over to Dad, who has come to the table. He's breathing heavy and uses his cane to clumsily pull out a chair to sit on. He turns sideways, lets go of the cane, hands swinging limply back and forth as he awkwardly sits, moving his feet back and forth until he's finally situated. In the corner of the living room is the wheelchair. It came. The fact that Dad's resisting it makes me love him even more.

"I wish I could. Drinking my dinner . . . tonight."

Didn't Dad eat something this morning? I can't remember. Have I not been paying enough attention?

"Where's Jaimes?" Whitney asks.

Mom looks at her watch. "Away soccer game."

"Why isn't Dad . . . ?" I look at Dad. The answer is obvious. How would he get on and off the bus, let alone coach a game?

"Golden," Mom says. She looks at the Squirrels and Benny, offering a small smile. "Dad's probably not going to be coaching soccer anymore. He's going to take a leave of absence from work as well."

Benny silently watches this exchange, which makes it a million times worse. I try to slow my breathing and heart rate.

"Daddy," Roma says, putting a jar of peaches in Dad's left hand, "can you open this?" Dad manages to put the jar between his knees with his left hand. He squeezes, his left hand clenching and twisting, his whole body contorting.

"Here," Mom says. "Let me help."

"Dad can do it!" I say.

"I got it," Benny says quickly. He opens the jar and gives it back to Roma.

"Than . . . u," Dad says.

Mom puts a smoothie in front of Dad. He leans forward and takes a sip. He then tips his head back to swallow several times.

Benny watches in fascination.

Mom watches like she's waiting for him to choke and fall over again.

"The muscles in his tongue and palate are starting to atrophy," she tells Benny. "They're getting too weak for him to swallow, especially food. His epiglottis is sometimes a little slow to close off the larynx."

"Where's that again?" Benny asks.

Mom pulls out an anatomy textbook she keeps on the counter at all times now. "There. If the larynx isn't closed off when you swallow, food can go down the trachea, which leads to the lungs. Then we have a problem."

Mom loves telling everyone our business, but Benny doesn't look grossed out or scared.

"Any . . . thing I eat . . . drink now can . . . kill me," Dad says matter-of-factly.

"Soon we'll be feeding him through his stomach," Mom says.

I tap my foot impatiently on the ground.

"And we won't have to worry about the choking," she says, as if this will pacify me.

"What will you eat, Dragon-Ball P?" Benny asks.

"Ensure, smoothies, any liquids," Mom answers for him.

A thick spool of drool mixed with smoothie drips out of Dad's mouth. I jump to wipe it.

"Sorry," Dad says.

Benny shakes his head. "It's okay. My grandma is getting old. I've had to clean up a lot of things—not that you're getting old!" he says.

Dad laughs. "My body is prob'ly shutting down at a faster rate than . . . Grandma right now."

"Can I have a smoothie, too?" I interrupt. "Both me and Dad have been lifting to gain weight, right, Dad?"

Mom and Dad exchange a look.

"What?" I say.

"Honey, lifting weights won't help Dad at this point," Mom says, sounding like Jaimes, who is sounding like Mom.

I look at Dad. Why doesn't he back me up? It *has* been helping . . . hasn't it?

"But *you* could use some weight gain," Benny says loudly.

"Yep," Dad says. "All good . . . Golden."

"Take a drink of Dad's first," Mom says. "See if you like it."

I take a sip, grimace at the taste.

"What's in it?"

"Beets, hemp, whole yogurt, protein powder, chia seeds, avocado, blueberries . . . stop!" Mom suddenly shouts as I swallow another big gulp and nearly choke.

"Geez, Mom."

"Laxative," she says.

"Laxative?" I look into the smoothie.

Mom and Benny and Dad begin to laugh.

"I'm sorry, Golden, I forgot," Mom says.

"What's a laxative?" Roma asks, coming into the room.

"Golden's going to be on the toilet tonight," Benny says, keeling over in his seat.

Beyond uncool.

There's a knock at the door.

"Don't answer it!" I say quickly, thoughts of the Dark Lord returning.

"Of course answer it," Mom says.

I sink down as low as possible in my seat.

"Hello!" I hear Lucy say. "Treats for our favorite neighbors! Mom just made them."

"Is the Dark Lord with her?" I whisper to Benny.

Benny looks at me, his eyes wide, and nods.

"Hi, Lucy," Benny says, standing. "Baby swap since I'm here?"

"Hi, Benny!" Lucy says. "Sure. Sweet Estelle is pretty cranky. Someone pulled up her favorite plant right outside her window."

"Oh no!" Mom says.

I sink lower. Dad eyes me, confused.

"Please tell Golden hello from me," I hear a deeper and darker voice say. "We had a bit of a tough day by the mailbox—nothing major," he rushes on, sounding all friendly. "I just didn't say the right thing and I wanted to apologize." *Puh-lease.* Tell me she isn't buying this nice-guy act.

"Golden?" Mom calls.

"Meow." Curtis came too.

I telepathically command him: *Curtis, attack!*

I stay low, head under the table, waiting for Attack Cat to make his move. Believe me, I know he can. Instead I see the furball curling his way around the chair that an unattended Sugar Ray sits on.

"Curtis!" Lucy calls. Curtis meows noisily at me and jumps on my head, then onto the table before sprinting off. "Please tell Golden hi . . . ," Lucy says. "Is he okay?"

"Oh, sure!" Benny says, a little too cheerfully.

"I'll tell him you said hello," Mom says. "Thank you, sweetie."

The door closes, and Mom walks over holding a plate of cookies.

"Don't eat those," I whisper. "They're likely poisoned."

"What happened at the mailbox, Golden?"

"Nothing."

She takes a bite. "Yum."

"If you value your life, you won't eat another bite."

"He's perfectly nice."

"Yeah, for a psychopath."

"You are acting very strange," Mom says.

I rise, stretch my neck, and pick up Sugar Ray. "If it wasn't for him, Lucy wouldn't be moving."

"Honey," Mom says, reaching out her hand to rest on my shoulder.

I shake her off. "I'm fine, Mom. And I have a plan. Right, Benny?"

Benny holds Estelle the Sugar Baby, looking skeptical.

Before I can execute, I dash to the bathroom. "LAXATIVES," I yell. "Uncool!"

"It's cool he didn't snitch on you," Benny says when I walk him home.

"It's all part of his evil design," I say. "To lure us over to the dark side."

Benny sighs.

"Benny, don't give in!"

"Look, I don't want Lucy to move either, but what in the world can we do about it? You're going to keep pulling up flowers, running over the mailbox, and what next— breaking windows? Knocking down the house? You're going to be in jail before the house sells."

"That's an idea."

Benny laughs like I'm joking.

"She's *not* moving!"

"Golden—"

"Maybe I'm focusing on the wrong thing. Maybe they need to see that *he's* the problem—not the house!"

"Oh wow. Golden, listen. You are definitely focusing on the wrong thing."

"I am?"

"Yes! Hello? Our soccer team. You're not at all focused like you should be. You're not thinking about our next game or talking about our next set plays. What's wrong with you, man? That's all you ever used to think about, talk about, dream about! Don't lose it now. It's only the middle of September and we've got nine games left before the championship, remember? We can't get there if we don't have our captain focused and helping us win games! We need you!"

"I think about soccer every waking moment!" I say.

Benny stops in front of his house. "You're distracted."

"Why aren't *you* a little more distracted? This is Lucy!"

"Dude . . ."

"You're jealous!"

"I'm not jealous! I'm trying to help you. . . ."

"You're jealous because . . ."

"Because what? Because you always put her before me? Because if you had to choose between the two of us, I know it would always be her? Okay, you're right. I am jealous! But that's not why I'm saying this." Benny blinks rapidly and kicks a rock.

"Benny, that's not—"

He pokes me hard in the chest. "Focus! You wanted to be captain so bad, but why? To wear an armband? You don't actually seem to want to BE captain. Captains can be replaced, you know."

"Is that a threat? You're supposed to be my best friend!"

"I am your best friend!" he roars. "That's *why* I'm telling you!"

His front door opens, and Mrs. Ho steps out. "Benny?"

Benny and I look at each other and fume.

Then, slowly, and stiffly, we do our handshake. As he pulls away, he also wipes his eyes with his arm, which makes me feel bad and kind of surprises me. It's been a long time since I've seen Benny Ho cry.

I walk home alone. Captains can be replaced? What's he talking about? I'm trying to keep everything together when everyone else, including Mom and Benny and Lucy and Jaimes, seems fine to just let everything fall apart.

I get home just in time to see Lucy pulling the pulley, Kermit the Frog waiting at my window.

Inside is a pink piece of paper folded into a tiny square. I carefully unwrap it and read:

Maybe it's not your job to make everything better.

I look outside my window. Lucy is staring at me from

hers. I lean out so I can see her better. Fireflies light up in the small garden below her window.

"It *is* my job, Lucy."

She tips her head to the side, hair falling across her shoulder.

Her hands reach out across the darkness, across the chasm that separates us. I reach my fingers out too, reaching as far as they will stretch, something we used to do when we were little and had to go to bed but wanted to keep playing. If we could only have reached a little farther, the tips of our fingers might have touched and we could have conquered the whole world.

"The only reason I'm forgiving you for what you did to the beautiful plant under my window is because I know why you did it," Lucy says.

"I'm sorry. I'm trying to help you! And I don't know why you're not trying a little harder to stay."

"Goldie, I *am* trying. I'm scared and sad to move, but sometimes I'm also excited—I can't help it."

"Two opposite things."

"And both are true."

"Lucy . . . I need you to believe."

She tips her head at me. "If there's anyone I believe in, it's you."

I feel a lump in my throat as big as a size 5 soccer ball.

"Good night, Golden."

She drops her hands, breaking the spell.

"Good night, Sugar Ray."

I hold up Sugar Ray—and accidentally drop him two stories below.

Luckily, he lands in a hydrangea bush and has only minor scratches and is a very forgiving baby.

Work Harder

You have to fight to reach your
dream... sacrifice. Work hard for it.

—LIONEL MESSI

Less than a week later it's game day against Kearsarge,
which means we need someone to watch our babies.

Whitney beams at the suggestion—and it gets her off
YouTube.

She squeezes both Estelle and Sugar Ray. "I promise
on my honor that baby Estelle and Sugar Ray will receive
only the best care!"

"Thanks," I say.

"Come on," Lucy says. "I've got snacks." Today her
hair is in braids with small red scrunchies at the bottom.
Her fingernails are painted a matching firecracker red.

As we run to the bleachers, I see Benny already on
the field warming up. I wave, but he stays focused on

dribbling. I swallow hard, still feeling bad about last night. Jealous of Lucy and me? I guess it's true that we always say we're the twins, that we found Benny later, but we're still three musketeers, not two plus one.

Lucy opens her lunch box and hands me a granola bar. She looks at me and sighs heavily.

"What's the matter?" I ask.

"I'll tell you later. We have a game to play."

"Tell me now so I can focus on the game—please?"

"Fine. Please don't be mad. Today George is taking down Kermit."

"*Our* Kermit?"

"Until like a couple of weeks ago we hardly ever used it anymore," Lucy reminds me.

"It doesn't matter. He can't do that! *My* dad put it up."

"We can still—"

"I notice you aren't calling him the Dark Lord anymore," I say. "So much for believing in me."

I turn my back and walk away from her.

I can't think about this right now. Benny was right. I have to focus.

When the refs blow the whistle, I look around for Dad. Jaimes was going to drive him over after a short practice session, but they're late, as usual.

I want to come out strong in the first five minutes, so I call for the ball.

"Pass!"

Mario passes me the ball, and without hesitating, I shoot.

It goes into the net!

Except it's the wrong net.

With horror I realize I've accidentally scored on C.J.

"Oh no!" I say, dropping to my knees.

"For real?" Slick says. "So lame. What kind of captain does that?"

Coach pulls me out, subbing Archie in for me. Even more embarrassing.

"Buddy," Coach says. "What's going on? You upset?"

"I'm not Buddy," I say. "It sounds like a baby."

"You want to cool off and come back to talk to me?"

I walk to our bench and sit down.

By halftime we've recovered and are tied 1–1—which Slick says is mostly because I've been on the bench.

"Good half, team," Coach says. "Now get some water and then go out there and finish it."

I look down at my magic Messi cleats, pound on his name taped around my calf.

"Captains?" Coach asks.

"Team of my heart," Lucy says, clutching her hands to her chest. "What a spectacular first half."

"Except for—" Slick starts.

"Never mind!" Lucy says. "Defenders, keep up the good work pushing the ball upfield. Midfielders—"

"If we want to win we've got to get some shots in," I interrupt. "We want to win, right?"

Lucy frowns.

"Defense, you have to step up and stop giving up when you get beat. Middies, run faster and shoot the ball! Forwards . . ."

"Don't shoot on our own net?" C.J. asks.

"Golden, Archie," Coach says. "You'll start our second half as forwards. Call for the ball, take the shots. Benny, Sunny, and Brady as middies. Remember . . ."

Remember, remember.

You can overcome anything, if and only if you love some-thing enough.

I want this win and I want it bad.

But . . .

"Where's Dad?" I ask Coach.

She checks her watch and scans the crowd. "Let's just get through this game."

The Magpies thunder back onto the field. I find Benny and lightly punch him on the shoulder. "We're good, right?"

"We're good," he says. I can't tell if he's just saying that, though, so I won't keep messing up.

The whistle blows and the game resumes, but my head doesn't quiet like it usually does when I play. Benny passes to me and I try to hesitate and wait for a half second, just like Coach always tells us, for the opposing team to make the first move. When Kearsarge attacks my left side, I lunge right so that I'm one-on-one with the goalie. Her hands are out, fluorescent orange gloves on them and a too-big yellow goalie jersey.

"Go, Golden!" I hear Lucy scream.

Her voice emboldens me, and I know it's my chance to impress everyone. Show them why they chose the right captain.

I Maradona, going over the ball with one foot, turning, and pulling the ball with my opposite foot, just as the goalie comes out. Unfortunately, I underestimate her speed and we run into each other before I can take the shot. I fall to the ground and—*No!*—the ball is loose, slowly rolling out of the box.

"See the field!" Coach calls as I get up. My face burns. She's right. I had a wide-open shot. Why did I have to show off with a Maradona?

Lucy sprints forward and intercepts the ball. "Archie!" she yells, looking for a striker, then passes the ball to him.

"Golden!" Archie yells.

I scramble up, realizing I was just watching everything happen.

Stumbling, I try to get back into the game, but the defender steals it from me after one touch and boots it toward C.J. in the goal.

I close my eyes and try to channel Messi.

But what comes to mind first is Dad. *Here with you.*

And suddenly everything finally focuses.

C.J. blocks the goal, and our defense has officially recovered from my show-off move. They pass the ball up, finding our middies. I grab a pass and send it perfectly to Benny.

With a minute left, a quick dribble, and a small flick, Benny puts it in the back of the net for a 2–1 lead.

A few seconds later the refs blow their whistles.

Game over.

It's a win! My stupid wrong goal and Maradona will be forgiven because we won.

Dad would be cheering and jumping up and down like crazy, if he could.

I notice the Dark Lord is doing just that. I hate him even more.

I Tell a Lie for the Good of All

How do you mark Cristiano Ronaldo? You try not to leave him alone, don't let him shoot on his right foot. And Lionel Messi? Just make the sign of the cross.

—GIORGIO CHIELLINI

I'm ecstatic all the way home. Off the field, in the van, out of the van. Can't wait to tell Dad and Jaimes and everyone that we're that much closer to the championship.

When we get home, Lucy's mom is outside sweeping the porch, arranging the wreath on their front door.

"Another showing!" she calls.

I bounce a little less into the house and shower but try to rebound while putting bread in the toaster. I even decide to be happy that we're having avocado toast for dinner again. Jaimes chops avocado into slices, salts and peppers it, and we sit and chatter about the game. Dad is resting on the couch, eyes closed, a smile on his face as we talk about soccer.

"What helpful children," Mom says. She's happy too, for once. That's what a soccer win can do.

In the window behind her, I see a familiar car pull up outside. *Another showing.* A chance to spy on the enemy.

"Back in a minute!" I call, and I step onto the porch to find Myra the Realtor—and she's got a family with her. While Myra goes inside Lucy's, the couple stays outside. The woman is pregnant. I squeeze Sugar Ray even closer to me.

"Hello," they say when they see me looking.

"Hi."

It's then that I see it—Kermit the Frog is staring at me from the lunch box sitting on my porch. I look up. The Dark Lord really has cut down Dad's pulley. Never again can I send Lucy a note in Kermit. The tears I feel coming down my face are unexpected and shocking. The couple looks alarmed.

I pick up Kermit and furiously wipe tears, trying to gain control of myself.

"Honey," the woman says, coming up the stairs. "Whatever is the matter?"

I gulp, swallow, try to talk.

"Is that . . . your lunch box?" she asks.

"There were these little kids who shared Kermit to pass notes back and forth in," I say.

The woman pats her heart. "How sweet."

"It *was*," I say bitterly.

"Was? What happened?"

I do something very bad, but very necessary. I tell a big fat preposterous lie.

"And—they died!"

She gasps, puts her hand on her heart.

"That man in that house over there?" I nod to Lucy's. "He *killed* them."

"What?"

I nod.

"Should we be . . . calling the police or something?" The woman looks at her husband, who looks equally alarmed.

"No, no, no," I whisper. "I've tried everything. No one listens. We'll just have to wait until he makes his next . . . mistake."

"Mistake?" She puts her hand protectively on her stomach as Myra's voice carries through the front door. "Can we help? What were their names?"

"Who?"

"The kids!"

"Uh. Sugar Ray . . . because he was so sweet. And Estelle." I pat my baby.

"Is that him?" she asks. I nod and show her Messi's face, praying she doesn't recognize the greatest soccer player in the world. She shakes her head sympathetically. Her husband tilts his head, studying Messi's face.

I turn the sugar baby back around. "I keep his picture here so I can remember. It's been a terrible time. We'd welcome you to the neighborhood, of course, but . . . I don't know that you want to live here. Some say they can hear the voices of the children crying during the night." I might be carrying this a bit far. Then again, the woman's eyes bug out in sympathy for my pathetic tale.

"Golden?" Mom opens the front door and smiles. It's good timing.

"Yoo-hoo!" Myra calls, walking over. "Did you meet your delightful new neighbors?"

The couple slowly backs down our stairs.

Mom waves, then pulls me inside and shuts the door. She looks at me suspiciously as she goes to sit by Dad on the couch.

I hold up Kermit the Frog. "Look what *the Dark Lord* did!"

"I'm sorry I forgot to tell you," Mom says. "They asked, and I was going to discuss it with you. I didn't think they'd take it down so soon."

"You said it was *okay*?" Unbelievable.

"You don't even use it," Jaimes says.

"That's what you think."

"Well, that's disappointing, but I do have happy news," Mom says.

"Exc . . . ing news," Dad says, opening his eyes.

Mom's eyes start shining. "You know how they're upgrading the turf field at the high school with new bleachers and lights for night games?"

Of course I do. Jaimes hasn't shut up about it all season.

"They're also having a ribbon-cutting ceremony, and we're all invited as the special guests of honor."

"Why?" Whitney asks.

"Because of what they're naming the field," Jaimes says, smiling.

"The Patrick Maroni Championship Field." As soon as Mom says it, she bursts into tears.

My sisters jump up and crowd around Mom and Dad. I feel hot and want to run away.

"Mom, it's okay!" the Squirrels say while Jaimes gives her a hug.

Dad has a helpless look on his face, like he wants to sit up and put his arms around Mom—but can't.

Mom looks at me, smiles, and wipes her face.

"Sorry, wow. I think I needed that."

She reaches over and squeezes Dad's hand. He's able to catch the ends of her fingers and squeeze back.

"Why are they naming a field after Dad?" Roma asks.

"Because he's the greatest of all time, of course," Mom says lightly.

"The man, the myth, the LEGEND," Jaimes says.

You have to die to be a legend. Isn't that what Moses said?

I feel a tightening in my chest.

"GOAT!" Roma and Whitney yell. "Daddy is the GOAT!"

"There's more," Mom says. "After the dedication, guess whose league gets to play their championship game on *the turf field.*"

"Turf. Bright lights," Dad says. "Fancy . . . bleachers. Big score . . . board."

The ball in my throat begins to loosen and my mouth drops open.

"Us? It's us, isn't it! This is HUGE, GINORMOUS! I have to tell Lucy and Benny right now!" Never in our lives have we played a game on turf before—let alone the championship.

"Well, first you have to make it to the championship," Jaimes says.

I scoot my chair out. I've got to refocus. Train hard for the next eight games. "I'll be in the garage working out. Dad? Coming?"

"No. I'm . . . wiped."

"Dad, you've got to try even when you don't want to try! You don't have to lift weights if they're too heavy—you can just practice walking!"

"Golden . . . ," Mom and Jaimes say at the same time.

"Tomorrow, then," I tell Dad. "No excuses."

"No excuses," he says. A shadow passes over his face.

I ignore Jaimes, who is looking pointedly at Mom, and make for the front door.

But I should have gone straight to the garage.

I should have run out the back.

I should have run away with Lucy and Benny.

Because when I fling open the door, Myra the Realtor is standing on our front porch. Arms folded, foot tapping. Yikes.

After an excruciating and totally one-sided conversation, I'm sent to my room for "telling expectant mothers tales about dead children crying in the woods. For heaven's sake, Golden!"

The Fight

A week after "the big fat lie," I open my eyes to find Sugar Ray staring at me from under the covers.

"Hello," I whisper excitedly, so Jaimes won't hear me. "Game day, little buddy. Are you ready?"

I swear mini-Messi smiles back at me.

I look out the window and see that Lucy's blinds are open and baby Estelle is sitting on the windowsill. I place Sugar Ray there so they can smile at each other—just like Lucy and I always have and always will.

Hours later, Gag Me delivers us to Lakes Middle School by hitting their front curb, followed by slamming the brakes so hard that Sugar Ray and three other sugar babies fall off their seats and crash to the floor.

I grab Sugar Ray. There is a tiny tear near his head. Poor thing. I'm soon holding four abandoned sugar babies on my lap. One doesn't even have a diaper on.

We unload off the bus, and since Ziggy's not playing due to shin splints, I place all the sugar babies on his lap. "You're on duty. Cool?"

"Thanks, Golden!" Ziggy says, like I'm doing him a favor.

I breathe in the crisp just-starting-to-be-fall air and reach down to secure the white athletic tape with "Messi" on it. I'm not going to let anything shake my focus today. I'll make the man proud.

Lucy and I run through the warm-up, and I try to give my best and most impassioned speech, but Brady and Slick aren't paying attention.

"Hey, your CAPTAIN is speaking!" I shout, but they just snicker.

"Let's go, team!" Lucy yells hastily, putting her arm in the center for a cheer.

The first half goes even better than I hoped. We're passing and scoring easily, like Barcelona. At halftime we're up by two. I walk off the field to grab a drink but notice Slick touching Sugar Ray's ripped head.

"Goldie-Locks," Slick says. "I can see his sugar brains."

He sticks his finger through the tear and then *tastes* our baby.

"Slick!" I grab Sugar Ray back.

"Were you, like, eating your baby?" Ava asks. "You are so warped."

The ref blows her whistle. "Five minutes!"

"So what's your halftime speech?" Sunny asks me.

"How about this? Slick is a jerk and he's eating my baby!"

"Team!" Lucy interjects. "We're up by two, but we can't let up. Let's keep passing and talking like we have been."

"That's right," Benny says. "Great saves, C.J. Their number five has a great shot. Defense, you got him covered?"

Lucy and the defense nod.

I nod too but look at Benny. Why is he chiming in? Does he think he could do better than me?

As we head out to the field, I realize I took my mouth guard out for water and forgot to put it back in.

"It was right here!" I say, rummaging around the bench.

The ref blows her whistle again.

"Golden—now!" Coach says.

"Someone took my mouth guard!"

Brady goes in for me as I search in vain, around all the strewn sweatshirts, socks, and gym shoes that should have been put away behind the bench.

"Look at the bench!" Sissy says to Sunny. "This is

practically a yard sale—our captains should totally be on this." She starts chucking stuff behind the bench like I'm not standing right there.

"Where's my mouth guard!" I say, turning to Slick.

He shrugs and starts whistling.

"You're lying! First you take my shirt, then my mouth guard."

"Dude, is that your dad?" Slick asks, pointing.

"Don't try to distract me."

"Dragon-Ball P!" Sunny shouts.

I turn and see someone and some*thing* coming onto the sidelines.

"Oh . . . ," Coach says, her voice trailing off.

It's Jaimes and Dad.

Except Dad's not walking.

He's in the motorized wheelchair.

Time slows down. The ball rolls back and forth on the field. I can't move or talk—not until Slick flicks me in the back of my knee.

"Goldie-Locks, can Dragon-Ball Pops not walk any-more?"

"Wow, you're so sensitive, Slick," Sunny says. "Just shut up."

"I was just asking!"

"Of course he can!" I say.

My hands begin to shake.

"Golden?" Coach asks. Her voice sounds far away, like the sound is coming out of a foghorn. "Dad's okay," she says very quietly. "Now he can be here with us—isn't that great?"

Great? Breathe in, breathe out. Shoulders back. Warrior pose.

Sure. We talked about the wheelchair.

But actually seeing him in it *at a game* feels . . . so wrong.

Using a little joystick that he controls with his left hand, Dad parks himself next to the other parents who have traveled to the game.

The ref blows her whistle when Mario accidentally trips another player and they go down hard. Mom runs out to the field.

I barely notice. I keep looking at Dad.

"That's sad," Slick says. "He was, like, the greatest of all time."

"No," I say, my voice rising. "He's still the GOAT. We're going to work out tonight. . . ." This time when I say it I know how . . . desperate and stupid I sound. "Where's my mouth guard!"

My hands clench.

"This is so stupid!" I yell. "Mouth guards are stupid! The pros don't even wear them!"

I look at Slick at the same time he lets my mouth guard fall on the ground—out of his mouth.

"Goldie-Locks, I found your mouth guard!" He picks it up and throws it at me. It hits my chest, spit bubbles flying onto my chin, onto my cheeks, and into my eyes before it drops to the ground.

"YOU!"

Slick's eyes go wide at the look in my eyes.

I take a step toward him.

"Take a joke, Goldfish!"

I take another step. "That's NOT MY NAME."

He holds up his hands.

"You don't deserve to be on this team," I say. "You don't deserve to wear that jersey. You're a terrible person and you . . . SUCK at soccer!"

The rest of our bench is up like dogs, ears perked for a fight.

"Golden!" Benny yells from the field, followed by Lucy. "Golden, don't!"

"Well, guess what?" Slick says. "You suck at soccer *and* YOU SUCK AT BEING CAPTAIN!" The insult was bad enough, but then Slick does something that flips a switch in my brain. A switch I can*not* ignore—he *spits* on my Battle Packs. The Battle Packs my dad gave me. My lucky rabbit's foot, my everything.

I react with the speed of a rattlesnake, kicking my left leg up to fling the spit onto Slick's shorts.

Slick grabs my leg and we both go down on the ground.

I feel his hands grasping at my shirt. Fists fly, feet kick, my nose starts to bleed. Benny comes off the field to pull us apart. Coach is suddenly in the middle of us, yelling, and grabs me by the jersey, her eyes wide with shock.

My teammates are staring at me like I'm an alien.

Lucy looks like I've punched her, not Slick.

"Coach?" the ref asks, hustling over.

"I'm so sorry," she says, her voice shaky. "Could you please escort these players off the field and to the bus?"

"Do you need to forfeit?"

"No," Coach says. "They just need a long time-out."

Gag Me opens the doors of the yellow school bus before we're even halfway across the field.

I can't bear to look at Dad—or Jaimes—as we go by.

I hold my bloody nose and march past Gag Me without looking at her fangs. My cleats click on the bus floor, grass and dirt dropping behind me. I punch every seat I pass and slide into a middle seat, where someone has left a Ritz cracker wrapper.

"Sit," Gag Me orders Slick. He plops down in the first row of the bus, far away from me.

I slump against the window just in time to see Sam score a goal, with an assist from Brady. The team yells and high-fives Sam. I steal a peek at Dad. He's still on the sidelines, watching the game. No longer smiling.

Jaimes stands with her arms crossed, chewing on her lip. She looks back at the bus a few times until she spots me through the window. She offers me a tiny smile and a wave. I shrink down below the window, listening to the sounds of the second half, trying not to think. When the final whistle sounds, I hear my team cheering without me.

It's only then that I remember Sugar Ray. I peek out the window and spy him sitting forlorn with all the backpacks and other sugar babies. Will someone think to grab him?

Lucy remembers. She picks him up after the handshakes, cradling him next to Estelle. What is she whispering?

"Where did Golden go?" I hear Mario ask through the open window as he makes his way to the bus.

I freeze.

"Do you think he ran away?"

"I'd run away before Mr. T found him," Ziggy says.

"Totally," Brady agrees.

"He shouldn't even be captain anymore," Dobbs says. "I say we impeach him."

"Come on, you guys," Sam says. "Slick stole his mouth guard and spit on Golden's cleats—you know how much Golden worships his cleats."

"We should give him a second chance," Lucy says.

"No," Sunny says. "He's done. The only reason we

237

voted for him was because we felt sorry for him . . . and because Benny told us to."

Benny? He told the team to vote for me? He didn't think I could do it? I don't know what's worse—everyone voting for me because they felt sorry for me, getting impeached because I really was that terrible, or my own best friend not even thinking I had a chance.

"That's not true," Lucy says.

"I like Golden," Ziggy says. "He was nice to me at preseason. That's why I voted for him."

"And he tried super hard," Archie said. "He got me across the finish line, remember?"

"But once he got elected, did he do one single thing to help you or anyone else?" Dobbs asks.

"He's trying," Moses says.

Even Ziggy goes silent, and I think of the Marvel movie I never really intended to see with him. All the terrible things I thought about Moses's smell. If I could, I'd vaporize into thin air.

I sniff back tears, but can feel waves of emotion coming up, up, and up. I sniff louder, trying to squash it down before it hits my nose and eyes, but it's no use.

I can't even be quiet about it, even though Gag Me and Slick are on the bus somewhere.

I hold my body so tightly I can barely breathe. I cry, realizing that all I want is a hug. From Mom *and* Dad.

It's been over six months since I've had a huge bear hug from him because guess what? His huge arm muscles can't squeeze around me. Lucy and Benny and I haven't had a squish hug since my birthday. I don't even have Sugar Ray to hug at the moment.

I lost my game.

I'm losing Lucy. Then probably Benny.

I'm losing the team.

I'm losing my dad.

My head hangs down between my knees so I'm eye to eye with the dirty bus floor. I rip the tape off my socks and crumple it into my fists.

If I lose him, I lose everything.

None of the rest of it will matter.

Footsteps start walking down the aisle. The footsteps stop in the aisle next to me and walk away again.

When I glance up, there is a tissue sitting on the seat next to me. Gag Me resumes her seat behind the steering wheel.

Ten minutes later, my team gets on the bus.

Benny sits down next to me, silent.

I look out the window and follow his lead, staying silent even when Lucy pauses at my seat. She places Sugar Ray in my lap before sitting in the row in front of me.

Coach calls my name. I ignore her until Benny pokes me, and I drag myself all the way to the front row.

Coach pats the seat next to her, but I don't sit. Gag Me starts driving and it lurches me sideways onto the seat anyway. I stare down at my Battle Packs. They're grass-stained, dirty brown, and slightly wet. They look as bruised and beat-up as I feel.

"Goldie."

I can't talk to her. If I talk, I'll cry again. If I cry in front of my team, I'll die.

"Goldie."

I pull my jersey up so it's covering my entire face except for my eyes.

"Golden, will you look at me?"

I turn slightly toward her.

She puts a hand on my knee. "Did that just happen?"

Shrug.

"Honey," she says softly. "I'm so sorry that life is so hard right now. I didn't mean to spring this on you. I'm dropping a lot of details these days. I'm sorry for that, too."

She's not forgiven.

I start shaking my head. "But remember when you said it was tendonitis?"

"It's not tendonitis. Golden. I'm doing my best. I'm trying so hard to keep this team and our family together, but you have got to start understanding that things aren't going to go back to normal with your dad. And you can't keep digging in and lashing out when something doesn't go right."

I don't want to *understand*.

"Your best is *not* working," I spit out. "You're not even trying. It's like you *want* him to die."

She looks struck.

I feel like a horrible troll. What I said isn't true. As much as Mom loves being my mom and coach—she loves Dad even more than that.

We ride in silence the rest of the way home. I don't even go to the back of the bus when Sam calls, "Secret Circle!"

I hear snippets of my teammates spilling their most intimate thoughts. They don't ask me to join in. They don't ask me anything. I don't wait for my team's inevitable impeachment. Instead, I slide my captain's band off my arm and drop it in Coach's bag. She doesn't object. No one does.

It's over, I think.

The Golden era is over.

Benched with Slick

Step over the white line. You're on the field now. Leave everything else behind. BE HERE.

—COACH KARL

Early-morning light wakes me the next day. I open my eyes, feel the sun on my face. My fingers touch my bicep, just in case the captain's band really isn't off my arm.

It's gone. It wasn't a nightmare.

I'm no longer captain of the Mudbury Magpies.

I may have taken it off myself, but I heard my team loud and clear.

Lucy's roller skates move up and down the driveway just outside my window.

Instead of trying to go back to sleep, I tuck Sugar Ray under the covers and go outside. Lucy smiles and waves as she holds Estelle. Lucy's hair is loose and she's still wearing her long white nightgown, with a sweatshirt thrown over it.

My heart grows two sizes. At least Lucy still likes me.

"Good morrrning!" I turn around and see Dad. He's standing in the grass with a soccer ball at his feet. His hair stands straight up because no one has combed it yet. He wears a jacket, but it's pulled at weird angles like he couldn't quite get it over his shoulders. I'm surprised to find he's not sitting in the wheelchair.

He's practicing: tapping his foot on top of the ball.

I take a soccer ball and begin to juggle. He pushes the ball back and forth between his feet.

When I dribble, he moves the ball an inch or two, forward and back.

I do push-ups and he attempts squats, making it down only a few inches.

When I see that Dad has hit his limit, I wipe his face, arms, and legs with my shirt. Lucy continues to skate up and down the driveway, even though I know she's watching everything.

"Thanks," he says. "Want to talk . . . about yesterday?" He swallows hard.

"I don't feel good," I say. "Can I stay home from school with you?"

His eyes crinkle into a smile. "I'd like that."

When Mom takes everyone to school (*Faker*, Jaimes says to me), Dad sits down in his wheelchair.

"Can you help . . . arm up?"

I put his left arm on the armrest but leave his right arm in his lap.

"Head . . . rest?"

I lower the headrest slightly, putting Roma's super-soft bunny blanket behind his head. He closes his eyes and smiles.

I pick up his heavy feet and place them on the foot-rests. "Anything else, Dad?"

"Fingers?"

I carefully unclaw his left hand and place his fingers around the joystick.

"Go for a walk?" he asks. "Blanket?"

I nod, tucking a fleece blanket around him, and put a hat on his head.

With his pointer finger, he pushes forward and speeds toward the front door. I grab Sugar Ray.

As much as I don't want to admit it, going for a walk with Dad in the wheelchair is actually fun. I can walk normally instead of crawling at a snail's pace. Dad doesn't get so worn out. He cruises down the driveway and takes a left down the road. I pause when we see the FOR SALE sign back in the Littlehouse yard, and briefly think about kicking it over until Dad says, "Come on."

"Are you sure you want to go down the hill?"

He pauses.

"Buckle me?"

I buckle him in and he's off! I run beside the wheelchair as Dad motors down the hill, the wind blowing his hair back, making us both smile. I remember him saying *I'm flying!* on the back of my bike. That's the look he has on his face. Maybe this wheelchair thing is okay.

We sail past the trees that line the road, past the small cemetery where Lucy's favorite dead person, Raymond Von Mousetrap, is buried. I hold my breath for good luck. Dad pauses at Benny's house.

"Good friends," he says.

Grandma Ho is at the window.

I wave and wave until she finally raises her hand.

I follow Dad as he motors all the way to the lake and parks in the sand.

"You swim. I'll watch."

"Dad, it's October! It's cold!"

"You're not scared of a lit . . . tle cold, are you?"

I place Sugar Ray in his lap. Kick off my shoes, peel off my socks, shorts, and shirt, and dive in. It's freezing, but I glide under the cold peaceful stillness until I'm out of breath. It's different without Benny and Lucy, but I can't wait to tell them. They'll be so jealous, me swimming while they're in math class.

But . . . will this be how it ends up? Me swimming alone forever? When I come up for air, I turn back to Dad. I know he can't, but I ask anyway. "Swim?"

"No. Happy watching . . . you."

"You're not afraid of a little cold, are you?"

He laughs, but I see him shudder a little, so I go to shore and shiver awkwardly into my clothes.

The walk home is harder. Dad's fingers tire more quickly.

I can see the effort it takes for him to make his pointer finger and thumb work together as he wills them to move.

"I can push when you get tired, Dad."

He blinks. Was that for yes? I don't know and he doesn't stop pressing. We slowly climb up the hill together.

"So. A fight yesterday," he says.

"Yeah."

"Why?"

"I don't know."

"I think . . . you do."

"Slick stole my mouth guard and then put it in his mouth and threw it at me and spit on my cleats so I couldn't play!"

"And?"

"That's what happened."

"And because . . . I showed up . . . in wheel . . . chair?"

I see the moment in my mind, how time seemed to slow, my ears ringing, vision clouding. Slick's drool coming out of his mouth with my blue mouth guard. His stupid questions. How my dad, who could walk, who was going to get better—was in a wheelchair.

"Dad . . . we're trying so hard. Why isn't it working yet?"

He pauses at the top of the hill, breathing as if he's sprinted a mile instead of his fingers having only pressed a small joystick for too long. I pluck an apple from Lucy's apple tree and take a bite.

We look out over our house, the way it sits beneath the mighty Mount Kearsarge. I chew and swallow. So very easily.

"That's the hardest part about life," Dad says. "When you try your very hardest, when you give everything . . . and can't give any more . . . and it still doesn't go the way you want it to . . . go."

We head up the driveway.

"But we get . . . skip school . . . together."

That's true.

"One more . . . day (*swallow*) with you."

I hold Dad's hand. This time we push the joystick together.

The next day Slick and I sit on the bench watching practice.

We've been benched by Coach.

Mom and I really aren't talking at all, which makes

me feel sick to my stomach. I wish I could take it all back. The fight. My mean words. I wish we could rewind to when life was perfect and I didn't even know it.

Lucy is captain by herself, wearing yellow-and-pink-striped socks and her red cleats. It's not going so well.

"I'm playing offense today," Mario says during the scrimmage. "And I'm not wearing a pinny. They smell." He wads up the yellow jersey and throws it on the ground.

Slick doesn't laugh like I'm expecting him to.

He clears his throat and doesn't look at me. "Hey, uh. I'm sorry about yesterday. About Dragon-Ball P."

I'm so surprised I almost fall off the bench.

"I hate sitting," Slick says.

I nod. I hate sitting too. I hate that my dad is sitting.

"Sucks, man" is what I muster.

"You'll be back on the field soon," Slick says. "You're the captain."

"Not anymore," I say. "I heard the team talking yesterday. I was only voted captain because . . . you felt sorry for me."

Slick shrugs an acknowledgment.

"And because Benny told you to."

"Actually, I didn't vote for you," Slick says.

"Gee, thanks."

I look up to see Benny walking over.

"Hey."

"Hey."

"Golden's mad now because you told everyone to vote for him," Slick says.

"Did you?" I ask.

"Yeah," Benny says.

"Because you felt sorry for me?" I wish I could sink into this bench.

"Dude," Benny says. "Why would I feel sorry for you?"

I stare at him.

"Oh, you mean because of your dad? No. That sucks, but he's still the most awesome dad on the planet, so no, I don't feel sorry for you. I voted for you because I knew how much you wanted it and because you're a really good friend and because I thought you'd be a good captain. How's that for a reason? Now, why don't you step up and start acting like one instead of making both of us look like idiots?"

"Geez, Benny."

"Geez, nothin'."

"Easy for you to say."

"Why's that?"

"Why? You're just better at everything. Everyone has always liked you more. Everyone does whatever you want—even voting for me because you said so. You score anytime the heck you want and—"

"Not true."

"True!"

"You know what, Golden? You think everything is so easy for me? I have *everything* to prove. See anyone else getting called Chopsticks on the field?"

"Nope!" Slick says. We both give him a look.

"Yeah, well, I'm Goldie-Locks, Goldfish, Golden Macaroni!"

"It's not the same and you know it. I'm Chinaman, Konichiwa, Rice Paddy. Want me to go on? I've heard them all and so have you. And you never let people get away with it because you're my best friend. But do you know what *everyone* has always liked about you?"

"What?"

"You try so hard, no matter what."

"Tryhard," Slick says, but this time it actually sounds like a compliment.

"You make people *love* soccer," Benny says. "You make us think everything is possible—like winning the championship—when it's such a long shot!"

"No it's not."

"Yes it is! Mudbury in the championship game? That's never happened before. We have to win the rest of our games or score enough points to be at least number two in the league. But there's Shaker *and* Merrimack and they're pretty much impossible to beat."

"No they're not!"

"This is exactly what I'm talking about. You believe more than anyone—and it's hard to beat someone who never quits. Remember preseason? How in it you were? How you clapped for people, how you came off the line and got Archie through the sprints? *That's* why we voted for you."

"Oh . . . Thanks, Benny."

"Well, boys, it was nice knowing you," Slick says.

"What do you mean?"

"Here comes Mr. T."

We freeze.

"Getting along again?" Mr. T asks.

Slick and I eye each other.

"Good. Because if you ever pull a stunt like you did the other day, both of you are off the team for the whole season, not just sitting out for one game, got it?"

We nod again.

"It's Golden Goal time!" Coach yells.

"See ya," Benny says. "Hope you can get it together soon, because I miss being on the field with my best friend. No offense, Slick."

I watch Benny run off to join my team.

"Benny," I call after him.

Benny nods, and I know we're okay again.

It's the hallowed Golden Goal time. Our favorite part of practice, when everything is on the line. When there are mere minutes to make the final, winning shot.

The team battles each other for a full five minutes until Sunny gets a pass from Brady and comes in with a sniper-like play to score on C.J. I look longingly after Benny and Sunny as they high-five. This is what happens inside the white lines: nothing else matters, not who's cool or uncool, just the team.

I decide then and there: I will do everything possible to earn a place on the field again. I'm going to believe in us. If that's my superpower like Benny says, then here we go.

"I hate not playing too."

"Then you better stop punching me," Slick says.

"Stop eating my mouth guard."

"Deal."

"Bring it in!" Coach yells.

"Come on," I tell Slick. We rise from the bench, walk to the circle, stand on the outside.

"MVP Gum of the Day goes to Brady!" Coach yells. "For the assist that made the Golden Goal possible!"

The team claps, pounds his back.

Coach pauses to look at me and Slick.

I clear my throat. The team turns. "I just want to say . . . I'm really sorry."

"What he said," Slick says. "I'm sorry too."

"And, uh, I hope I can gain your trust back," I say. "I haven't been the captain you deserve. I'm going to work harder and do better." No one says anything about being captain again, but in my heart, I hope that someday I'll be sliding the armband back on.

"Mudbury on three!" Lucy yells.

"One-two-three Mudbury!"

I pull Lucy aside afterward. "I've got the best idea you've ever heard!"

"Oh no," she says.

"No, really. It's the best!"

When we pull into the driveway, we see that all of the Maroni and Littlehouse trash cans have tipped over. Trash is strewn all over our yard and the Littlehouses'. Lucy's mom and George are scrambling to pick it up as a family stands looking at the house.

"Oh dear," Mom says. "Myra is showing the house. Bad timing."

"Or good timing?" I suggest as we pile out. This isn't my great idea, but it's almost as good.

Curtis Meowfield is in heaven, licking a tuna fish can.

I suppose I deserve it: all adult eyes, plus Lucy's, turn to eye me suspiciously.

"I was at practice!" I proclaim, hands in the air.

The Dark Lord has been giving me the benefit of the doubt—until now. His smoldering glare laser-beams right at me.

Mom looks flustered, Myra's face frowns, and the visiting couple sniffs, making a face.

"It's usually not like this," Mom says. "The Littlehouse family is very clean."

"Actually . . . ," I say.

"Golden!" Mom barks.

"Is this your house?" the couple asks.

Mom laughs uneasily and looks around like she's not really sure. "Uh, yes. We're kind of dealing with a lot right now. My husband is sick and . . . we've got four kids . . . all great and really active. . . ." Eyes sweep across our property, at the bikes on the lawn, the goalie nets, the soccer balls, the two-day-old laundry hanging on the line. A pair of underwear swims through the air and lands on a hosta plant. Mom's face turns pink as she grabs it and stuffs it into her pocket.

I can't help myself. I fall on the ground, hysterical.

Lucy looks around, her eyes wide with wonder. "Do you think the ghost of Raymond Von Mousetrap sent a tornado through here?"

"Maybe," I whisper. "Destiny is finally starting to make its move."

Sugar Ray and Estelle high-five.

Psyched

We go back for those left behind,
don't we, Golden?

—LUCY LITTLEHOUSE

My great idea? Secret Psychs. I don't tell Jaimes, but I totally got the idea from when she did this with her team a week earlier.

After the trash is picked up, Lucy and I spend the rest of the evening writing a secret note to every single person on the team. Jaimes, Whitney, and Roma help too, drawing hearts and soccer balls in every imaginable color.

"We'll secretly put them in lockers, before we play Sunapee," Lucy explains to them excitedly.

"It will psych us up to win, and really get ready for our next game, against Winnisquam," I say.

When we're done and Lucy's leaving, Nurse Verity comes in holding a black zippered bag.

"What's that?" Roma asks.

Verity sits down and shows us an oxygen machine. "This will help your dad get a little more air while he sleeps."

"Like, for later?" Whitney asks.

"Maybe it will help him now. Let's go see."

I'm skeptical, since Dad has no trouble breathing from what I can see, and follow her upstairs, where Mom and Dad are.

Dad is lying on top of his covers and smiles when we enter. Verity sits on a chair next to him.

"Hi, Patrick."

"Hi. New machine?"

She nods and turns to us. "Your dad can't turn over anymore, so we need to be careful to not pull the covers up too high, in case they cover his face."

I realize that if Dad can't move his arms much, he can't get the covers off his face. The thought makes me squirm.

"What if you have to turn over or get cold or too hot?" Jaimes asks.

"Your mom," Dad says.

"So Mom probably isn't getting a ton of sleep," Verity says.

"Oh, I'm fine," Mom says. I look at her, but she does look tired. And not like normal I'm-not-a-morning-person tired. I think of all the other things she says are fine. Like Jaimes needing new cleats and Dad's expensive equipment. Like me breaking the door molding even though Dad can't fix it anymore. Mom says it's fine but it's not.

Maybe I should get a job.

Do the grocery shopping.

Jaimes could drive.

Terrifying thought.

Verity puts the oxygen mask on Dad's mouth and nose. He closes his eyes.

"Better?" she asks.

"Yes," he says, his breath fogging up the mask.

Huh. I'm glad he can breathe better—but how did I not know he couldn't? What else have I not been seeing?

I sleep in my uniform, Battle Packs and all. It will make the morning routine easier, plus I'm needing a little Messi Magic right about now.

Tomorrow is game day. Also the day we give back our babies.

It's only a bag of sugar, but I've grown unnervingly fond of Sugar Ray. I squeeze him, feeling him crinkle. After Slick tried to eat him, I taped him up so well he's pretty much indestructible. Like Messi. Like . . . Dad?

I squeeze Sugar Ray to me and turn over on my side. Such a small thing I've never thought about before—being able to turn myself over. Maybe I could invent a sleeping-turning machine for Dad.

I hear the creak of my door and pretend to be asleep.

It's Mom. She pulls my covers up and tucks my fleece blanket under my chin and even pats Sugar Ray. My blanket is two pieces of green-and-dark-gray fleece, tied together on all four sides. We made it together a few years ago when I liked sewing—when Mom had time for projects.

I'm not mad at her anymore. I see how hard she's trying. Even now, when she's so tired, she didn't forget about me.

She lies by me for a few minutes. "I love you, buddy."

Sometimes when she says this it almost feels like she's saying "I'm sorry for everything."

Me too.

During science Mr. Mann congratulates us on our parenting skills. Most of the class is relieved to be free of caring 24/7 for a bag of sugar. But my foot taps on the ground like a rabbit.

No one's taking my baby.

"How many of you found caring for a 'child,' twenty-four hours a day, stressful?" Mr. Mann asks.

A couple of kids raise their hands.

"Be honest, how many of you forgot about your sugar babies a couple of times?"

More hands go up.

"Remember—" Slick starts.

"Ah-ah-ah," Mr. Mann says. "No more stories of neglect."

Only one "couple" failed, Mario and Sissy, after Mr. Mann found their sugar baby, Savage, propped up in a tree branch during recess while we played an epic game of four square.

"Time for lunch," Mr. Mann says. "But before you walk—not run—to the cafeteria, say thank you to your sugar baby, for the experience he or she's attempted to provide, and then place your baby on my desk."

The whole class files forward and puts their baby on Mr. Mann's desk. Except me.

There are some wistful good-byes.

But I can't do it.

I cannot say good-bye.

I slip Sugar Ray into my backpack.

"Hey!" Slick says.

I whirl around.

I put a finger to my lips and growl through my teeth, "Not a word or I promise you this: You WILL regret it."

Slick backs up. "Whoa, dude. Chill."

I give him my most scary hairy eyeball. Coach would be proud.

When he runs to the lunchroom, Lucy and I quickly distribute Secret Psychs.

This is Slick's:

> *Roses are red*
> *Violets are blue*
> *Give me my jersey*
> *Before I pound you*

Okay, okay, that's what I wanted to write. The only nice thing I could muster was: *Good luck today!* But I also include my last piece of gum, so I figure that's good enough.

Sunapee is a home game so we have to get through the whole day before it's time to get ready.

Cool: I'm no longer benched.

Uncool: I do not run out to meet the refs and the opposing team's captain with Lucy.

Cool and uncool: Lucy captains on her own.

"Come on," C.J. says. "Warm me up."

Grateful for the job, I take a shot on goal.

"Ten on the ground, right and left," C.J. says. I practice shooting with my left foot. The leather ball connects with my leather Battle Packs. My right leg plants, my left leg swings, all my leg muscles tightening and releasing, my abs and back twisting, adrenaline and endorphins coursing through my body. It feels so good, even though C.J. blocks it from hitting the net.

"Nice save," I tell C.J. as he dives on the ground.

"Who gave me the note today?" Sam asks behind me.

The team buzzes, talking about their Secret Psychs.

"Love this energy today!" Coach yells.

That good energy carries us all the way through the game for a win!

Even without being captain, even without Dad at the game today, I actually feel happy.

Because oh yeah, I get to play FREAKIN' SOCCER.

A week later that energy is still there as we take the field against Winnisquam Middle School. Our passes connect, teammates are talking on and off the field, and Benny gets a wicked corner kick goal.

We leave the field with another win, which puts us one step closer to the championship game.

Maybe it's the endorphins again or another week of Secret Psychs or the humongous smile from Coach, but it feels like nothing can stop us now.

Bitter and Sweet

Now that you've melted my heart, will you go to the dance with me?

—JAIMES'S SUGGESTION. IS SHE FOR REAL?

"Are you going to ask Lucy to the dance?" Jaimes asks.

"We always go together—with Benny, too."

Tonight I'm loading the dishes that Jaimes rinses. Dinner was Whitney's turn: slightly burnt quesadillas that I helped her make, and a can of green beans, which was the last of our vegetables.

"What if Slick or Brady asks her?"

"No way."

Jaimes raises her eyebrows. "Aren't you the one who always says you have to fight for what you want?"

I frown. I *am* fighting for Lucy—to stay in Mudbury. But the thought of Slick asking Lucy to the dance does make my stomach feel weird.

"How would I even—"

Jaimes pounces. "Write a note on a little red heart and freeze it in the middle of an ice cube heart. Put it in her locker and it will begin to melt. Totally something Dad would do."

"What does the note say?"

Jaimes pauses dramatically. "'Now that you've melted my heart, will you go to the dance with me?'"

I can feel my face turn warm.

Jaimes smiles. "I'm brilliant, right?"

"It will melt all over her locker and Mr. T will pummel me."

"Hmmm. How about honey? Something like 'Honey Bee, will you buzz buzz buzz over to the dance with me?'"

"Not in a million years."

Verity the nurse pokes her head around the corner as she prepares to leave. "It *is* pretty brilliant. See you tomorrow bright and early!" she says, walking out the door.

"I like her," Jaimes says. "Do you?"

"Sure."

"Anyway, my idea is Gucci golden. Lucy will melt in your arms."

I make a face even though melting in my arms doesn't sound *so* bad.

Mom and Dad walk into the kitchen. She helps him

sit in the wheelchair, adjusts his head, puts his feet up, and tucks a rolled blanket under his elbow.

"Mom, Jaimes and I can go to the grocery store if you want." It's the first time since our big fight I've spoken to her directly.

Jaimes and Mom couldn't look more surprised than if I had turned into the Easter Bunny.

"Such a nice offer," Mom says. "But I'd love to go and spend time with you."

Jaimes lowers her voice and hands me the last plate. "You should also apologize. And not a lame, mumbled, unintelligible eighth-grade-boy apology. Like a real one."

In response, I flick Jaimes on the leg with a dishrag.

Mom steers me toward the front door before Jaimes can retaliate.

I know I owe Mom an apology.

I'm thinking of what to say on the way out when she takes a phone call.

"Oh no, we're doing fine," Mom says.

"But if someone wants to clean the bathroom . . . ," Jaimes yells from the kitchen, "that's awesome!"

"Meals?" Mom hesitates. "Well . . ."

We all pounce. "SAY YES!"

"I'll let you know," she says before hanging up.

"That was Mrs. Ho," Mom says.

"Dumplings for life!" I yell, fist-pumping the sky.

"You should let her help," Dad says.

"A good captain knows when to delegate," I say sweetly.

"That's why you cooked tonight," Mom says, totally not getting it.

Meanwhile Roma has climbed into Dad's lap to read a story. "I've become very smart in first grade," she says, looking up at Dad. "And in second grade I'll be smarter and in third grade I'll be even this smart! Right, Dad?" She holds out her arms wide. Dad nods but begins to swallow hard.

Whitney skips over and begins to rub Dad's head. "Can you buy popcorn?"

I almost say Dad can't eat popcorn except now it doesn't matter. Now Dad only drinks his food.

Mom walks back to Dad, puts his face in her hands, and plants a big kiss on his forehead. "Love you. Maybe don't eat or drink anything while I'm gone?"

"'Cause Dad could choke and die?" Roma asks.

"Can I watch Sugar Ray?" Whitney asks. I notice she's doing what I've been doing: distracting Roma from her obsession with death. She shares a room with Roma. I wonder how many conversations and worries Whitney's had that I don't even know about.

"Thanks," I say, even though the assignment is over and no one needs to watch Sugar Ray. "He's on the couch."

"For five bucks. I want to buy a violin."

"What? No! I'm saving up for Slick to give me his jersey."

"You're what?" Mom asks.

"Nothing."

"Fifty percent possession of Sugar Ray, then," Whitney says.

Luckily, Mom and I escape to the van without me making any promises to Whitney.

"I need deodorant," I say, because I still haven't figured my apology out yet.

"Write it on the list," Mom says, tossing it over to me. It's a well-known fact that Mom won't remember *anything* if it isn't on the list.

I smell my pits. "Do you think I'll smell more when I get pit hair?"

"Definitely."

"Everyone in eighth grade has armpit hair except me."

"No they don't."

"Yes!"

"How do you even know that? Do you guys say 'Show me your armpit hair'?" She pulls into the supermarket.

"We just know—we see it. Even Moses has it."

"He's a big kid," Mom says. "Anyway, Moses has other things to deal with."

True.

When we get there she walks briskly into the super-market like it's a mountain she's about to summit.

"You know, Mom, it's more fun at the grocery store if you enjoy the food. I mean, look at all these awesome bags of chips." I point hopefully to the toasty cheddar variety.

"Go get your chips," Mom says.

I practically cartwheel down the aisle.

Dad was way more fun to go grocery shopping with. He loves food and cooking. And when we went shopping he'd always throw in cookies and other "junk" Mom has banned from our diet because it's not good "brain food."

After I find the chips, I wander into the all-natural homeopathic and vitamin aisle. One of the packages catches my eye—"improves brain function by stimulating the growth of new neural pathways." I take it.

"Look!" I say when I see Mom. "New neurons is what Dad needs."

She reads the label, looks at me.

"It's worth a try."

"Golden, I will buy this for your father. But look at me. This is not going to be the miracle cure. You *do* know that, right?"

I nod half-heartedly.

She tosses it into the cart, stockpiled like we've had a huge food shortage—oh yeah, we have.

Mom's quiet on the way home, recovering after a

record-breaking whiplash Olympic-speed grocery shopping sprint.

I take a deep breath. "I'm sorry, Mom."

She glances at me.

"For what happened. For the fight. For what I said to you on the bus."

She turns onto a road that definitely does not go past our house. "I'm sorry I didn't prepare you well enough for the wheelchair."

I look out the window. "I didn't think it would be this hard."

Mom pats my leg. "I know. Golden, that's life. Things break, dreams crumble, teammates lick your mouth guards."

"Drool," I say. "He *drooled* on it."

Mom laughs loudly. "Yeah. That's gross."

"You think . . . I could be captain again?" I ask hopefully.

She smiles. "I don't know, Golden. But doesn't everyone deserve a second chance?"

A second chance. Does my team think that?

"You know what a lot of people say about Barcelona?" Mom says, driving even farther away from our house. "They think Messi is the whole team. He's *not*. You can take any of them out of the mix and guess what? The game goes on. Life does too."

I furiously start rubbing at my eyes, then punch my seat. I didn't know I could feel so sad and angry at the same time. "Life's not going to go on without Dad."

Mom pulls into the parking lot of our favorite doughnut shop, Rollin' in the Dough. She turns off the ignition as we sit in the dark. "It's okay to be sad, Golden. It's good to cry." Her voice breaks.

"Mom?"

She furiously wipes tears away from her face before mine can start falling. "I'm fine. I'm just . . . so tired."

And suddenly I feel we've switched places. If she's falling apart, I can't.

"It's going to be okay," I say awkwardly, putting my hand on her shoulder. "Anyway," I go on, wanting her to smile. "Weren't we talking about soccer? The greatest topic in the world? And me being captain?"

"Yeah." She sniffs. "That's right."

"How about you sleep in tomorrow?"

She finally laughs, her eyes shiny. "You are such a good boy."

Embarrassed, I ask, "Doughnut?"

"You know it."

Inside, we breathe in the sweet smells of warm fried dough. My stomach clenches and my salivary glands start wetting my mouth. And wouldn't you know? The girl behind the counter gives us a dozen for free because once upon a time, Dad was her soccer coach. "He was the best," she says.

"Still is," Mom and I say at the same time.

"Jinx!"

In the car she takes a bite and chews with her eyes closed. "Sometimes I really miss eating doughnuts." She takes another bite. "So good."

"Doughnuts should be on the dinner menu once a week."

"Poor Dad," she says. "Can't eat these anymore."

"How about a doughnut smoothie?"

She nods. "Golden, tell me. What's your contingency plan?"

"Contingency?"

"What if you don't get what you want, Golden? What if Dad isn't going to get better?"

"Not an option."

"It should always be an option."

I give just a little bit. "I'll think about it."

But I don't tell her about my deal with God.

I'll take Dad exactly the way he is right now, remember? The downhill just needs to stop.

I don't tell her about my deal with Dad.

You don't give up on me and I don't give up on you.

Ten minutes later Mom pulls into the driveway.

"Oh no," I say.

"What?"

"The For Sale sign," I whisper. "It's gone."

"Sometimes people wait to sell until spring if the house doesn't sell right away."

This news perks me up, just a little.

Mom pulls into our driveway and pops the trunk. I'm beginning to get out of the van when I suddenly see a large dark shadow lurking outside my door.

I yell so loudly the shadow jumps back and yells, "Woah!"

The Dark Lord. Lurking around in the dark.

Mom runs to my side of the car holding an armful of groceries. "Golden?"

"So sorry to scare you," *George* says. "Can I talk to Golden for a minute?"

I get out of the car and face him while Mom goes inside. He looks even more evil in the dark—the whites of his eyes and his teeth glow. My heart beats hard in my chest, making me feel short of breath. I hear a meow, see the glowing eyes of Curtis Meowfield. Would he protect me or eat my dead carcass?

The Dark Lord folds his arms and stares down at me. I gulp and back into the car.

"The sign *and* the new numbers on the mailbox?" he says, raising his bushy eyebrows.

I shake my head.

"Okay. So you're telling me you don't know the sign is gone."

"I didn't . . ."

"And I just replaced the numbers—you were with me."

I open my mouth.

"Golden, I'm sorry, but if you remove them again, or take the sign again, I'll have no choice but to tell your parents."

"I didn't—"

He squeezes my shoulder like he's trying to be friendly for Mom's benefit, who's coming back outside.

"Golden, we're going to sell the house. I need this job and I really want Lucy and her mom to come. I'm not forcing them. We want to be a family and we want to stay together. And you can come visit anytime!" He actually sounds sincere, but I'm not buying it.

We're Lucy's family. And I will never visit the Dark Lord in this lifetime.

"So, please," he says. "Please stop sabotaging us."

I open my mouth to deny it, but then it occurs to me. Lucy! It must have been her. She's finally taking action! I won't rat her out. We're a team. We've always been a team. This guy can't break that up.

I suppress a smile. His eyes narrow.

"Are we . . . good?" Mom asks, coming up beside me.

"I hope so," he says. "Let me help you with the groceries."

When they go inside, I look up at Lucy's light in the window, then at the black night.

The universe is so big.

And I'm so small.

Messi was small and discounted. Nobody thought he would become the greatest of all time.

But he did.

George thinks he's won . . . but the game's so not over yet.

A Great Big Crack

I have no doubt:
we all have our shining moments.
—COACH DAVID FLEMING

Days later I'm still dreaming of doughnuts when my alarm goes off super early. Time to get my family on board with my new morning plan of attack.

"Get up!" I say to Jaimes. "You wake Whitney and I'll take Roma?"

Jaimes rubs her eyes at the clock. "For real?"

"Come on!"

"Goldie!" Roma says when I get her up and piece together a matching outfit. "Can you do braids today?"

While I wrestle with Roma's snarls, she says, "I'm going to die and you're going to die and everyone is going to die."

"Um."

"Because when we're born all of our cells are already dying."

"Look." I turn and face her toward the mirror. "Look at that girl. Who is that?"

"Roma."

"And look how big you are! Remember when you were a baby?"

"No."

"Well, I do. You were teeny tiny like a baby tomato. But you've gotten so big! And you're going to keep growing until you're bigger and stronger and taller. So instead of thinking about dying, how about you think about how awesome it is to be alive? Dad can't run right now, but you can. Dad can't jump right now, but Roma can! Before you die you get to LIVE! A LONG, LONG TIME, got it?"

Roma smiles and nods.

"Think positively, right?"

"Yes, Golden, I will!"

In a mere twelve seconds Roma is rocking some lame braids, but hey, it's effort, man.

Jaimes and I successfully tidy the living room and kitchen, pack snacks and lunch, and feed the Squirrels breakfast, all before Mom and Dad get downstairs and Verity is knocking on the door.

"Wow," Mom says, looking around the kitchen. "I'm speechless."

"Good man," Dad says, shuffling to the barstool and perching.

I stand straighter. *Good man.*

"See you at the game today?" I ask.

"Wouldn't . . . miss."

"I'll bring him to Jaimes's practice," Verity says. "And then Jaimes can drive them both to your game?"

"You're a lifesaver," Mom says.

In the van I close my eyes and focus on the next order of business: winning against Shaker School. Known for its huge players. Slick already said we're dead meat.

"Goldie?" Whitney says, interrupting my visualization. "Can you do my hair next?"

I do Whitney's hair while getting in the zone. It ain't easy, but where there's a will there's a way, right?

It's a perfect New England October afternoon as we travel to Shaker after school.

Mr. T is driving behind our school bus. We wave and make hand signs until he gives us the *Turn around and sit or you're dead* face.

Minus Dad and Jaimes, the whole Maroni family is on the bus. Unfortunately, Sugar Ray is at home, as it would not be socially acceptable to be seen with him in public. I'm ashamed of my weak constitution, but Sugar Ray totally gets it.

I close my eyes to channel my best moves, my best passes, my best compliments. I'm slightly heartsick that the captain's armband is still not around my arm today, but my Battle Packs are on my feet and "Messi" is written on my tape.

You're going into battle. You've got to be ready. You have to work hard. If you love something enough . . .

I see the ball at my feet. It's brand-new, an f50, green and white. My Battle Packs are molded to my feet. I hear Dad . . . *Bend your knees . . . fake left, take the ball right . . .*

"Goldie, we're here." Sam elbows me in the shoulder from across the aisle. I realize everyone else is standing.

"Whoa," Archie says, looking out the window.

I stand and look. The athletic fields are immaculate, green, perfectly mown, with white lines that shine in the sun.

"SIT!" Gag Me roars, hitting the curb as she attempts to park the bus.

We lurch forward, and I end up on the floor next to Benny.

"Come on, you guys," Lucy says crossly.

"What's wrong with her?" I ask Benny, jumping off the bus. I grab the med kit and ball bag out of habit.

Lucy turns around. "You know what!" she says.

I stare at her.

She takes a deep breath. "Golden, it's time to stop."

"Stop what?"

"Stop! Stop taking the numbers off. Stop throwing the sign into the woods. It's not helping. It's just making everyone really mad."

"I didn't—"

"Golden, please. You think you can fix everything, but you can't fix this. It's happening whether or not we like it. I'm making the best of it and so should you!" She turns around and begins to march away in green-and-yellow-striped socks that totally don't match our uniform.

"It's not over!" I call after her. "And for the record—"

"Shh!" Benny says, grabbing my arm.

Lucy calls the team in, and together we walk in two lines to our side of the field, taking in our opponents, their uniforms looking like they're right out of a Nike catalog. The players look super athletic and coordinated, like they've already had ten thousand hours of ball touches.

"For the record," I whisper to Benny, "I didn't do it." I'm close enough that I'm pretty sure Lucy can hear me.

Benny suppresses a grin. Making me suddenly suspicious. *"Benny?"*

He shrugs.

My eyes bug out, but we silently do our handshake.

"Bros for life," I say.

"Bros for life," he says.

"And we can't lose Lucy. The Three Musketeers. Not two plus one."

From the way her shoulders soften, I know Lucy hears that, too.

"Captain," Coach says.

Lucy runs to the middle to consult with the ref.

I shake off the loser feeling. I just gotta play. For my team.

I'm thrilled to get a starting position again, even though I'm facing a legit striker giant, #8.

My Battle Packs don't look so shiny next to his Ronaldo-inspired Nike Mercurial Superfly Elites: a high-top black-and-white-spotted safari design with an orange Nike swoosh. Retail price: $239, and the cleat Ronaldo is wearing this season.

Still, we play our guts out. And though we play well, we're just outmatched.

When I pass to Hannah, Shaker's foot skills are so quick she never even touches the ball.

"Nice try," I say encouragingly, trying to recover the ball.

"Push up the field!" Coach yells.

We do, but Shaker is so fast they beat us almost every time.

"Ref!" Coach yells when a Shaker player slide-tackles Brady. "You gotta call that!"

I remember something I saw Iran do against Spain in the World Cup. Spain was clearly a superior team, but they couldn't score because Iran pulled all their players back in the defensive area. We're not going to score against Shaker, but maybe we can prevent them from scoring.

I drop back to middle defense, pulling my midfielders back with me.

I'm scared. I'm not a great defensive player. That's Dad's position, the great defensive master.

His voice comes into my head.

Anticipate. Wait for the offensive player to make a move. Now!

Number eight comes at me, fakes right. I watch his hips turn and go left with him; he gets a shot off, but it goes wide.

C.J. dives for the ball, yelling, "I GOT IT!"

"YES, C.J.!"

"Nice defense," he says.

We fist-bump, and C.J. boots the ball out past the half line.

I start to run. And the more I run, the more my heart starts to pump like a crazy happy person. I was meant to play this game. My fear and doubt back off like a retreating pack of vultures. Adrenaline rises. Dad, Battle Packs, my team.

With one minute before halftime, Lucy gets tripped, but not before she passes the ball.

Brady and I make eye contact.

He takes off for a run.

I send the ball to the right corner flag.

Sprint up the field.

Archie is breathing hard but covering my back.

Brady channels his inner Mbappé, French soccer star.

He pulls a sick move, fakes right, draws the defense with him.

Then fakes left.

He sends the ball. It sails through the air, looking like it's going to go wide of the goal.

The goalie relaxes.

But at the last second, the ball bends: upper-left ninety.

Score!

We are in this.

At halftime we grab water and take a knee. That's when I notice Coach isn't on the sideline anymore.

"Where's . . . ?" I look around.

"Golden," Mr. T says quietly. "Hey, your dad has had an accident—your mom has gone to the hospital."

"What kind of accident?"

My first thought is Jaimes. She finally did it. She crashed that big white whale of a van.

"He fell," Mr. T says. "But he's okay."

"How?"

"Listen. Coach thought you'd want to finish the game, but I can take you to the hospital right now if you'd like."

"The hospital?"

"He's okay," Mr. T says again.

I look at my team. My grass-stained gladiators, silently watching me.

"Who's going to coach the team if we leave?"

"There are lots of parents who would be happy to help out."

Help out?

"No," I say. "I gotta stay with my team."

"You sure?" Mr. T asks.

"Coach and Dad will understand."

Lucy and I nod at each other.

"We got this if you do, Golden," Benny says.

"Yeah," Archie says. "You're our captain. Right, team?"

He looks around our tight circle. To my amazement, my team is nodding in agreement.

"Really?" I say.

"We got this," Lucy says, fist-bumping me.

The team takes a knee beside me. *What would Coach say?*

"Coach is gone right now," I start. "She's with my dad

and, um, I think they'd tell us this: No one thought we'd be up by one at half against Shaker—look at 'em! We are *in* this. We're the team to beat. If we go out and keep playing with this intensity? We're gonna pull out a win! Right?"

"Right!" my teammates yell.

When my team claps, I start to feel the energy again, the soccer gods rallying.

"Defense, awesome work. Remember to stay wide—and listen to your goalie. He's the boss."

"Yeah, Golden!" C.J. says, rubbing his gloves together.

"Middies!" Lucy yells, blue eyes lit up. "Watch the empty middle. Everyone—trap the ball with your body. Slow it down and look for a pass."

"Let's do this for Coach—and us!" I say.

They are actually listening. Maybe because I finally have something worth saying.

We huddle together, arms wrapped around each other's shoulders.

"Team," Archie says in his preacher voice. "We are gathered here on this holy ground to play the game we love."

"Yes!"

"We're here to beat those Shaker School dirtbags. . . ."

"Archie!" Lucy whispers.

"Sorry," Archie breathes. "Uh . . . we need our coach."

I wipe my nose on Benny's shoulder.

"She can't be with us right now, but we know she's with us in spirit. So let's rise to the occasion and make her proud. Let's make Dragon-Ball P proud 'cause he taught us this great game of soccer, too. And we also ask that he's gonna be okay."

The whistle blows.

Gonna be okay.

I hand Moses the ball. He looks at me in surprise, then elation.

"I ask you now, TEAM, what time is it?" Archie roars.

"Game time!"

"WHAT TIME IS IT?"

"Game time!"

"AHHHHHHHHHHHH!" Archie yells. Moses throws the ball up high, and we go.

The second half is tenser than any soccer game I've ever played in my life.

I'm working so hard, sweat pours down my face, soaking my jersey. Shaker still scores on a fast break, and then again when Hannah hesitates and trips up C.J.

"Communicate!" I yell.

"Easy," Benny says.

"Let's go, team! Win it back!" I say, trying to stay calm.

Sometime in the middle of the second half, Chase scores, and we're tied 2–2.

But we get in trouble when C.J. comes too far out of the goalie box.

C.J. is fast and he's got mad skills, but he's trained to dive and save goals. He gets beat in the middle of the field, and suddenly we have an open net with no goalie. C.J. sprints as fast as he can, but in desperation, he does something stupid: he pulls on #8's jersey so hard that #8 falls.

Number eight pushes C.J., and the refs start blowing their whistles. I have *never* seen a goalie get red-carded. But that's exactly what happens.

C.J. is out.

Mr. T calls me over. "Get his jersey. You gotta get in the goal."

"Me? Goalie? No way." I've only played goalie at recess or in practice, never when it's mattered like this.

C.J. walks dejectedly off the field, drops the gloves in my hands. "I messed up," he says. "Golden, you gotta do it. Don't let them score, okay? Whatever it takes!"

"Go get 'em, shrimp," Slick says.

There's no time to protest.

I run to the net, putting the too-big goalie gloves on my hands.

"Cover me!" I yell.

My team, seeing my fear, steps up. They keep the ball away from our net as best they can.

But in the final minutes, #8 gets a breakaway. My defenders sprint back, neck and neck with him. I come out of the goal, defensive stance: slight squat, hands out, laser focus, on my toes.

Number eight comes at me. I can see it in his eyes: no mercy.

He outsprints everyone until he's facing me, one-on-one.

It's me against the giant.

Whatever it takes. If you love something enough . . .

My team.

Coach.

Dad.

My eyes lock with the striker's. His laces connect with the ball. It flies at me so hard and fast, I sense that something is going to break if I don't duck.

But I can't do that.

I jump as the ball slams into my arm, doing exactly what I feared: breaking it in two.

The Day I Big-Time Break Middle School Boy Rule #1

Something deep in my character allows me to take the hits, and get on with trying to win.

—LIONEL MESSI

I hear the crack and topple to the ground.

The ball bounces off me and into #8's extended foot. He looks at me on the ground and takes a lazy shot right into the net.

The refs blow their whistles as I writhe on the ground, making a sound I've never heard come out of me before.

My arm feels splintered and shattered into a million pieces.

My team races over, surrounds me as I lie on the grass.

"Golden!" Lucy yells.

"Hey, Goldie," Ziggy says. "Knock knock."

"Back up!" Mr. T barks.

"Interrupting cow," Ziggy says.

"Interrupting cow who—"

"Moooooo."

"Ziggy!" Mr. T says.

The athletic trainer moves in.

"Hey, kid, you're going to be okay." She picks up my arm. "How's this feel?"

I moan.

"It might be broken."

Upon hearing this confirmed, something else breaks inside me: my heart.

"No!" Benny says.

I respond by laughing hysterically.

"See?" Ziggy says. "I cheered him up."

"Shock," the trainer says. "He needs to get to the ER."

"No." I try to get up. I see my socks, the athletic tape around them, the name "Messi" written in black Sharpie. My scuffed-up Battle Packs.

"Season's over, son."

"You can't say that!" Lucy yells. "You can't say that to Golden!"

The world goes still.

I turn my head. My eyes meet Lucy's.

Her eyes fill with tears, and I can feel mine start to follow.

Middle School Boy Rule #1:

YOU CANNOT, UNDER ANY CIRCUMSTANCES:
CRY.

I can't help it. I break the rule. Big-time.

I lose it.

When I cry, my whole team goes silent.

I cry for the goal I couldn't stop. The championship that's further out of reach. My season. My team.

Lucy.

Dad.

Messi said: *If and only if you love something enough.*

Didn't I love them enough?

Didn't I try my hardest?

Mr. T drives me to the hospital after all.

Mortified by my sobbing, I finally go silent.

I hold my arm, feeling so much pain I wish I were unconscious.

When we arrive, Coach is standing outside the emergency room. Coach's face crumples into Mom's face when she sees me. "Oh, Golden."

"I'm not crying," I say, fighting fresh tears all over again.

She tries to laugh.

"Dad?"

"He fell. I'll take you to him after your X-ray."

"If I can't play soccer . . ."

"You're going to play again," she says fiercely.

I cling to these words while we're waiting for my X-ray results. I realize Mr. T is still here, and I scoot a little farther away from Mom's lap. Geez.

"Thanks for, uh, bringing me here."

"No problem. You've been holding yourself together pretty well."

I nod.

"But there's nothing wrong with asking for a shoulder to cry on." He suddenly grins. "Not that you have any problem with that."

I can feel my face go lobster red.

"Ah, come on now," he says. "You created a chain reaction out there. Even the boys were crying buckets for you."

I look at him skeptically, hopefully.

Mr. T leans in close. "And I'll be the first to pound anyone who gives you grief about it," he adds, giving me a fond look. "'Cause you know, us bros have to stick together."

I grin just as the doctor comes in.

Turns out, my arm isn't completely broken.

"Just a hairline fracture," the doctor says, putting a soft cast on my arm.

"So I can still play soccer?"

"Not this season."

My heart sinks again, but I decide he's not even close to being right.

Dad and I are both discharged a couple of hours later.

He was trying to get in the van with Jaimes, after Verity left, when he fell out of his wheelchair, headfirst. And since he can't hold out his hands anymore, to break the fall, he smashed into the concrete headfirst and broke the orbital bone around his eye and got nine stitches in his forehead.

"Your mom says I have to stop my boxing career," he says. "You too."

"Mom's right."

When we get home, Jaimes looks like she's all cried out but still manages to burst into tears. "I'm sorry, Dad."

"It wasn't your fault," Mom says.

"I'm good," Dad says. "I'm groovy." His voice slurs and his head lolls back and forth. The pain meds are taking effect. He doesn't ask for a sip of water, but Mom brings the straw to his lips anyway. He barely makes an effort to take it. Or maybe he just can't.

"Ice is your best friend!" Mom says, holding up frozen peas. "Both of you."

I hold my own bag of peas.

She holds Dad's.

When I trudge up to bed, Jaimes is already in hers, covers pulled up over her head. There are soggy wadded-up tissues all over the floor. I stare out the window at Lucy's, then at Jaimes, wondering what to do.

Finally I just lie down next to her and put my good arm around my sister.

"I heard what you did. That was really dumb," she says, voice muffled under the covers.

"Thanks."

"And totally wicked."

"Thanks."

Later that night I can hear Lucy's roller skates and Benny's voice. While Roma and Whitney tuck me in, I can hear Mom saying I need to rest.

"Our poor, poor brother," Roma says.

Whitney clucks tragically and tucks five stuffed animals under my neck. They're soft.

I told Roma that even though her cells are dying, there were new ones being made every single second of the day. Isn't that what's happening to my arm? Cells are broken and dying but also trying to heal me. New cells every single second. So that means I will play again.

With four games left of the regular season, I *will* be on that field, so help me.

By the way? Did breaking my arm even mean anything? We still lost the game. That last goal counted because the ref hadn't blown his whistle yet.

The World Is Short on Finishers

You think soccer is just a game?
Well then, you've never played it.
—GOLDEN

A week later and I'm still not playing.

I can't even practice.

Not even wearing the captain's armband makes me feel better. I watch as Mudbury Middle plays against Kearsarge again and pulls out a win with me on the bench. Four days after that we lose to Lakes Middle School, a game we should definitely have won. However, Benny calls to tell me both Shaker and Merrimack also suffered heavy losses.

"Don't give up," Benny says. "We're still in this."

Are we? I try to rally while I sit glumly on a barstool in the kitchen.

"What's up, Golden?"

Dad turns his chair around in the kitchen and looks at me. His right eye is swollen shut and the entire right side of his face is starting to turn into one dark-purple-blue-black bruise. The skin around his stitches looks red and itchy. He opens and closes his eye at the irritation.

"I feel useless. I can't play soccer. Can't help my team. I can't *do* anything."

Even as I say it, I realize it sounds ridiculous while facing a guy in a wheelchair. We look at each other. Dad's mouth twitches.

"Dad, how . . . how can you stand it?"

"Hardest thing I've ever done."

"I couldn't stand it."

"No . . . choice."

Sigh.

"Walk?" Dad asks.

He doesn't wait for an answer. He turns his chair around and heads for the door.

Before going out, I one-handedly put a load of laundry in, remembering all the steps without Jaimes being my boss. I put a hat on Dad's head, then a straw to his mouth. His lips tighten around it. Up, up, up comes the water, with big gulping sounds. I imagine Dad's brain telling his tongue to move, his throat to swallow. I see the epiglottis covering the trachea to prevent water from entering the lungs.

He leans back in his chair, concentrating on the swallow.

"You okay, Dad?"

"Yes," he gasps.

"Do you need a suction?" The suction is our newest machine because it's so hard for Dad to swallow his own spit now.

"No."

Dad taps the arm of the wheelchair with his left fingers as I open the door. He wiggles his two fingers, trying to inch them forward.

"Help?"

Swallows. "Yes."

I carefully move Dad's arm and arrange his fingers to fit around the joystick. We make it to the porch.

"Hey, Dad? Why don't we just stay on the porch?"

"'Kay." He sounds relieved. A long line of drool comes out of his mouth.

I wipe his mouth with my sleeve, take his swollen, banged-up head in my two hands. It feels so heavy. I gently place it back on the headrest.

We take in the forest that lines our shared driveway, the evergreen tips that sway in the breeze, the bright blue sky holding clouds the shapes of dragons.

"Love fall," he says. "Nice air."

"Yes."

"Coach needs you," Dad says.

"How? I'm useless."

"No," he says. "You have a choice . . . to make."

I look down at my arm.

"Anyone can be . . . negative . . . discipline to be positive. Your superpower. Remem . . . ?"

He takes big gulps of air and swallows several times. "Don't . . . give up," he says. Swallow.

"It's okay, Dad. You don't have to talk."

"Lead from bench. Wambach . . ."

I know who he means. Abby Wambach, #20, one of the best players in the world, two-time Olympic gold medalist, FIFA World Cup champion, top international goal scorer. During her last game she didn't start, but she cheered so hard and so loud—from the bench—that the US won anyway.

Oh yeah, and she was captain.

Lead from the bench.

"Gold . . . en?"

"Yeah?"

I lean in—I can barely hear him.

"Don't give up on me . . . (*swallow*) either."

Dad wiggles his two left fingers until they grasp the end of my shorts. That left hand. Those two fingers. Fighting so hard to hang on.

He struggles to sit as straight as possible. And it is

a struggle—I can see the fight for every single muscle fiber in his body. Sometimes I've felt he was too accepting, when all I wanted was for him to put up a fight. But right now I see the fire that flares up in his eyes, the look I've seen countless times when he was pushing me to be stronger and better.

I've been wrong. Dad has never given up.

"The world . . . is short on finishers," he says. "Finish . . . this!"

Dad sinks back, exhausted, struggling to breathe, making small gasping sounds in his throat until he stabilizes. His face goes from a purple to a healthier pink. He smiles for my benefit as his vessels loosen their squeeze on his heart and the desperate pumping slows.

"Let's get you a shake," I say as confidently as I can. "More fat 'cause we have to gain weight. Avocado, whole milk, and how about that chocolate ice cream? Don't tell Mom."

I put my hand on his wheelchair as he turns it around with his fingers.

"Such a . . . good boy," he says.

"Such a good dad."

Gag Me Almost Kills Me with a Bread Knife (Worth It.)

Maybe it's not your job to
make everything better.

—LUCY LITTLEHOUSE

The next week I still haven't been cleared to play and I stay home with Dad for two days when Nurse Verity is sick.

Mom doesn't even protest.

She says "How's Dad?" a lot, tries to work a few hours from home, cleans the house, runs errands, and coaches soccer. I help Mom give Dad medication and get him in and out of his wheelchair. When I watch her feed Dad, she reminds me, "Soon Dad's going to have a feeding tube in his stomach."

I try to remember how the wheelchair made his life easier. A feeding tube will help Dad eat more. Anyway, I would prefer to never ever hear the sound of choking again.

Dad and I go outside for walks. I put the straw to his lips, suction out his mouth, and practice my touch outside while he watches. I log five hours in two days, carefully making marks on my chart. Sugar Ray watches from the back porch. Curtis watches from Lucy's porch, tail swishing, occasionally chasing my ball just to remind me how annoying he is.

Lunges.

Squats.

Juggling.

Crunches.

Bigger stronger faster.

Most of the time, Dad stays parked next to me. I say "parked" because Mom and Dad both agree that the wheelchair is the safest way for him to move around now—even in the house. He rarely gets out of it except to go to the bathroom and go to bed.

We watch a lot of soccer. Sometimes Dad closes his eyes when I'm celebrating a great play.

"Sorry, Dad. Do you want me to change the channel?"

"No," he always says. "Love . . . soccer."

Only one gross thing happens. Dad gets a hair stuck in his mouth.

"Thowwy to ask—hair." He moves his tongue around, bends his head down, but can't get his fingers to reach his mouth. I adjust his head as he opens his mouth.

"I don't see the hair."

I touch his tongue, fish around the inside of his mouth, my fingers becoming coated with saliva. He gags twice and coughs. "Ew," I say, pulling out a long brown hair coated with spit. "Jaimes is a health hazard."

I shake it onto the ground, wipe my hand on my pants, and wipe Dad's mouth off. He grimaces.

"You. Taste like sweat," he says. "But . . . thanks."

On the second day home, I begin to wonder about my team.

What drills are they running?

Do they miss me on the field?

Do they notice I'm gone?

I miss my team.

And Coach. Even her Hulk ways.

I miss Lucy and Benny.

I can think of only one productive Operation Lucy tactic: I fill up every single balloon I can find with water, load them in my hamper, and hide them in my closet for just the right Dark Lord moment.

I wait impatiently for the Squirrels to get home.

"Who got the MVP Gum of the Day?" I demand when they burst through the front door.

"Mario," Whitney says. "And guess what!"

She pulls a navy-blue Mudbury Middle School jersey out of her backpack.

"Number ten!" Whitney shouts. "Messi's number!"

"Slick's going to—"

"He gave it to you," Whitney says. She lays it reverently on the floor for us all to admire.

I kneel down, finger the edge. "No way."

"He says you still have to pay him one day," Whitney adds.

Jerk.

"But I gave him my lunch money."

"Ah, Whit." She looks so pleased I give her a high five and a hug.

"Golden Macaroni!" I look up to see Lucy and Benny crashing through the front door, followed by Mom, followed by Grandma Ho and Mrs. Ho, who's wearing hot pads on her hands and carrying a glass dish. I almost melt into a grateful puddle right then and there.

"Surprise!" Lucy says.

"Hey, man," Benny says.

"Thank you," Mom says. There's a look of grateful resignation in her eyes.

"Hi, Grandma Ho!" I say.

"This is Golden," Mrs. Ho says like we've never met before. "You remember?"

"Of course she remembers me!" I peer closely at her face. Doesn't she?

Grandma Ho pats my cheek.

"Come here, Ma," Mrs. Ho says, leading her over to the barstools.

"Is Grandma Ho okay?" I ask Benny.

He shrugs. "Sometimes. Sometimes not."

"I'm sorry," I say. And I mean it. For everything.

Benny nods. "I know."

"You finally figured out a way to get the jersey," Lucy says to me. "By breaking your arm."

She smiles, all sweaty from practice, her face bright red, hair pulled back in a ponytail, big feathery earrings in her ears.

Dad drinks a smoothie while the rest of us eat minced beef and tofu rice, pan-fried Chinese spinach, clay pot eggplant, bamboo leaf sticky rice, and Benny's favorite dessert, called *tang yuan:* rice-flour dumplings filled with black sesame.

"I've died and gone to heaven," I moan after stuffing myself and falling to the kitchen floor in a glutinous stupor.

Whitney giggles at me.

"I think I gained ten pounds," Mom moans.

"That's awesome," I say dreamily, thinking of my growth chart.

It's a great dinner, all of us together. Even if Dad has to drink it.

* * *

The next morning I'm awoken to Jaimes yelling.

"Mom! Golden dyed all my whites pink! I told him—I specifically said to separate the whites from the darks—especially when it comes to the color red."

"He was trying to be helpful," Mom says. "Be kind."

"My white pants!" Jaimes yells.

I bury my face in my pillow so she won't hear me laughing—but it really was an accident!

When I finally do get up, since I can't shower easily with my cast, I wipe myself down with a wet wipe and go to school smelling like a freshly bathed infant. Dad sits in his chair, his broken face still healing.

He looks after me, watching until I'm all the way out the door.

"I'll be back in a few hours!" I say. "And I'll tell you everything."

Even though I can't play soccer—and I'm wearing pink underwear—the day turns out okay.

My friends take turns drawing on my soft cast, Lucy signing with her sparkly pink pen and swirly penmanship.

"Guess there's no dancing for you, huh?" Slick says, signing his name obnoxiously big. "So sad."

"That's what you think!" I say. I'd forgotten—until Slick practically dared me.

Oh, I'll be going to the dance.

In a totally impulsive moment, Benny and I sneak

away during lunch break. I pull him over to a flower patch where a patch of blue flowers grows.

"I want to give Lucy some flowers," I say without looking him. "Lucy loves flowers and she's been kind of mad at me and I want to dance with her at the dance. . . ."

Benny looks at me sideways but thankfully doesn't laugh.

"Okay. Minor detail," Benny says. "Those are Ms. Gag Me's flowers. She comes outside after lunch and waters them. You have to decide if the dance is worth your possible demise."

"Maybe she won't notice?"

"Remember when we were told she's the witch in 'Rapunzel'? If you pick her flowers she'll come for your firstborn child. Think of Sugar Ray," he says, trying to keep a straight face.

"Dude . . . not funny!"

The late bell rings.

I quickly and savagely pull on the flowers.

"Go!" Benny says, stomping on the dirt. We make a dash for the door, only to find we're locked out. Slick sees us, waves, and walks away.

"For real?!" Benny yells.

"Lunchroom doors," I say.

"That's where Gag Me is!"

"Do you want to get back in or not?"

We're through the lunchroom and halfway down the hallway when an awful pterodactyl screech fills the middle school hallway, echoing off the walls and into our ears.

We whirl around.

Gag Me is marching down the hall wearing an apron and pointing a lunchroom bread knife at us.

"Weasels!" Gag Me says, waving the knife around. "I want them back!"

We back up, hitting the locker doors.

"Uh, I'm really sorry, Gag—Mrs. Gagne. B-but—" I stammer.

At that moment, saving us from certain death, Mr. T intervenes.

"Thank you, Ms. Gagne," he says looking down at us. "I'll handle this."

"See that you do!"

While she marches away, Mr. T fixes his eyes on us, unsmiling.

"Nice scarf," I say. "New pattern?"

"Nice try."

"It was for a really good cause—" I begin.

"We will discuss this later. Get to class."

I stop to stow them in my locker until the bell rings. After class, Mr. T and I have a "discussion" about taking flowers from school property. I try to look repentant while heading to and opening my locker, but then Lucy comes down the hall.

"Here," I say, thrusting the flowers at her, ignoring the fawning sounds from Sunny and Sam. Lucy reaches out to take the flowers, her bracelets tinkling. By now the flowers are not nearly as impressive: pathetically wilted and droopy. "They're forget-me-nots," I say. Sunny melts, hand to heart.

"Forget-me-nots," Lucy says. "Don't worry. You're kind of unforgettable, Golden Macaroni."

I don't know how I make it out to the field, watch practice, or go on living, since I'm a puddle on the middle school floor.

Maybe I should have been more careful with the laundry, because I'm going to need Jaimes to keep giving me pointers. I gave Lucy flowers, but forgot to ask her about the dance.

The Best Things Come in Threes

What are the qualities of a hero?
Loss. Defeat. A comeback.
—COACH PATRICK MARONI

A week later I'm cleared to do the warm-up and a few drills, but over the next two weeks Coach keeps me mostly sidelined with Shin-Splint Ziggy, who prefers to sit on the bench with candy Coach can't see. He's actually not so bad, and he's totally generous with his stash of Jolly Ranchers.

It's growing colder as November nears, much chillier now that I'm not running down the field or making shots on goal. The whole soccer field is surrounded by trees of red, orange, and yellow, and the humidity has all but blown out.

I can feel the muscles in my right arm shrinking to a tiny baby toothpick.

I flex my fingers, just to make sure they're still working.

Squeeze my hands into balls.

Twiddle my thumbs.

Everything's working.

To be absolutely sure, I repeat the sequence many times.

During practice I chase the balls that fly over the fence, put down and pick up cones, and am the most cheerful one-armed soccer player on the planet. I remember what Dad said: *Lead from the bench.* I can be cheerful on the bench instead of the field because we *are* getting to that championship game.

And my cast will be off by then. The doctor has kind-of-almost guaranteed it. I have an appointment booked the day before the game.

"If that isn't a sign I don't know what is!" Lucy says. Speaking of Lucy, I haven't seen anyone tour her house recently, and Mom says winter can be a tough time to sell—so we're almost there.

"What are you so pleased about?" Jaimes said when she found me looking out the window last night.

"Nothing. Just that I pretty much single-handedly kept my best friend from moving a couple of states away. You're welcome."

She rolled her eyes and shook her head like she wasn't super impressed, then went back to strategizing her team's path to the championship with Dad.

* * *

With that off my mind, I refocus on our upcoming games. Lucy leads the warm-up of the last two games of the regular season like a pro. Benny pulls off a hat trick against Pittsfield, scoring three goals in a row, with Moses even getting an accidental assist.

When I yell, "Way to go, Moses!" I hope not to sound pitiful and jealous. "Nice finish, Benny!"

And when Dobbs makes a terrible pass during the Newport game, I swallow a groan and yell, "That's okay, recover!"

We manage to blow out Pittsfield and pull out the slimmest of wins against Newport, 1–0.

YES!

"We needed that," Benny says, walking off the field after the game.

"It's got to be enough," Lucy says.

I cross all my fingers.

The only reason I can stand not playing in the last games of my middle school career is because of our one chance at that final championship game. We won't find out who makes it until the end of the week, so we practice as if we're already in. I do the warm-up and drills every day, but no scrimmaging, which is practically impossible—the Messi Magic Battle Packs are so ready!

On Friday afternoon, Coach looks at her watch.

"In one hour we should know."

"Know what?" Ziggy asks.

"Ziggy!" I say. "Whether or not Mudbury Middle has qualified to play in the biggest matchup of the season: the championship game? What else is there?"

"Oh yeah," he says. "I knew that."

During the last scrimmage, a ball gets kicked over the fence.

"I got it," I say, making my way under a sticker bush just as Coach yells, "Grab another ball. It's Golden Goal time! Next goal wins!" My team plays while I wrestle under the bush.

The thorns snag my shirt and prick me all over until I can feel small drops of blood appear, dotted across my face and legs and arms. I can hear the team play, can hear the happy screams when the Golden Goal is scored. I missed it.

I roll out from under the sticker bush just as Coach says, "Mr. T!"

He's walking onto the field holding a piece of paper. I scramble up.

We run to the middle of the field and surround him. I can hardly breathe. Benny bites his lip. Lucy squeezes her eyes and fists together.

Mr. T shakes his head. "Sorry, guys," he says.

A collective shock ripples across the team. *No.*

"Hold up," he says. "I came out to tell you we don't have the results yet and probably won't have them until tonight. Hopefully we can announce it at the dance. Go home and shower. Y'all stink."

"So we still have a chance?" I say.

"We still have a chance!" Benny pounds on my back.

"But first the MVP Gum of the Day," Coach says, raising it into the air.

"Golden, obviously," Archie says. "The man's covered in blood *and* he found our Nike Pitch EPL soccer ball."

"Thanks, Captain," Slick says.

When he smiles, he's wearing my mouth guard.

I decide to let it go.

Coach hands over the cinnamon gum, my favorite.

We rush home from soccer practice so that we can go back to school in two hours for the Big Dance. Not only will I get to dance with Lucy, but it's where our championship fate will be announced: so basically the most important night of my whole life.

I take a hot shower, covering my wrist with a plastic grocery bag. Real classy. Afterward, I pat my face down with Dad's smell-good aftershave.

"OW!!!" I yell.

I apply hair gel to what little hair I'm starting to get back, pushed up in front. Then I kiss my fingers and point them at the sky, just like my man Messi.

Or bathroom ceiling. Whatever.

I wear jeans, a white T-shirt, and a blue-and-white-checkered button-down shirt. It's long-sleeved so I can slide my captain's band onto my bicep without anyone noticing. It's slightly sweaty and smelly, so I sprinkle it with more of Dad's smell-good juice.

I won't take it off until after we win the championship with Dad front row.

When Dad walks or rolls across the field and we hold up the trophy together.

That will be a sign.

A sign that Dad's the exception.

That I've worked hard enough.

That I gave everything.

That I loved him enough.

Jaimes chatters on about my dance etiquette. "Don't burp or do those other disgusting boy things."

"Like I was going to burp in Lucy's face."

"Dance the waltz," she says, gliding across the room with her arms outstretched. "One-two-three. She will love you for, like, *ever.*"

"Yeah, no."

"There she goes."

I peek out the window to see George and Lucy's mom getting in the car to take Lucy to the dance. Which means the house is empty. Between a cracked arm, Dad, championship dreams, and laundry, I realize I'm off my Operation Lucy game. Now's my chance to regroup.

"Don't even think about it," Jaimes says.

"What?"

"Whatever you're scheming."

I make a scoffing sound.

"I thought you said you were almost sure it wasn't going back on the market till spring, so why are you still doing this?" she challenges me.

"Extra insurance!"

"You know, Golden, maybe you'd be a better friend . . . if you let her go."

"You don't even know what I'm going to do!" I say, backing away.

"Golden—"

I slide down the banister before she can say anything else, slip on my shoes, and sprint across the driveway to Lucy's house.

The door is unlocked as always.

I walk in and look around, adrenaline coursing through me. What can I do?

Break a window?

Clog a toilet?

How do I prevent Lucy from moving without getting grounded for life or permanently infuriating her?

There's duct tape on the counter.

I grin and remember one of Dad's April Fools' tricks. I place a little piece on the faucet so when it's turned on it will spray the Dark Lord in the face. It won't prevent a home sale, but it will really tick him off.

I hear my front door open and close, the keys jangling as Jaimes walks to the van.

I sprint to the front door, but that's when I see something else on the counter—a phone.

Don't do it.

But I do. I slip it into my pocket and race to the car.

We pull out of the driveway . . . just as Lucy's mom's car is pulling back in.

Jaimes slows and rolls down her window.

"Forgot my phone," Lucy's mom says. "Expecting an important house call."

I keep a perfectly bored look on my face, but my heart is hammering inside my chest. House call? Does that mean the house didn't go off the market?

"Can we take Lucy?" Jaimes asks. "It's kind of tradition anyway."

"And you can just pick me up, Mom?" Lucy asks.

"All right—thank you. Have a great time!"

The Dark Lord smiles at me. I play along and raise my hand in a wave.

A few minutes later, when Lucy runs up the Hos' driveway to get Benny, the phone in my pocket starts ringing. I immediately silence it.

"What was that?" Jaimes says.

"Nothing."

"Golden . . . you didn't."

I can't help myself. "I also put duct tape on the faucet."

Lucy and Benny get into the car.

Jaimes rolls her eyes at me. "Buckle up."

We hold our breath when we round Cemetery Corner. Everyone, that is, except Jaimes.

"Now you're going to be haunted," I tell her.

"Uh-huh," Jaimes says.

"Because the ghost is jealous he doesn't have a body," Benny says.

"It's true," Lucy says. "Once I didn't hold my breath, and I heard the ghost of Raymond Von Mousetrap whisper, *You lucky, lucky thing.*"

Jaimes slowly nods. "And I thought you three were weird before today."

When we arrive, Mr. T stands out front, arms crossed.

"Yo, Mr. T," I say. "Any news yet?"

"Patience! I'll let you know when I know."

"Nice scarf."

"Thanks," he says proudly. "Just finished it."

I try not to laugh.

"Not cool enough for you, Goldie-Locks?"

"Uh . . ." *No?*

"Hand-eye coordination, calming effect, sense of accomplishment, not to mention a fashion statement. You should try it."

"Maybe I will," I say. "If we make the championship!"

When we walk through the doors, Ziggy and half the team are chugging Mountain Dews.

"What are you doing!"

They freeze.

"Uh, championship game?"

"Lighten up, Goldie-Locks," Slick says, pounding me on the back. "You only live once."

"Exactly," I say, walking into the gym.

The lights are off except for the large disco ball on the ceiling that spins white light around the room. I'm feeling light-headed for three reasons: sometimes I hate my friends, there's a stolen phone in my pocket, and I really, really want to ask Lucy to dance.

The phone starts to buzz again in my pocket. I run to the bathroom and lock myself into the stall, panicky.

The name on the screen says "George." I stare at it until it stops ringing.

I splash water on my face.

The phone buzzes again.

Back into the locked stall.

On the screen is an unidentified number. Lucy's mom did say she was expecting an important phone call about the house.

Do I dare?

I have to. Because I love Lucy that much.

Taking a deep breath, I answer. "Hello?"

The bathroom door opens. I peek through the crack and get a view of the gym.

I spy Lucy across the dance floor. Her light blue dress is flecked with white disco light.

"Golden?" Benny says, the door closing behind him.

"Ms. Littlehouse?" the voice on the other end of the phone says.

"No," I say, making my voice as deep as I can.

"George?" the voice asks.

I hesitate one second. "Yes. The house isn't for sale any longer. Sorry." I hang up, my face burning, my hands shaking.

I open the stall door.

Benny's standing with his mouth open.

"Yo, let's dance," I say.

"You're so dead. You know that, right?" he says, following me out to the gym.

"Yeah." My hands are sweaty. I'm so scared, I might barf.

The phone is burning a hole in my pocket, so I place it underneath a chair to forget about it, at least until the dance is over. Also so I won't get caught.

Lucy is with a group of girls when I attempt the worm. I make sure she can see me when I get down on the floor, but it turns out you can't do the worm *or* break-dance with a cracked arm without looking totally pathetic. Uncool.

I wander around to walk it off, admiring blue-and-white homecoming balloons and WELCOME ALUMS banners. Some ninth graders are back visiting, but they only stay long enough to let us know how cool they are before exiting.

The mood is light and loud, with baby sixth graders huddled in corners, seventh graders laughing, and eighth graders dominating the dance floor. Chaperones are chatting and gossiping. I'm supposed to call Mom and Dad as soon as the championship news is announced—if it's announced. I look around the gym for Mr. T.

As if on cue, I spy him walking to the middle of the gym, the disco lights bouncing off his head.

The music stops.

"I'd like to make an announcement."

Suddenly, both Benny and Lucy are by my side. We hold hands.

Please please please.

"For you soccer players, we've just received some news about the championship game."

He pauses for effect.

We hold our breaths.

I flex my bicep, feel the sweaty captain's band.

"The goals were tallied, the level of play was taken into consideration, and the league vote was unanimous . . . for the first time in history, Mudbury Middle School is going to the championship game!"

The entire gym erupts. My knees go weak. Benny and Lucy hold me up.

"Not only that," Mr. T says above the noise, "but we'll be making history by being the first team to play under the lights on the *Patrick Maroni* field!"

Benny and Lucy pull me to the middle of the room, where the whole team jumps up and down as the DJ plays "Celebration." It's wicked fun.

Two songs later, the tempo slows and the DJ says, "Ladies and gentlemen, boys and girls. Here's your last song of the night."

I look everywhere for Lucy.

She's not in the huddle of girls. Slick's alone, so he hasn't found her yet. She's not in the hallway. I run back into the gym, sweating profusely, frantic, and almost call her name out loud.

And suddenly she's there.

Right in front of me.

Smiling her big smile.

She bows with a flourish.

I bow back.

I put my casted hand in hers and my other on her waist. With my cast so close to my face, I realize how dirty and smelly it is. I gulp, hoping she doesn't notice.

"Do you waltz?" I ask.

"Waltz?"

"I'll show you." I start counting, "One-two-three." Soon we're turning around in a squarish circle.

"One-two-three," she says. "Good things come in threes, right? Like you, me, and Benny."

"Right," I say.

"Your dad told me that once," she says. "A long time ago, and I've been happy ever since."

I nod, even though I can't help thinking, *How can it be the best if you're not here with me?*

Of course it's Lucy and she can read my mind.

She smiles, her eyes shiny. "And no matter what, we'll always be together, Golden. No matter where I travel, no matter who buys our house, no matter where you go. We were born on the same day in the same hospital, remember? And then we found Benny . . ."

". . . in preschool," I finish. "Of course I remember."

"Golden . . . are you wearing your captain's band?"

I nod.

We stop dancing; there's a mischievous look in her eye. She pulls up her sleeve to reveal her red-and-white captain's band.

Twins. For life. And I get it now.

Maybe Lucy won't move.

Maybe she will.

I kind of don't think I can do anything more to stop what's already begun.

I just have to believe that no matter what, we'll always be Lucy and Golden—and Benny, too.

I don't think about what it will be like to say good-bye. I don't ask about her leaving. I don't think about how sad I'll be without her, or say I'll miss her or how life will be a perfect graveyard without her living next door for the rest of our lives sending notes in Kermit the Frog. Lucy's eyes, deep and blue and flecked with light from dancing disco stars hanging from the ceiling, remind me of the sky, but also of water. I've never been to Maine, but I imagine that the color of the ocean there looks something like Lucy's blue eyes.

We dance.

One–two–three. One–two–three.

The whole time, I don't let my mind wander to what might happen next, not the soccer field, not the FOR SALE sign, not Dad's clawlike left hand. I don't think. I make myself stay right here, living in this one perfect happy moment under a disco ball with my forever best friend, Lucy Littlehouse.

I'm so busy not thinking, I don't even remember the phone left under the chairs.

The Covered Bridge

It's hard to beat someone who never quits.

—BENNY HO

I wake up early the next morning still smiling.

There's hammering outside, cars driving into our drive-way.

Jaimes looks over at me. "You know who you're play-ing in the championship, right? Merrimack."

I sit up. I was so excited last night I didn't even ask.

Merrimack! Biggest Mudbury rival there is.

"You know why Shaker isn't playing against Merri-mack in the championship game? Because they got beat by Franconia."

"What! How? We beat them six-zero and Shaker demolished us."

She shrugs. "Who knows. Off day? Or maybe number

eight was at the dentist. Or maybe there are more forces at play than we know."

My eyes open wide. Forces at play? Like what? Like whom? Grandma Ho's dead ancestors? Raymond Von Mousetrap?

"I remember going to the last regular-season game against Merrimack when I was in middle school," Jaimes continues. "It was the first time Mudbury Middle had ever even had a chance at making the championship. We lost by one in overtime—remember that?" She shudders. "It still haunts me." She leans forward. "Golden, you've *got* to beat them."

Geez, no pressure.

"Mindset," Jaimes says, tapping her head.

Okay. We *will* beat Merrimack the way Jaimes's team couldn't.

She appraises me, hearing my competitive thoughts. "And remember whose shoulders you stand on. Mine."

We're interrupted by Mom calling us to come downstairs. It's there that we will prepare to watch the entire town descend on our lawn.

We can't just build a normal ramp like normal families.

The small ramp that Slick's dad put down is being converted into a timber-frame covered bridge that requires a contractor, builders, and the entire town of Mudbury. We do this because Dad has always wanted to build a covered bridge, and because Mom says a covering will protect Dad from rain and snow and mud season. I'm glad to hear she's finally thinking long-term. You know, at least three seasons from now.

Mom says Dad's going to show everyone how to build it. Since he can barely speak more than a couple of words at a time, I'm wondering how exactly he's going to show everyone anything.

"Someone's here," Dad calls from outside. Roma, Whitney, and I look out the window, and my mouth drops in a horrified O.

"The witch," I whisper. "Gag Me."

"On her broom?" Roma whispers.

"She's driving a car—obviously a cover," Whitney says. It's a little white Subaru with steel-studded snow tires—probably so it will hurt more when she runs over small children.

She gets out, looking tiny and harmless. I suddenly remember the tissue she left on my seat.

"I think she *might* have a heart," I say.

"That'ssss the spirit," Dad says.

Thankfully, the rest of Mudbury isn't too far behind Gag Me, including many of my soccer teammates and their parents. I even invited Ziggy and Moses. When Mom and Dad go out to greet everyone, Jaimes corners me.

"Golden, Lucy's mom is *freaking out*. She still can't

find her phone!" She puts her hands on her hips and raises her eyebrows.

My mind goes blank.

Phone?

THE PHONE.

"They're downloading an app to find it and they're going to know you have it, so I suggest you put it back right now."

I search my memory. Where's the phone?

Car.

Dance.

I had it in the bathroom.

But not when I did the worm.

Not when I danced with Lucy.

I didn't come home with it.

I . . .

In the gym . . . under the chairs.

"It's at the school!"

"Well, they're going to find it and know you took it and you'll be so busted," Jaimes says. "Your fingerprints are all over it."

"Help me! You have your license. You have to take me there before the Dark Lord gets there first."

"You seriously still call him that?"

"Please, Jaimes," I beg.

"Oh, now you want to drive with me?"

"Please."

Her eyes soften as I clasp my hands together. And I don't mean to, but I'm close to tears.

She looks out the window.

"I don't know how we're going to get out of here."

But we do because Jaimes tells Mom we should have drinks and snacks for everyone.

"DRIVE!" I yell as soon as we're out of the driveway. She presses on the gas. "Ahhhh! Slow down!"

On the way down the hill, we see Benny walking up.

Jaimes slows and rolls down her window.

"Get in!" I say. "Rescue mission!"

He climbs in and Jaimes guns it.

"Rescue mission?" Benny asks. "Can I call my parents? They're going to your house right now."

"Don't tell them where we're going!" I yell.

"Where are we going?"

I tell him about the phone.

Benny's phone dings.

"Text from Lucy," Benny says, holding up his phone. "George is driving to the school right now."

"Stall him, Benny!" I say.

"I'm in the car with you! But it gets worse, dude. They think Lucy took the phone but won't admit it."

I smack my head with my hand.

"The janitor probably already found the phone,"

Jaimes says. "You're busted either way. If you don't get expelled or sent to jail or grounded for life it will be a miracle. You've probably just written *yourself* out of the championship game."

Not once has this consequence ever crossed my mind. I was only trying to sabotage the Dark Lord. Was I really sabotaging myself?

I feel a pit in my stomach, wishing I could get a twenty-four-hour life do-over.

"Golden, you've got to stop—"

"I know! I swear. But first the phone!"

We get to the school in one piece.

It's Saturday morning. The doors are locked. There is only one car in the parking lot. Mr. T's.

We run around to every window and door, banging on them.

Finally, a door opens.

Mr. T steps out and lets us in. I run to the gym without explaining.

The phone isn't there.

"Looking for this?" Mr. T asks. He holds up Lucy's mother's phone.

I reach my hand out just as it begins to ring.

"It says 'George,'" Mr. T says.

"Don't answer!"

"I think *you* should answer," Mr. T says.

"I definitely should NOT answer."

He slides the open button and hands it to me.

There is a deep voice on the other end.

The Dark Lord speaks my name.

"Golden."

When we get outside I realize our mistake. We parked our huge white whale of a van in the parking lot! We couldn't be more conspicuous.

Fear the size of a lightning bolt courses through my head, along my spine, and all the way down to my toes.

I walk to the Dark Lord.

"Phone found!" I say. "In the school—I heard you were looking for it, so we thought . . ." My voice trails off as he shakes his head.

"This doesn't make any sense," he says. "Lucy *has* a phone."

Lucy is in the front seat looking miserable. She knows I took it and yet there she is—covering for me.

I stay mute.

He shakes his head and walks to the car. "Thanks for finding it. See you at the house? Big project today."

I nod, feeling a terrible pit in my stomach.

He climbs in.

"Wait!" I yell.

Lucy watches me.

"Oh boy," Benny says under his breath.

I trudge to his car. "Well, the thing is, Lucy didn't take the phone. I did. And I'm really sorry. It was a mistake. I mean, it wasn't a mistake, but I shouldn't have done it. It was me who left the phone here—that really was a mistake."

He tips his head at me, looking even more confused.

"I can prove it was me. You'll find my fingerprints on the phone."

"I don't think we'll be taking—"

"Also," I say, "I may have . . . told someone on that phone last night that . . ."

"Yes?" he asks, raising his eyebrows.

"That the house was no longer for sale?"

He doesn't say anything for an excruciatingly long time.

"I'll see you at the house," he finally answers.

Jaimes was right.

I have so stupidly put my fate in the hands of the Dark Lord.

By the time we get back home, I'm about to barf from all the trouble I'm going to be in, and the covered bridge project is in full swing. Dad has everyone staining big pieces of wood. We drop off the snacks and drinks before carrying wood from one place to another—and stealing potato chips from the lunch table. All the while I do my best to avoid Lucy's mom and *George*. I keep waiting for them to go over to Mom or Dad, but so far they don't.

As the cover is assembled, we're told to back off and let the adults do the heavy roof lifting.

There are about forty adults on the ramp, wood laid down across it. Dad sits in his wheelchair at the end like the captain of a ship.

"No one moves until I . . . say so," Dad says, struggling to project his voice.

The adults freeze, lean in to hear.

"We're trying to lift an entire side all together at the same time," Mom explains. She glances at Dad. "Ready?"

"ONE," Dad says. "Two. Three . . . lift together."

There is push and there is pull, like how we get Dad to stand up. Mom is on one side of the frame with a dozen people, Jaimes on the other side with another dozen. Very slowly the frame starts to rise.

It's so quiet I can almost hear the hearts beating, foreheads perspiring.

They do the same thing for the other side.

Again, the push and the pull.

I watch how everyone listens to Dad. He's in total control though he's hardly moving or speaking.

He knows how to build a bridge. And everyone on the bridge trusts him to tell them what to do and how to do it.

"I hope I can be like that someday," I say.

Benny and Lucy look at me.

"Like what?" Benny asks.

"In command, confident. Everyone has complete respect for what he has to say, even in a whisper."

"Probably because he's not a thief," Lucy says, folding her arms.

"Lucy, I'm so sorry, I—"

"He defended you, you know."

"Who?"

"George. My mom was super mad and he totally talked her down, even said it was partly his fault because you've been playing pranks on each other."

"Say what?"

"And I'm pretty sure the pranks are one-sided," she says. "This is after he got sprayed in the face yesterday by the faucet after a piece of duct tape was mysteriously placed there."

We can't help it—Benny and I bust up laughing.

"Sorry, sorry, sorry," I say, holding up my hands.

"They got engaged last night."

My face falls.

"It's good, Golden. I know we called him the Dark Lord at first, but he's really nice and my mom's been so lonely for so long. I just want her to be happy."

I nod because I want that too. I just want them to be happy *here*.

"Dude," Slick says. "Look at Gag Me. She looks like she's a thousand years old."

"She reminds me of a tree," Lucy says. "A wise old tree like Grandmother Willow." She spins with her hands out like she's feeling all the colors of the wind.

"Wouldn't it be bad?" Ziggy says out of nowhere. "If a beam fell down and, like, crushed a little kid?"

"Be quiet, Ziggy," we all say at once.

We watch as the frame goes up. The logs on top get fitted into the sides.

"Hammer nails," Dad says.

Those assigned quickly hammer nails into wood so that it fits into the frame. Ropes come out to pull and secure. More nails and hammering until Dad surveys the work and nods.

"Okay. Let . . . go," Dad says.

Everyone steps back from the bridge. I hold my breath.

The supporting beams stay standing.

Dad rolls across the ramp, stopping underneath the cover.

He smiles amid the claps and whistles.

Slick's dad looks at Jaimes and points. "Up next? Your bedroom."

"Cool," I say, but inside I'm screaming: HALLELU-JAH!!!

"Let's eat!" Mom says.

While everyone heads off to the snack table, though, I find Gag Me, who's standing alone.

"Mrs. Gagne?" Thankfully I remember to say the right name.

She turns to face me. We're the same height. Her face is lined with deep wrinkles. She kind of does look like a wise willow tree.

"I wanted to say sorry for picking your flowers. I didn't think anyone would mind."

Her eyes narrow as I rush on.

"They were for . . ." I lower my voice. "For Lucy."

Gag Me says nothing.

"She liked them a lot," I say hopefully.

"Of course she did. Forget-me-nots," she says curtly, eyeing my arm in a sling. "Heal fast. That game's a once-in-a-lifetime."

"I'll try!" I call after her. Confirmed—she does have a heart after all.

A few minutes later she zooms off in her car, passing our soccer game in the driveway. She drives so fast we have to jump out of her way.

When she rolls down her window while passing, I think that finally, she's going to say something nice.

Instead she yells, "Next time I hit ya!" before zooming away.

Unbelievable.

I run to get the ball and find myself facing my house and the new covered bridge. I see my whole life from here. My sisters, bikes, teachers, neighbors, soccer balls, teammates, Lucy's roller skates, so many trees. All the people I've grown up with. They're here for us. Laughing, eating, and pounding nails. They still love Dad even though he can't play soccer or coach their kids. This day feels special, like a reunion, and that wouldn't have happened if Dad weren't sick. It feels weird to actually be thinking of silver linings for a disease I've hated with all my guts.

But today? It just feels exactly like it should.

Life is so weird.

Head Up, Wings Out

Impossible is nothing.

—LIONEL MESSI

The day before the big game, Jaimes drives me to the doctor's office to get my cast cut off.

It's a chilly November day, but I shiver with excitement, skipping inside.

"Hi there," the receptionist says with a smile. "I'm sorry we didn't reach you earlier, but Dr. Arun was just called into a surgical case. He can reschedule you for Monday if that's convenient."

I gape at her. Convenient?

"Uh," Jaimes says, "we *really* have to get his cast off. He's playing in *the* championship soccer game tomorrow. You may have heard of it? Mudbury against Merrimack?"

"I'm sorry," the receptionist says. "But the doctor's

not even here to take a peek. And we're not here on the weekends."

"Can you make an exception?" I ask.

The receptionist blinks.

"Is there anyone else here that could do it?" Jaimes asks.

"Can *you* do it?" I ask.

She laughs like I'm joking.

"A nurse?" Jaimes asks.

"No. The doctor really has to."

I feel my face getting really red and really hot.

"I *have* to see Dr. Arun today," I say.

"I'll put you on the schedule first thing Monday."

"That doesn't help. Please, you have—"

Jaimes puts her hand on my arm, steers me through the waiting area and out to the van.

"Jaimes," I say. "We can't just leave—do something! What if you couldn't play in *your* championship? You wouldn't just give up!"

She opens the door and pushes me inside.

She says nothing while we drive home.

She says nothing when she steers me into the house and into our room.

"Jaimes!" I say. "Find me another doctor."

She hands me a pair of scissors.

"Do it," she says.

I stop shouting.

"What?"

We stare at each other.

"Really?"

"You don't always get to control your destiny," she says. "But today you can."

And so I do.

I take the pair of scissors and cut the cast off myself.

My arm looks smaller, skinnier, and freakishly white.

Like Dad's deteriorating muscles.

"Mom's going to kill both of us," Jaimes says. "But not till Monday."

She starts juggling the soccer ball to calm herself down.

I put on a long-sleeve hoodie so no one will notice what I've just done with destiny.

Benny is waiting outside. He's gotten Lucy out of her roller skates, and they're passing the ball barefoot. I have to hand it to George and Lucy's mom. So far, my parents haven't said a word about the phone theft—and believe me, they would if they knew!

Dad comes out to watch wearing a coat and hat, wrapped under a blanket, and Mom guides us through some last-minute drills.

"Let's get you inside," Mom says when the temperature drops and the light of the sun is almost gone. "And you three—you need lots of sleep tonight, okay?" I exhale.

She still hasn't even asked about the doctor's visit.

"Okay, Coach!" Lucy and Benny say.

"One thing," Dad says.

Mom stops, waves us over.

Lucy, Benny, and I huddle around Dad, arms linked together.

Dad is shivering, his lips turning blue, but he keeps going. "Sometimes . . . only get one ch-ch-chance. This is yours."

"Yes, Coach."

Mom puts his hands on the joystick and helps wheel him inside.

"Are you ready?" I ask my friends.

"Biggest night of our lives," Benny says.

"Squish hug," Lucy says.

I squish-hug Benny and Lucy even tighter until we can barely breathe.

You see, I can't even think about letting go.

When I go up to bed, I stare at my ten thousand hours chart. I'm still a lot of hours short of mastery, but it's led us to this moment.

It's really happening.

In less than a day, we play the championship game against Merrimack, number-one-ranked team in the league. We're a distant second place, with fewer overall goals and wins—but it doesn't matter. We are the two teams who have risen to the top. Everything else is behind us. The championship game is all or nothing. Winner takes all.

My hands feel clammy, my brain jumpy as I try to visualize the ball at my feet, see the field.

To get mentally prepared for game day, I lay out my jersey. I am Messi #10.

When I rummage in my drawer for shorts and socks, I find my old jersey. Tracing the number five, I wonder if this is the one I should be wearing on the biggest night of my life. Instead of relying on Messi's magic, maybe I have to rely on myself and my ten thousand hours and my Magpie teammates. And Coach. Dad.

I carefully fold #10 and place it in my drawer.

The Battle Packs? Oh, you better believe they'll be on my feet.

Shorts.

Socks.

Shin guards.

White athletic tape.

Captain armband is already on my arm.

I'm fighting the nerves big-time.

It's going to take a miracle to win. That's what everyone is saying.

But I've faced those odds before.

When I finally climb into bed, I find I can't straighten out my legs.

"What the . . . ?" I push and push with my legs, but the sheet is messed up.

"I didn't do it," Jaimes says.

"Do what?"

"Short-sheet your bed, obviously."

Peering down into my bed, I see that it's true. Someone came into my room and folded the sheet so I can't get in. I've been pranked!

I look out the window. George is in Lucy's room with Lucy and her mom pointing at me. And laughing! Wait, is that Curtis Meowfield? Even he's laughing!

I quickly turn out the light so they don't see me smile, but I think they do anyway.

It's the start of November and already, the first snowflakes of the year are falling, leaving a light white dusting on our yard. After I'm dressed, I get Dad ready. Mom and Dad argued about whether or not he should even stay for my game.

"It's going to be so cold," she said. "I worry that you're going to freeze. Maybe—"

"I'm gggoing," he said.

Mom looks at me now. "Dress him for a blizzard."

He's lying on his bed waiting for me.

"Ready, Dad?"

"Question issss, are you?"

"I'm so ready!"

I put my arms around his middle and manage to pull him up to a sitting position while also supporting his head. Touching the faded brown and-yellow bruises on his face, I ask, "Does that hurt?"

"Not much. Almost . . . healed."

He's wearing soft warm sweatpants with elastic waistbands almost all the time now. They're more comfortable and much easier for us to dress him in. I lift his right arm and put it through a winter thermal top, slide it over his head, bend and put his left arm through the other sleeve. His arms are heavy, like dead weights that hang limp if I leave them.

"Sweatshirt?" I ask.

"Fleece," he says.

I lay him back down and walk slowly to the closet, one eye on Dad in case he decides to fall off the bed. He stays put as I grab his warmest fleece and winter coat.

"Sleeping . . . bag too."

"At the game?"

He blinks one deliberate blink.

"Was that for yes?"

"Yes."

"Are you practicing your blinks?"

Dad blinks once for yes and smiles.

I slide warm wool socks onto his feet and pull them up as high as they'll go, followed by fitting his feet into his warm work boots.

"Ready to get downstairs?"

"Hat."

"I'll get it."

I put his right arm around my neck and my left arm around his body; my right hand grasps his. On the count of three we stand.

"Good," I say.

Dad concentrates, putting one foot in front of the other, his feet barely coming off the ground. Jaimes jumps in and helps us get down the stairs.

"One more step, Dad," I say.

"Just like you. Champion-ship."

"Under the lights. And a field being named after you!"

He smiles with his whole face. "Let's go."

"Warm up!" I say.

We start at 5:15, just as Merrimack shows up in a big yellow bus filled with soccer players and screaming fans. Literally screaming. They carry signs and at least one bullhorn.

It's so cold I keep my jacket on, my uncasted arm especially chilled.

"Look!" Sunny says. "The bleachers are already totally full."

Jaimes waves at me, her hair in a high ponytail. She's shivering in tight black leggings and a short black puffy jacket—the uniform she and all her friends wear. She's standing where I'll be next week, when she has playoffs.

Real refs show up. They're actually getting paid for tonight's game, versus most of the volunteer refs we get in middle school. They wear black pants and official-looking white-and-black-striped shirts, with whistles hanging around their necks. They also have a little book in their shirt pocket that holds yellow and red cards.

The hugely bright scoreboard says thirty minutes to game time.

My heart pounds.

Coach and Dad are on the field. He's in his wheel-chair wearing his wool hat, a scarf wrapped around his face, a down jacket, and mittens that I put on him. Atop all his winter wear, he's also encased in a giant orange sleeping bag.

Fifteen minutes later, after Lucy and I lead our warm-up (flawlessly, by the way), I adjust his hat, making sure it's not in his eyes, and scratch his nose.

"Thank . . . u," he says, looking into my eyes.

The refs blow the whistle, and the small marching band stops playing.

Mudbury High's athletic director, Wendy Whitmore, walks to the center of the field, shakes the refs' hands, and speaks into a microphone.

"Thank you for being here on this very historic night!"

Mr. T walks out with a large amount of red ribbon and the dance squad.

"Dance squad?" Ziggy says. "I can't wait to go to high school."

I join my family, and we walk to the middle of the field.

"We'd like to dedicate this new field and name it after our beloved high school soccer coach," Wendy Whitmore says. "Coach Patrick Maroni. A man I've known for a long time. Patrick has dedicated his entire life to Mudbury. Together with his wife, Rayna, Patrick has coached hundreds of kids, including my own. The lessons he's taught our children on the field—kindness, unselfishness, grit, and a resolve to never ever give up on your dreams—transcend the athletic field. We are so grateful to know and love a living legend."

You have to die to be a legend.

And yet there he is. The legend. Wrapped up in a puffy orange sleeping bag.

Apparently, legends take many forms.

The big red ribbon is cut. The Mudbury High chorus sings the national anthem. The crowd cheers.

And then? It's time to play.

"What time is it?" I yell after the field is cleared.

"Game time!"

"What time is it?"

"Game time!"

"I can't hear you!"

"GAME TIME!"

I gulp. It feels like a giant, wiggly porpoise is flipping through my stomach. The Merrimack squad looks taller than they did a month ago.

"Take a knee," Coach says. "Look at me. Focus."

We encircle her, take a knee.

"You'll likely hear some whiners complaining about the weather," Coach says, jutting her chin toward Merrimack. "That's what whiners do. They whine about stuff. They can't help it. Sad."

We straighten.

"It's going to get darker and colder before this game is over. The wind is going to blow. More snow will fall. But we don't have to hang out with the whiners because that's not what we do. Tonight we are only here to play!"

We pull in closer and start clapping.

"Captains?" Coach says.

"All of these people are here for us," Lucy says. "Hold hands."

"Lucy," Slick says with an eye roll.

"Do it!" she commands. We reach out and hold the

hand of the person next to us. Lucy's hair is in two braids, and she's painted black stripes under her eyes like some sort of warrior.

"Feel the energy of your teammate," she says. "Feel the magic that's going to happen tonight under the lights on Patrick Maroni Championship Field. He's here for us. Can't you feel it?"

We nod. Totally feel it.

"Merrimack is going to try to throw us off our game by chirping," she says. "But that's not going to work for them tonight. Tonight," Lucy says, raising her voice, "tonight is *our* night!"

She looks at me.

"We're going to respond to every attack and every setback we've ever had," I say. "Tonight is the night we control our destiny. We dream big and play big, and we're GONNA WIN BIG!"

"YEAH!" the team cheers.

Coach turns to the defense.

"Settle before you pass. Always outside, right?"

"Right!"

"Midfield, you're going to run like you've never run before. C.J., call your team back when you need them."

"Got it, Coach!"

"Captains!" the refs yell.

I hear Roma scream my name.

"At least you've got one fan," Slick says, elbowing me.

In the captains' circle, we face Merrimack's captains. They nod, tuck in their shirts, shake our hands. They've beaten us once and tied us once. The look on their faces is pure confidence, like they've already won. Rookie mistake. Never underestimate your opponent. They don't know what's coming.

I glance at Dad. He's watching me. His left hand turns just enough. Thumbs-up.

Lucy and I call tails at the same time. We win the coin toss and pick the side we warmed up on.

"Starting lineup," Coach says. "Go get 'em."

Benny and I handshake: palm, palm, backhand, backhand, slide, elbow, finger lock, pull away. Lucy and I high-five. I wince at the pressure in my right arm.

Still, I high-five each starting player with my left hand, running down the bench.

Anytime, any weather, we play best when we're together.

The Golden Goal

Coach doesn't start me.

She eyes my uncasted arm worriedly. "What did the doctor say?"

Lucky for me, I don't have to lie. Coach gets distracted by the start-of-game whistle.

Lucy would say this serendipitous intervention is a sign.

I was meant to play this game tonight.

Not only that. I will score.

We will win.

Dad will witness.

Together we'll lift the trophy high in the air. Way above his head!

Because he's the exception.

Because I've never worked so hard for anything in my life.

After eighteen minutes of battling, Merrimack turns up the pressure and attacks, gets through our defense, and scores.

I swallow hard. Clench my hands. It's a fluke, a temporary setback.

"Recover!" I yell. "Everything's okay."

I get up and jog in place to stay warm. *Come on!*

When Archie, playing forward, raises his hand for a sub, I seize the moment.

"Coach! I'm ready!"

"Your arm . . . ?"

"Totally fine!" I yell, already running onto the field.

It's aching. She's going to kill me.

Worth it.

I run onto the field with my lucky Battle Pack cleats. My fists clench as I run to my starting position, the position I was meant to play. My legs and arms are once again in sync without a cast reminding me of pain and brokenness. The wind carries me forward. I think of how much I love my fast legs and my beating heart and my breathing lungs. Of course the ghosts are jealous. Of course they whisper *You lucky, lucky thing.*

That's how tonight feels. Lucky.

As the whistle is blown again, I pull up my socks. Wrapped around them is athletic tape like usual, but I've written a different name tonight: "Patrick Maroni." I look to where he sits, motionless except for his eyes, the eyes that follow my every move. I pound on his name so he'll notice.

And I know, like I'll always know, that when Dad's got his eyes on me, I will never—ever—give up.

You have to fight to reach your dream.

Make the impossible possible.

We got this, Dad.

On the turf, under the lights, in front of a couple thousand people who want us to win, we battle for another twenty-two minutes straight, until Benny finally scores our first goal in the final seconds of the first half.

When the ref whistles for halftime we're down 2–1.

"Get a drink," Coach says, giving us all a high five when we come off the field.

We take a knee and circle up, arms around each other.

"They're so good," Sam says, looking at the scoreboard.

"They haven't lost this whole season," Chase says. "I don't think we're going to win."

Lucy's head and my head snap up. "What!"

"We have a choice now," Coach says fiercely. "We always have choices. In tough, stressful situations, there are two choices. We can let the stress consume us and respond with self-doubt and fear. We can shut down. Or we can choose to respond with our best selves. Choose to focus on what we can control. We can discipline ourselves to do what we know how to do."

Coach looks right at me, and I know that I have to choose right now.

That no matter what happens on the field and off, now is the time.

Choose my best self or not.

Choose to focus on what I can control, or not.

Choose to be happy that I gave everything I had—or not.

No matter what happens next.

"Listen carefully," Coach says. "All the preparation for this very moment is behind you. You've practiced and sprinted in hot and humid weather until you thought you were going to barf. You've worked on your touch, your through balls, your shots. You've psyched each other up. You are ready to win this game because you are the best-conditioned and most unselfish team out there. Let's go do what we do!"

We start moving on our toes. "Yeah, Coach!"

"Go out there and smile," Coach says. "This is your moment. Play like this is the last game you will ever play. Play like this is the last time we will ever suit up as Mudbury Middle School soccer players. Leave nothing on the field."

Sam sniffs. "Is it really the last time?"

"Cry later," Sunny says. "We've got this!"

The whistle blows. Game time.

Archie takes a deep breath and yells, "One, two, three . . ."

"Magpies!"

As I run out with Benny, I am one with the field, feeling every bead of artificial turf under my cleats.

I don't let my brain tell me my arm hurts, because tonight I can run—I can play!

I look over at Dad. One blink for yes.

YES.

Cold wind blows across my face. The roar of the crowd is loud in my ears, then fades. I fake left and pass to Brady, who's made an overlap play.

Sunny looks to Benny and Benny takes off, but he collides with a defender and goes down hard, grabbing his ankle.

"Benny! Get up!"

"I'm not flopping," he says, his voice full of pain. "It hurts so bad."

The ref blows his whistle. Coach runs out to the field with the trainers.

"Archie!" Benny says when he's carried off the field by Coach and Moses. "Play tough!"

"I got it, Benny!"

Oh no. Archie in for Benny?

Archie is already breathing hard when he joins me as striker. "We can do this, man. I got you."

Lucy's eyes find mine. *You've got to believe, Golden.*

"Okay, Archie," I say. "Let's do this!"

Twenty minutes in and we've had very few shots on goal.

Step it up! Dad coaches me with his eyes. Coach paces on the sidelines, using her hands to push us forward or pull us back. But really, the time for coaching is over. It's up to us to execute.

With ten minutes left, Merrimack #2 shoots a killer shot to the right lower corner. C.J. dives to the ground, and we hold our breaths until he shouts, "I GOT IT!"

Save!

The crowd screams his name. He boots the ball out. Brady brings it down out of the air with his feet.

My heart is pumping hard and fast.

I want a shot more than I've ever wanted anything. For Dad.

Paige dribbles the ball, passes back to Lucy, who passes it up to Dobbs. On a corner kick I get a head on the ball, but it goes wide and Merrimack gets the ball for a goal kick.

"Win this ball!" Lucy shouts. "Mark up!"

But Merrimack boots it up the long turf field, way over my head to the defense.

We keep battling, and with six minutes on the clock, we're finally tied 2–2, after Sunny makes a penalty shot. I look over at Dad, desperate. I look at my socks, see the name "Patrick Maroni." *I will do this for you, Dragon-Ball P!*

"Pull up!" I yell to the defense. They push up until they're all the way to the half line. It works, and Merrimack gets two offsides calls in two minutes.

We follow up offensively, battling back and forth on Merrimack's side of the field for a full five minutes, meaning Merrimack's getting no shots on goal—but neither are we. Brady takes a shot, but he's way past the eighteen-yard line, and the goalie easily catches the ball, giving it back to the defense.

With one minute left, Chase passes the ball way over my head.

I take a run.

All the Merrimack midfielders and defenders have pulled up close to the midline, so when I get past the center mid I'm past all four defenders, too; they've gotten caught flat across the field.

Fast break!

Suddenly, no one is in front of me except the goalie.

Watch this, Dad!

The goalie crouches in anticipation.

Make this shot, I win the game. I win everything.

Archie is coming up behind me, huffing and puffing.

The crowd is going crazy! I can hear the Squirrels.

The cold air whips at my ears, through my hair.

I turn on the wheels, passing the eighteen-yard box, dribbling faster than I've ever dribbled in my life.

The goalie's Adam's apple moves up and down as he swallows hard.

The crowd screams louder.

My team bench is on their feet.

"Go . . . Golden!"

The goalie makes his move, coming at me fast.

"Shoot!" someone calls.

I shoot at the same time the goalie slides into me, taking me out. I land hard on my bad arm and scream out in pain.

But the ball bounces out of the goalie's hands.

I manage to touch the ball back with my toe.

I see the fear in Archie's face.

"NOW!" I say.

Archie shoots. Fires like a loaded gun.

I duck.

The ball rockets past me.

Into the net.

GOAL!

There is a small moment of silence.

Right before the crowd goes crazy.

Archie stands still, his mouth open. He falls to his knees. "Goal!" he whispers. "Goal!"

I look at the ball in the net, just to make sure it's still there. My heart fills with too many feelings.

"Goldie! I got my first goal—the *Golden* Goal!"

The scoreboard lights up.

2–3.

The clocks ticks down to zero. The refs blow their whistles.

Against the odds, Mudbury Middle has just won the championship game against Merrimack Middle.

My team runs to Archie.

I sit up, holding my arm.

They pick Archie up.

He fist-pumps into the great big sky and yells, "Yeah! My life is complete! Greatest moment of my life! That's it—I'm done!"

You think soccer is just a game? Well then, you've never played it.

I stand, bent at the middle, catching my breath. The refs shake Coach's hand as she comes onto the field. One of them jogs over to me.

He approaches as I finally stand.

"The assist is so often the unsung hero," he says, reaching out to give me a handshake. I wince as he squeezes my right hand and arm. "But tonight? That's as good as it gets."

I hear Archie yelling for me. "Golden Macaroni! Where the heck are you?"

Last I read, Messi had scored a total of 671 goals and assisted 275 goals in his career. On average, he scores a goal every ninety-nine minutes and twenty-three seconds. But for all the goals he scores, he's also one of the top assist players in the world. Another reason the world loves that guy so much—he helps others feel the glory too. It's an amazing feeling.

I search the crowd for Dad, almost afraid, I'm hoping so hard.

There. He sits unmoving amid the chaos, an orange puffy dot in the cheering crowd.

I wait for it—for him to sit up straight. To push himself to the edge of his wheelchair.

But he does not walk to me. And I finally have to concede, *He's not going to*.

Every great athlete has at least one moment that will forever haunt them because of what might have been. After years of literal sweat and tears, a dream can be over in seconds.

This is my moment.

Coach reaches me, pulls me to her. "It was a great battle," she whispers. "He couldn't be more proud of you."

We walk to Dad.

He pushes with his pointer finger. The wheelchair rolls forward to me.

His eyes take in my socks, his name written with black Sharpie on white athletic tape.

"Gold . . . en," he says, his voice thick.

I don't know if he's emotional or just cold, but I find a tissue and wipe his eyes and nose.

He can't lift his arms, will not lift the trophy.

But he stretches out the two fingers on his left hand.

It's not exactly what I wanted. Not how I always pictured this moment.

But I know that just like I've given my all for him, he's giving everything he has to give.

To me.

His Golden Boy.

And that makes it perfect.

Paper Plate Awards

We can't let our team down if we are trying to
do the right thing.

—COACH KARL

Every year for our end-of-season soccer banquet, Dad,
Benny, Lucy, and I make paper plate awards. They're just
what they sound like—awards on paper plates. Easy on
the nonexistent athletic budget.

Benny is bringing a picture of a professional soccer
player to put on them this year for each of our teammates
because he has a wicked good printer.

It's been almost a week since the under-the-lights
game. Dad's about the same. My arm is back in a soft
cast.

Mom is salty with me.

Still worth it.

Lucy and Benny walk in together. Lucy is carrying

a bucket of markers, but I still haven't found scissors or markers, and the only glue stick is nearly out of glue.

"Aha!" I say, holding up a pair of kiddie scissors.

Dad wheels over to the barstools.

"Your face is better," Benny says. "No offense."

Dad nods, smiling, barely a touch of greenish-yellow bruising under his eye.

I'm glad he can still smile, that the muscles that pull his mouth upward are still working, that the skin around his eyes still crinkles. *You know why?* Whitney said. *Even toward the end, ALS patients can usually still move their eye muscles, still blink, AND smile. Isn't that so great, Goldie?* I think she got that last part from YouTube, but I grudgingly agreed with her.

"Who gets . . . Ronaldo?" Dad asks.

"Benny," I say. "Both have mad skill."

Benny grins.

"Brady?" Lucy asks, holding up his paper plate.

"Mbappé," I say. "Great ball control, right?"

"C.J.?"

"De Gea."

"Mario?"

"Silva," I say. "Nobody gets past him."

"Slick?"

"Suárez," I say. "Because he bites other players. And me."

"What about Lucy?" Coach asks, coming into the room after putting the Squirrels to bed.

"Rapinoe or Hamm," Lucy says, and I grin. Of course she gets to choose her own.

Dad moves his nose up and down. "Can you scratch . . . nose?"

I reach over and scratch a small speck of his nose.

"Low. High. Over . . . right. There. Good. Thanks."

He wiggles his nose around until he's good again.

"Archie?"

"Maradona." Messi's childhood hero.

"Golden?"

Dad makes a sound in his throat.

"Suction?" Coach asks. "You don't have to watch this," she says to Benny and Lucy. "Golden, want to take them to your room?"

"Come on," Lucy says.

We walk out of the kitchen and up the stairs, past the newly installed wheelchair lift that goes all the way to the top.

"Want a ride?" I joke.

Benny touches it, slides his fingers all the way up.

Jaimes is playing her music loudly, the door shut. So we sit down at the top of the stairs, hearing the suction noises—spit being slurped and sucked from around and under Dad's tongue, teeth, and gums and into a giant straw so he doesn't choke to death.

"Is your dad going to be able to stay here until . . . always?" Lucy asks.

"In Chinese culture," Benny says, "no one goes to a retirement home. Parents live with their children until they pass, like my grandma. My parents always say, 'We will be together forever until the end.'" He pauses. "And I think the end is coming pretty quick."

Lucy nods like she already knows.

"Grandma Ho?" I ask. "Why didn't you say anything?"

But I know why. I've been so super focused on only me. "I'm sorry, Benny."

He just nods. "Me too."

Lucy looks deep into my eyes and puts her hands on mine. "Are you scared?"

"I guess. Sometimes. Yeah."

"Me too," Lucy says.

"Me three," Benny says, putting his hands on top of ours.

The suctioning stops.

"Good?" we hear Coach say.

Jaimes suddenly opens our bedroom door and sees the three of us sitting.

My face goes red.

"Just tell him," Lucy says.

"Tell me what?" Benny asks.

Sigh.

"We have to share. Okay? I share a room with my sister."

Benny laughs. "That's cool."

"Um, no way!"

Jaimes walks back into our room and pulls out the hamper filled with my forgotten water balloons.

"Why don't you go use these? They're cramping my style."

"Those are for George," I say.

"Well, he just pulled up."

We rush to the window and wouldn't you know? She's right.

"Serendipitous moment, right, Lucy?"

Benny grins. Lucy giggles.

"Hey, George!" I yell.

He looks up, sees what I'm holding.

"Don't even think about it, Golden Macaroni."

"What did you call me?"

"I said, GOLDEN CHEESEBURGER WITH PICKLES MACARONI!"

I launch the water balloon at him. He jumps. The balloon smashes on the ground, soaking his foot—and Curtis Meowfield, who meows noisily at me.

George points at me. "Oh, it is so on."

I turn and smile at my audience. "You know, I've always liked that guy."

Banquet food at Mudbury Middle School is sometimes stellar and sometimes . . . not. You never know what kind of potluck you're going to get. Of course the Maroni family is hoping for stellar because, as usual, we are late and rushing, down to weird food choices at home.

But at least Roma and Whitney's matching French braids (I *know*) are looking stellar—and so is Dad's shaved face. Not a cut or rash anywhere. Who's the man now?

"Ah, I remember this place so fondly," Jaimes says in her superior older-sister voice as we walk into the school.

"Yeah, it was a mere four months ago," I say, discreetly shanking her in the back.

"It was like two *years* ago—did you just seriously *shank* me?"

"Childre . . . ," Dad says as I open the door for him. He wheels in, giving me a warning look to get along with the beast.

Mr. T stands at the podium with Coach, arms folded in an intimidating *Don't mess with me* way. He's got a new haircut: three shaved lines on the side of his head. Around his neck is one of his funky-colored scarves.

"Golden."

"Sweet haircut," I say, pushing up my own hair. "Maybe I should shave some lines too. We could be twins."

"You couldn't pull it off."

While I try to think of a comeback, he cracks, "Anyway, it's a little Ronaldo, don't you think?"

I cover my face in horror and shrink away. I can't admit it or anything, but Ronaldo might be growing on me.

While we eat pretzels and some sort of Jell-O salad with Cool Whip, Mr. T says, "I'd like to thank Coach for another great soccer season. We are lucky to have her expertise, especially in light of the . . . hardships her family is going through."

Clapping and whistling fill the gym.

"What hard . . . ships?" Dad whispers.

"Jaimes," I whisper. "She's such a hardship. And we have to share a room."

Jaimes purposely tosses her hair into my eyes, blinding me.

"Thank you, Mr. T," Coach says, smiling at the audience. "Thank you all for being here this evening. It's been a wonderful season. This team has surpassed my expectations with their hard work and effort. The stats are impressive: forty-four total goals scored by fourteen different players. Assists by sixteen separate players.

"Winning is fun and rewarding," Coach continues. "But the best part of coaching this year was witnessing the love these teammates have for each other." I start squirming at the mention of love and glance over at Lucy and Benny. "Soccer is not an individual sport, but there are certainly moments when one can be selfish. This team was pretty special."

Coach looks around the room, somehow able to make eye contact with each of us.

"Early in the season I asked for leaders to step up. There are many scenes that stand out, but my favorite moment was on the last Wednesday in August. Preseason. We were sprinting on the hottest day of the year. Remember?" There is a collective groan. "Some of you finished the sprints quickly. When you saw your teammates struggling to finish, all of you stepped off that white sideline and brought your teammates in. That was the moment you became a team."

Coach smiles and pats her heart. *Come on, Coach. Hold it together.*

"The end of this season is particularly bittersweet as our eighth graders move on. My husband and I have coached you your entire lives; we've seen you grow up. And we are so proud of you."

Everyone claps, but Dad can't. He's swallowing hard.

"Okay?" I whisper.

He blinks once for yes.

"Now for the awards," Coach says, back to her business voice. "Captains?"

We go to the front, and my voice cracks only once through the microphone as I call everyone's names. The Squirrels giggle. Most of the boys give me a half hug while discreetly shanking me so the parents can't see.

"Suárez?" Slick says. He leans over and tries to bite me.

Archie fist-pumps the air when he sees his Iniesta paper plate award.

Coach makes eye contact with Dad as we finish. It's like I know what they're thinking: everything changes after this moment. Our season together is over. And Coach? She's pretty much indestructible 'cause she's had so much practice holding it together, but tonight it looks like we're headed down Breakdown Lane.

I save the day by yelling, "To the Mudbury Magpies!"

Coach laughs as we have our last big group soccer-banquet hug, and all the parents take a zillion pictures.

"Guys, come on," Benny says.

The team heads over to Dad, Dragon-Ball P, clapping him on the back, telling him stories.

I hang back, watching. Coach is by his side, with Lucy, Roma, Whitney, and Jaimes. They all turn and beckon me to come, take my place on the dream team.

Epilogue: The Dream Team

I have come to learn that I am not perfect, nor will I ever be. Perfect is too hard. I'm perfectly fine with being perfectly imperfect.

—ATTRIBUTED TO LIONEL MESSI

I play this soccer game on my Xbox called *FIFA* (when Mom isn't taking away my electronics and saying "You're going to become an addict"). The more points you earn, the more coins you have to buy players or packs, contracts, and fitness boosts.

If I had enough coins I could buy my dream team.

There's no way I could make this happen on *FIFA* because there's no way I could get 200 million coins unless I played for like twenty-four hours a day, which, you know—Mom.

But this is what my dream team would look like:

David de Gea as goalie, anchoring Mom and Dad's favorite 4-4-2 strategy. Marcelo, Luiz, Hummels, and the great Patrick Maroni at defense. My midfield is pretty sweet: Ronaldo, Iniesta, Sánchez, and Willian. Yeah, I allowed Ronaldo on the same team as Messi.

My attacking forwards are me and the next-greatest player in the world: Lionel Messi, of course.

So that's my dream team. But in real life, if I had to choose which team to play on, and which players I'd want next to me on the field, I'd always choose the ones I had at Mudbury Middle School, the team who believed in me and made me a captain and took us to the championship game under the lights on the turf so Dad could see us play one more time. Before Verity became Dad's full-time nurse, before Mrs. Ho organized a town-wide meal delivery system. Before Lucy Littlehouse moved.

You know what Lucy left me? Her CAT. Curtis Meowfield is now a permanent fixture in my life. He still chases me and tries to bite my ankles. What gives?

You know what Lucy left Roma? Her roller skates.

So every time Roma skates up and down the driveway I think maybe it's Lucy. The wheels always sound like they're coming back for me. And she does whenever she can.

Some friendships have short life spans. Like Sugar Ray, who I eventually had to retire. Still, what a kid.

Others are GOAT: Greatest of All Time. Like me, Benny, and Lucy.

Like Dad.

He didn't live to see another fall soccer season—but I think he saw me at my very best, when I managed to pass the ball to a player who had a better shot under the lights on a turf field named after Patrick "Dragon-Ball P" Maroni. What more is there?

Toward the end, Mr. T came and sat with Dad, keeping him company, reading out loud, crocheting. Yeah, for real. He taught my Squirrel sisters how to crochet a scarf. Okay, he taught me, too. It's, like, wicked fun.

The last day with Dad we were gathered around his bed: me, Mom, Jaimes, Whitney, and Roma. His bed was a hospital bed moved into the living room. And even though he couldn't talk anymore and his left fingers had long since stopped moving, I could tell by the look in his eyes: he couldn't love another team any more than the one we had. His body wasn't strong anymore, but his mind and heart were. And in the end, that's what we needed most; I never once thought about his bench press stats. He was still the man.

There was something better—this feeling—that engulfed our entire room.

You don't give up on me and I don't give up on you.

And I didn't. I swear I never did—not even at the very end when he had lost so much weight and the only things he could voluntarily move were his eyelids. One blink for yes, two blinks for no.

"I love you," we said.

One blink for yes, for each of us.

He also smiled. I saw it with my own eyes.

Dad would say, *In the end, what is soccer?*

It's just a game.

It's air in a leather ball.

It's kicking a ball across lines painted on a field.

Just a game.

But for us, it was always more than that.

It was how Patrick Maroni and Coach taught us how to live.

How to be a team.

How to say good-bye.

I'm still working real hard on my ten thousand hours, getting closer and closer by the day.

And even now, when Benny and I are running down the soccer field and the wind is blowing through my Messi hair (which finally grew out) and the crowd is chanting my name (hey, I can dream, right?) and the sun is shining on my face and I'm going so fast I feel like I'm flying—he's with me.

My dad.

I feel him everywhere, but especially on the field.

With me.

His Golden Boy.

Acknowledgments

Something I've learned while watching a friend battle an incurable disease is that the human body, like a family, is both resilient and fragile. I'm so grateful to have both.

Thank you, Eric, Heidi, Annika, and Britta Johnson, for teaching me so much about life and love and silver linings. To learn and read about ALS advances and research, visit www.als.org.

This story was also inspired by my son, who, as a middle schooler, idolized soccer star Lionel Messi. Like Messi, he was small. Like Golden, he zeroed in on the idea that hours and hours of practice would lead to greatness. To later watch him and his middle school teammates play together in high school "under the lights" was simply awesome. Also: they may publicly deny ever shanking and "get wrecked," but we know better.

Thank you to the AEMS seventh-and-eighth-grade

soccer team: a rotating cast of athletic characters. The wins and losses, goals, penalty shots, cleats, Secret Circle, captain's band . . . it's the best. You keep growing up, which is annoying, but I adore you all. Thank you for making fall so glorious for so many years.

In his 2008 book *Outliers,* Malcolm Gladwell wrote that "ten thousand hours is the magic number" to achieve greatness. Popular culture has seized upon this notion, as did my fictional character Golden. While Gladwell was clear that this number does not apply to sports, I wasn't about to tell Golden that, geez. Anyway, I believe that enough practice will get you just about anywhere.

Thank you to my first readers: Andrea McDonald for your attention to detail; Kate Johnston for your ability to push me on story structure; Jon Beard; Julia Tomiak #thewordnerd #writingbuddy for holding me accountable every Monday morning; Heidi Johnson for your final-pass reading, ALS fact-checking, and extraordinarily positive outlook. And to my very last readers: Nelson and Paige for "you can't say that" and the final green light.

Paige, thanks for keeping me fed during the long writing and editing stretches.

Nick Ho, thank you for lending your name to one of my favorite characters, Benny Ho, for insight into Chinese and Western culture, and for being one of the really good guys.

Thank you to my editor, Alexa Pastor, who stuck with this story when it took nearly ten thousand tries to get it right! You made it so much better. In addition, thanks to Justin Chanda, Barbara Perris, and the wonderful Simon & Schuster team for bringing books into the world. Once again, Abigail Dela Cruz, I love the cover you created.

Thank you to literary agent Zoe Sandler, who champions and empowers me on the daily; I am so grateful.

Thank you to the coaches who spend hours volunteering and mentoring our youth; many of your inspiring pep talks and coaching moments were woven throughout this book. Female coaches, you have a special place in my heart.

Thanks to my parents, Steven and Mary Nelson, and their enthusiastic role as unofficial publicists. Thank you, best father-in-law Arthur, who helped grow Nelly Mak with nightly bowls of oatmeal.

Thank you, Meredith, Mindy, Lindsey, Chloe . . . my girls on the field. I'll meet you there. Anytime, any day.

And to Gregor, the original Dragon-Ball G. You're an amazing teammate, my other half. Furthermore, to our children, Cope, Nelson, Brynne, and Paige. The moments spent with you on and off the soccer field have been the best of my life.

Ten-year-old Guinevere St. Clair is determined to find her missing neighbor, but the answers just might lead her to places and people she never expected—and maybe even the one she's running away from. . . .

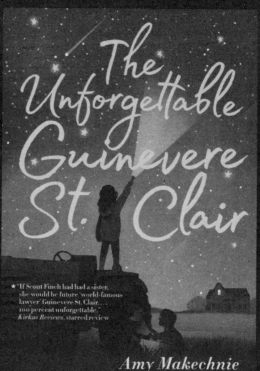

The Unforgettable Guinevere St. Clair

★"If Scout Finch had had a sister, she would be future 'world-famous lawyer' Guinevere St. Clair. . . . 100 percent unforgettable."
—*Kirkus Reviews*, starred review

Amy Makechnie

★"Part mystery, part study of the human heart, and one pierced with rays of hope."—*Booklist*, starred review

"5/5 stars . . . Rich and complex, filled with extraordinary characters and gorgeous writing."—*San Francisco Book Review*

> "A bighearted story that's as sweet
> as it is awesome."
> —R. J. Palacio, author of *Wonder*

Meet Ellie, a smart and funny girl with cerebral palsy who is determined to follow her dreams, no matter what challenges life sends her way.

A Kirkus Reviews
Best Middle Grade Book

A Bank Street College of Education
Best Children's Book of the Year

★ "Ellie is easy to champion, and her story reminds readers that life's burdens are always lighter with friends and family."
—*Publishers Weekly*, starred review

★ "An honest, emotionally rich take on disability, family, and growing up."
—*Kirkus Reviews*, starred review

★ "Ellie takes on life headfirst . . . A feisty, dynamic character surrounded by well-rounded characters just as appealing as she is."
—*Booklist*, starred review

PRINT AND EBOOK EDITIONS AVAILABLE

From atheneum
simonandschuster.com/kids